DOLLED UP

FOR MURDER

OTHER JOSIE PRESCOTT ANTIQUES MYSTERIES BY JANE K. CLELAND

Deadly Threads

Silent Auction

Killer Keepsakes

Antiques to Die For

Deadly Appraisal

Consigned to Death

DOLLED UP

FOR MURDER

31221000763438

JANE K. CLELAND

MINOTAUR BOOKS ✷ NEW YORK

www.minotaurbooks.com

Library of Congress Cataloging-in-Publication Data

Cleland, Jane K.
    Dolled up for murder / Jane K. Cleland.—1st ed.
        p. cm.
    ISBN 978-1-250-00184-9 (hardcover)
    ISBN 978-1-4299-4250-8 (e-book)
    1. Prescott Josie (Fictitious Character)—Fiction.   2. Kidnapping—
Fiction.   3. Appraisers—Fiction.   4. Murder—Investigation—
Fiction.   5. New Hampshire—Fiction.   I. Title.
    PS3603.L4555D65 2012
    813'.6—dc23
                                                    2011045374

First Edition: April 2012

10   9   8   7   6   5   4   3   2   1

For my oldest friend, Liz Weiner, who knew me before I was born. And for my newest, Christine de los Reyes, who found me through Josie. And, of course, for Joe.

DOLLED UP

FOR MURDER

CHAPTER ONE

Gretchen, administrative manager of PRESCOTT'S ANTIQUES & AUCTIONS, spread the photographs over her desk. "I can't decide," she said. She looked up and smiled at us, her expressive green eyes reflecting her pleasure. "What do you think? Should I go with the blue hydrangeas and paperwhites? Or the veronicas and baby's breath?" She angled the two photos so we could see them.

"I love hydrangeas!" Cara, our receptionist, said. Cara was grandmotherly in appearance, with curly white hair and a round pink face that grew pinker when she felt pleasure, embarrassment, or sadness.

"Me, too," I said, leaning over to see the images. "Especially the blue ones—and the paperwhites in this bouquet are beautiful." I looked at the other photo Gretchen was holding and laughed. "You're going to hate me because I'm not going to be of any help at all. I love these veronicas, too!"

"They're so delicate," Cara agreed. "Really lovely."

"I don't know," Gretchen said. She gathered up the photographs and jiggled them together. "Luckily I have a week before I have to decide."

The wind chimes Gretchen had hung on the back of the front door years earlier jingled. Lenny Einsohn stepped inside.

"Josie," he said. He nodded at Gretchen and Cara, then looked back at me. "Do you have a minute?"

Lenny looked awful, pasty white and too thin. I wasn't surprised. Wes Smith, the incredibly plugged-in local reporter, had just broken the story that Alice D. Michaels, the founder and CEO of ADM Financial

Advisers Inc., was being investigated for running a mega-Ponzi scheme, with or without her associates' knowledge. The associate most often mentioned as the brains behind the scheme was Lenny. Alice had fired him three months earlier, at the first hint of trouble.

I knew Lenny because his oldest son, now away at college, had caught the stamp collecting bug in junior high school, and after witnessing his elation at several tag sale finds, his parents had joined in the fun. Lenny started collecting Civil War maps and ephemera and his wife, Iris, fell in love with Clarice Cliff jugs.

"Sure. Let's go up to my office."

I pushed open the heavy door, stepped into the warehouse, and led the way to the spiral staircase that led to my private office on the mezzanine, our footsteps echoing in the cavernous space. I considered directing Lenny to the yellow upholstered love seat and Queen Anne wing chairs but didn't. A little voice in my head warned me I should keep our interaction all business.

"Have a seat," I said, sitting behind my desk as I pointed to a guest chair. "What can I do for you?"

Lenny looked as if he'd rather be at the dentist getting a root canal without anesthetic than talking to me.

"I was going through my Civil War documents the other day. I've acquired some nice things over the last few years. Some original maps showing forts and so on. I have two letters signed by Lincoln, too. I paid thirty-five thousand for one of them—a thank-you to Ulysses Doubleday for information about Fort Sumter." He crossed his legs, then uncrossed them. "I'd like to sell the entire collection."

I didn't want any part of it. If Lenny was charged with larceny or fraud or anything related to financial improprieties at ADM Financial, the courts would freeze his assets until the case was settled one way or the other. In situations like this, the authorities often went back ninety days or even longer, trying to recoup monies for victims.

My window was open, and a stack of papers fluttered in the soft, warm breeze. I moved a paperweight—a water-smoothed gray rock my boyfriend and I had picked up from a purling brook during a hike in the White Mountains last summer—onto the top of the pile. Lenny kept his eyes on me, waiting for me to speak.

"Do you want me to appraise the collection for you?" I asked.

"No. I'm hoping you'll buy it."

If I purchased his collection and he was subsequently convicted, the courts might decide that the proceeds of the sale should have benefited his victims, not him. Thinking through the worst-case scenario, the powers that be might even confiscate the collection on the theory that it had been originally purchased with stolen money. I'd be out the cash I'd paid him, and the public might think I'd conspired with Lenny to snooker them. That scenario had ugly written all over it. I tried to think how I could extricate myself without offending him but couldn't. There was no easy way out.

"Sorry, Lenny. I have to pass."

He bit his lip and tapped the chair arm. "I'll give you a good deal."

I shook my head. "Sorry." I stood up. "Let me walk you out."

Back upstairs in my office, I picked up my accountant Pete's good-news quarterly report, then put it down, my interest in revenue streams and profit margins waning as the breeze wafted through my window. I put the report aside and started reading my antiques appraiser Fred's draft of catalogue copy for an auction we were planning for next fall on witchcraft memorabilia, thinking it would be more engaging than financial data, but within minutes, I found myself staring at the baby blue sky. I was suffering from a serious case of spring fever.

"Come on, Josie," I told myself. "Concentrate."

I reached for a media release we planned to send to doll magazines, blogs, and book reviewers announcing the purchase of Selma Farmington's doll collection.

Selma Farmington had died just a week earlier in a horrific car accident, and now her daughters, up from Texas, were facing the daunting task of clearing out the sprawling home that had been in their family for generations. When they'd called me in to buy some of the antiques, they'd been frank about feeling shell-shocked and overwhelmed. I'd encouraged them to let me take the time to appraise the doll collection so they could sell the dolls individually at full retail, the best way to command top dollar, but they weren't interested.

They hadn't even wanted to consign the dolls. When I explained that in order to buy the collection outright, I had to offer them a wholesale price, they'd understood. After a brief discussion, they'd asked me to raise my offer from one-third of their mom's carefully recorded expenditures to half, and I'd agreed. The $23,000 sales price was fair. Once the dolls were properly appraised, cleaned, and repaired, I'd be certain to make a good profit, and they had one less collection to worry about. While Selma's doll collection wasn't of earth-shattering quality, I thought it was varied enough to be of interest to collectors and dealers. My fingers were crossed that we'd get good media coverage. I finished reading the release, e-mailed Gretchen that it was good to go, then considered what to do next.

Nothing appealed to me. I was about to struggle through another few pages of Fred's catalogue when Gretchen IM'd me. Alice Michaels had called for an appointment, and she'd scheduled her at three. *First Lenny, now Alice,* I thought. I glanced at the time display on my computer monitor. It was three minutes after two. I gave up trying to work, pushed the papers aside, and headed downstairs. I decided to walk to the church about a quarter mile down the road to the east, in the hopes that indulging my need to be outside for a little while would enable me to buckle down when I returned. Cara was on the phone giving someone directions to Saturday's tag sale. I told Gretchen I'd be back in half an hour or so.

I stood for a moment in my parking lot enjoying feeling the sun on my face and listening to the birds chat to one another, then started down the packed dirt path that wound through the woods, a shortcut from my property to the Congregational Church of Rocky Point. Everything was blooming or in bud, filled with the promise of renewal, of hope.

May was my favorite time of year in New Hampshire. The wisteria and lilacs were in full bloom, the wisteria hanging low over lush green grass and the lilacs scenting the roads and fields. Violets and lilies of the valley dotted the forest floor. Queen Anne's lace and heather grew in wild abandon near the sandy shore. May was idyllic. So was June when the dahlias and peonies were in bloom. September was dazzling, too, with its fiery colors and crisp evenings. As was

October, with pumpkins as big as wheelbarrows proudly placed on porches and golden and cordovan colored Indian corn hung on doors. The fresh-fallen snow in January created a winter wonderland that to my eye rivaled the postcard-perfect Alpine slopes. I smiled, realizing how much I loved New Hampshire in all seasons, how fully my adopted state had become my home. I paused to admire a clutch of Boston fern, their new fronds just unfurling.

As soon as I stepped onto the church grounds, I spotted Ted Bauer, the pastor, standing by the side garden. I walked to join him.

"Hey, Ted," I said as I approached.

He looked over his shoulder and smiled. Ted was of medium height and stout. His blond hair was graying, and he'd gained some weight over the last year or so. He looked his age, which I guessed was close to fifty.

"Hi, Josie. You caught me playing hooky. I have an acute case of spring fever."

"Me, too. I don't want to do anything but wander around outside admiring plants and flowers and birds."

"I understand completely. I've been standing here looking at the impatiens for way too long. I should be inside preparing next Sunday's sermon."

"It's only Monday. You have time. I should be reviewing catalogue copy Fred wrote. He can't continue his work until he hears from me."

"I wish I had plenty of time, but the truth is that it takes me all week to write a sermon. When's the auction?"

"September. Which, despite being months away, will be here before we know it. We have to start promoting it soon."

"We share a good work ethic, Josie."

"That's true," I acknowledged.

"But you know what?" he asked, his smile lighting up his eyes. "It's all right to take a little time now and again to appreciate things like flowers and birds."

"I know you're right, but I still feel guilty."

"Me, too. How's this? I won't tell on you if you don't tell on me."

"Deal," I said, grinning.

I circled the church and waved good-bye to Ted as I entered the pathway for my return journey. I stepped onto the asphalt outside Prescott's in time to see Alice Michaels pull into a parking spot near the front door. I walked to join her. I felt the muscles in my upper back and neck tense as I braced for another difficult conversation.

CHAPTER TWO

I don't know what it is, Josie," Alice Michaels said, gently stroking the antique doll's feather-soft auburn hair, "but just touching this little beauty takes my mind off my troubles."

The Bébé Bru Jne doll from Selma's collection *was* a beauty, marred by a poorly repaired ragged crack on the back of her head. I tried to think how to respond to Alice's comment. Her troubles were no longer private, that was for sure, not after Wes published all the gory details, yet I was surprised she was talking about her situation so openly. She sat across from me at the guest table in the front office where everyone could listen in. From Gretchen's expression, I could tell that she was all ears. She loved being in the know. Maybe, I thought, Alice didn't care what anyone thought. Or maybe she felt that she was among friends, that at Prescott's, she'd be safe from criticism. Regardless, she looked fine, the same as always. Her dyed blond chin-length hair was newly coiffed. Her makeup was subtle and flawless. Her navy blue gabardine suit and white silk blouse fit her like a dream.

"Have you heard anything more?" I asked, hoping my tone conveyed my genuine concern, not just my curiosity.

She looked up from the doll and met my eyes. "No, but they always say the victim is the last to know, right?"

She thinks of herself as a victim, I noted, wondering if it was true. Was she being set up as a scapegoat? Was Lenny? In his article, Wes had quoted an unnamed senior official in the district attorney's office as saying the two of them, and maybe additional employees and vendors as well, were going to be indicted within days, maybe within hours. Grim. Alice was watching me, gauging my reaction to her words. I tried to think of something kind or supportive to say.

"It's no fun waiting for someone else to make a decision about your future."

"Especially for a control freak like me," she said, trying to smile. "Whatever. Instead of spinning my wheels, I'll admire this young lady's complexion—classic peaches and cream. What talent the makers had! Tell me about her."

"With pleasure. How about a cup of tea? Would you like one?"

Her nose wrinkled. "Tea—awful stuff. Maudles your insides. I never go near it. I'll take a coffee, though, if any is available."

"Absolutely," Gretchen said. "I'll bring some gingersnaps, too."

"Thanks, Gretchen." I turned my attention back to the doll. "This doll, which is one of twenty-three that make up the Farmington collection, is a Bébé Bru Jne." I pronounced the tongue-tangling word as a cross between June and gin. "Her coloration is typical for the style, and as I'm sure you know, nineteenth-century dolls in unused condition are as rare as all get-out. Her head is made of bisque, pink tinted and unglazed, a proprietary formula. Her wig is made of human hair, probably original to the doll. Ditto her clothes—the white underdress appears to be fine cotton. The blue overdress is probably made of silk. Once we complete the appraisal, we'll know for certain what the materials are and whether they're original. Both dresses are hand-stitched. Unfortunately, at some point her head got cracked and someone repaired it, not well. They didn't use archival-quality products, and significant yellowing has occurred. The only good news is that the crack is hidden by her wig."

"A cracked head! The poor girl. Still, I think she's spectacular, cracked head and all. I look forward to holding her very frequently." Alice paused and sighed. "My mother never let me play with her doll collection, did I ever tell you that? They were to be admired from afar, but never touched." She snorted, a humorless sound. "Now here I am doing the same darn thing, building a collection to give to my granddaughter, knowing that her mother, Ms. Attila the Hun, won't let her play with them." She shook her head. "Funny how what goes around comes around, isn't it?" She waved it away. "Old news is boring news—throw it out with the trash. All I can do is hope that Brooke loves the collection as much as I do—even if she won't be allowed to play with it."

"I bet she has other dolls, not collectibles, that she can use," I said, hoping it was true.

"Dozens," Alice acknowledged. She looked at me as an impish smile transformed her countenance from polished adult to mischievous child. "When I was about seven, I sewed myself a sock doll. I used cotton scraps from my mother's quilting basket for the stuffing and for her dress. I named her Hilda, after my favorite teacher, Miss Horne. I painted Miss Horne's face on her, too—big blue eyes and a bright red heart-shaped mouth. I even stitched brown yarn on her head for hair. I loved that doll. I loved that teacher." She smiled wider. "When my sister saw it, she wanted one, too." Her eyes twinkled. "I charged her a dollar." She chuckled. "I left a little opening in one of Hilda's seams, a hidey-hole under her dress for my diary key. My sister searched and searched for that key and never found it. Ha!" She shook her head, a rueful expression on her face. "Jeesh! That's more than fifty years ago, Josie, and I remember it like it was yesterday. Fifty years ago. Life was simpler then, that's for sure. All I had to worry about back then was hiding my diary from my sister."

"Hilda wasn't included in the collection we appraised, was she? Do you still have her?"

"You betcha! And she's still my favorite. I didn't include her because I know she has no value—she's just a handmade kid's toy." Alice handed over the Bébé Bru Jne with a sigh. "I know you can't say what you'll charge for Selma's dolls until you've finished the appraisal, but are you confident it's a good investment?"

"Absolutely. While there's no guarantee, prices on dolls have been going up steadily for years, and I have no reason to think that will change anytime soon." I smiled at her. "I know you're impatient, but these things take time. We'll know more soon."

Gretchen set a tray on the guest table. As I thanked her, Alice reached for her coffee.

"Do you think my granddaughter will like them?" she asked.

"Of course!" I said, surprised at the question. "What little girl wouldn't?"

"I suppose." She sounded unconvinced. "Can you guess which doll is most valuable?"

"Until the appraisal is complete, I really can't. That said, Selma kept meticulous records, so I know how much she paid for each doll and where she purchased them. It appears that none is unique, and most of them have flaws, like that Bébé Bru Jne's poorly repaired head. Of course, you know what a lack of scarcity and poor condition do to value."

"I sure do." Alice turned to assess the dolls lined up on Sasha's desk. Sasha, my chief appraiser, was about to begin the complex appraisal. "Those are Selma's dolls, too, right?" Alice asked, pointing at the far end of Sasha's desk where a rugged-looking, decked-out-for-jungle-combat male doll leaned against Sasha's monitor next to a dramatically carved and boldly painted cottonwood doll with a fierce expression. "What are they?"

"According to Selma's inventory, this one is a second-round prototype of G.I. Joe."

"Which I suspect is less valuable than a prototype from the first round."

"Much. Assuming it is what I think it is, instead of being worth a quarter of a million dollars, which is what an original prototype would sell for, it's worth about five thousand."

She whistled softly. "That's quite a difference. Isn't it amazing that collectors are willing to pay that much for a doll?"

"Dolls have proven to be a solid investment over the years. By the way, as an aside, G.I. Joe has never been called a doll. G.I. Joe is an action figure." I smiled. "When this fellow was made, he wasn't even called G.I. Joe. Three prototypes were created: Rocky the Marine, Skip the Sailor, and Ace the Pilot."

Alice smiled, too, a small one. "He looks like a Rocky. How about that other one? What is it?"

"It's called a kachina. It's native to the Hopi." The doll's face was hand-carved with an open mouth and bug eyes. It appeared to be half mythical beast and half bovine. Horns and feathers shot out from its head like rays of sun. Green serpentine swaths were painted across the nose and cheeks. The chest was dark red. The doll had presence, conveying drama and a sense of danger. "The dolls were created to represent and honor ancestors. The elders used them to teach younger generations about their ancestors' spirits and to solicit their blessings."

"It looks like you'll be expanding my horizons, Josie. Up 'til now, I've limited my collection to European dolls."

"Nothing says you have to buy the entire lot. I'll let you cherry-pick."

"Thanks, Josie! That's sweet of you, but I want the whole kit and caboodle. Who knows which ones my granddaughter will fall in love with. For all I know, it might be that kachina. Just because I prefer traditional dolls, traditional, that is, to me, doesn't mean she will." She sighed, maybe thinking of her granddaughter. "How much is it worth, do you think?"

"Not so much. It's about a hundred years old, but only kachinas that are three hundred years old, or older, have significant value. Kachinas from the seventeenth century in fine condition go for nearly three hundred thousand dollars. I expect that this one will sell for around a thousand."

"The differential is astonishing."

"Supply and demand."

She kept her eyes on the dolls. "Poor Selma," she said. "Did you ever meet her?"

"No. I just met her daughters this week for the first time."

She nodded. "That's how I knew to contact you. I asked about buying the collection directly from them. They told me they sold you the dolls. Smart girls, I told them. Josie's the best. I'm just as glad, to tell you the truth. I hate doing business with heirs."

"It can be challenging . . . all that emotion. Jamie and Lorna seem to be having a tough time deciding what to keep and what to sell, and who can blame them? Clearing out a house is difficult enough under any circumstances. It's extra hard when your mom's only been dead a week and everywhere you look you see memories."

"Especially when she dies so suddenly. Drunk drivers . . . they make me so mad I could spit."

"Me, too," I agreed. "It's got to be extra challenging for them so far from their own homes. They need to get everything settled this week so they can get back to Houston."

Alice shook her head. "It's a terrible situation no matter how you cut it. So the girls called you in and now they're having a hard time deciding what to sell. I bet Lorna's the holdup, isn't she? She's a weeping-willow sentimentalist. Jamie's no waffler, that's for sure."

I laughed. "In your job, I guess you have to be able to read people in nothing flat, right?" I said, using the trick my dad had taught me back when I was in junior high school and found myself scrunched between a gossipy rock named Cheryl and a tattletaling hard place named Lynn. Never gossip, he warned me. When in doubt, talk about process, not content.

"In less than nothing flat," she said. "So what did they decide?"

"To sell a collection of cobalt glassware that had been packed away in the attic forever and some old wooden tools, you know, planes and levels and the like. The tools belonged to their grandfather who dabbled in carpentry, and just as with the glassware, they feel no emotional connection to them. An old collection of teapots, too, nothing rare."

"I know those teapots. They're ugly, if you ask me. I never understood why Selma liked them. That's why they make chocolate and vanilla ice cream, right? Who knows why any of us like anything in particular. One of the mysteries of life." She shrugged. "And the girls sold you the dolls?"

"Most of them," I repeated, nodding. "There are some they're holding back, sentimental favorites, they said, like your Hilda."

"Good for them. What do you think, Josie? Shall I give you a check now?"

"Let's wait until we know how much we're talking about before we do anything," I said, wanting to avoid agreeing to a deal that might soon be voided by a court.

"Sounds reasonable," she said.

Eric, my facilities manager, stepped into the office from the ware-house. In his midtwenties, he still looked and carried himself like a teenager; he was tall and gangly and reed thin. Eric had worked for me since I opened Prescott's Antiques and Auctions seven years earlier, part-time while he was still in high school, then full-time as soon as he graduated. He was conscientious and dedicated, sometimes too much so, treating even the most routine or mundane task as if it were his top priority.

"I just unloaded those rocking horses," Eric told me, after saying hello to Alice, referring to a set of three I'd just bought from some empty nesters looking to downsize. "I'll head to the Farmingtons' now."

"Great. Bring plenty of newsprint for the glassware and tools, and wrap each doll in flannel, okay?"

"And I'll cushion everything in peanuts."

"Eric!" Gretchen called as he turned to go. "I wanted to let you know that Hank loved Grace's catnip heart."

He flashed an awkward smile. "I'll tell Grace."

Gretchen giggled as Eric, obviously embarrassed, slipped away.

"What's that about?" Alice asked.

"Grace is Eric's girlfriend," Gretchen explained. "Hank is our cat. Grace made Hank a big, heart-shaped, burlap toy, filled with catnip. With a feather." She laughed. "Eric is a complete dog person, or he used to be." She turned to me. "You should have seen him tossing the heart to Hank this morning and chattering away as if Hank and he were old friends."

"Eric?" I asked in mock amazement.

"I know!" Gretchen said. "It must be Grace's influence."

"Combined with Hank's charm," I agreed. I turned to Alice. "Hank's a lover-boy, a real sweetheart."

"Nice—but can we veer back to the central issue?" Alice asked. "My radar is beeping. Did I hear Eric say he was going for more of the Farmington dolls?"

I smiled. "Yup! I only had enough packing material to bring back the teapots and eleven dolls this morning. Eric will get the rest now, along with the other collections I bought—the glassware and tools."

"I don't know how you do it, Josie. Glassware . . . teapots . . . tools . . . you seem to know everything about everything."

I laughed. "Hardly! I just know the questions to ask and have secret weapons in the form of Sasha and Fred, my appraisers."

"Modest as ever." She turned to Gretchen. "Your big day is close, I hear."

"Three weeks, five days, and three hours—but who's counting!"

Alice calculated for two seconds. "That's June fifteenth, around six thirty. I love June weddings!"

"Me, too," Gretchen said, giggling. "It's going to be fabulous—homey and intimate—about fifty people in my fiancé's folks' backyard up in Maine."

"They toyed with eloping to Hawaii," I remarked, "and robbing all of us who love them the opportunity to witness their marriage."

"A thousand years ago, I eloped," Alice said. "Not to a beach, cry shame, just to City Hall. Back then, girls who got pregnant got married pronto." She shook her head as if she were shaking off a bad memory. "I don't recommend it, but it's probably better than those pretentious megaweddings, all staged pomp and no personality. Better to be with people you love, and no one else. Fifty people sounds about right."

The chimes sounded as Sasha stepped inside.

As soon as she saw Alice, she said, "Sorry," her voice barely audible, as if she'd intruded into a private conversation and expected to be chastised.

"No problem," I said, just for something to say.

Sasha's manner changed as abruptly as if a switch had been flipped the second she spotted the eleven dolls lined up on her desk. Place an antique in Sasha's orbit and she was transformed from scared mouse into confident expert.

"Wow!" Sasha said. "Are these from the Farmington collection? They're gorgeous!"

"Eric just left to get the rest."

"I'm buying them all from Prescott's," Alice said.

"Which means that appraising them is your new top priority," I told Sasha.

"Okay," Sasha said with a quick smile. She tucked a strand of lank hair behind her ear.

"So where do you start?" Alice asked her.

"By authenticating and valuing each doll." Sasha picked up a character doll, another Bru. "She's spectacular, isn't she?"

"Well, I look forward to calling them my own. Right now, though, I've got to mosey. I'm off to my lawyer's office, no doubt to hear more bad news. Are you sure you don't want some earnest money to guarantee that I get first dibs? I don't want someone else to swoop in while I'm not looking."

I laughed. "You collectors! There's no need."

"I insist," she said. "I'll sleep better if I leave a deposit. How about if we label it a refundable right of first refusal, so if there's some problem with provenance or you discover one of the dolls had been owned by Queen Victoria, or something equally lofty, you're not on the hook for any certain price, or even to sell it at all, and if I change my mind for whatever reason, I'm not committed to buy something I no longer want."

I thought about it for a few seconds. Until I knew which way the prosecutorial wind was blowing, I didn't want to commit to selling her the dolls even with a we'll-figure-it-out-later price, and this seemed to be a face-saving, nonconfrontational way to achieve that objective.

"Done!" I said.

She pulled a brown leather checkbook folder from her purse and sat at the round guest table to write out the check. I asked Gretchen to prepare a receipt. The second Gretchen's eyes were fixed on her computer monitor, I turned to Cara, caught her attention, and winked.

"I have an errand," I said and winked again. "I'll be back in about an hour."

Cara, her blue eyes twinkling, winked back. She knew what I was up to—I wanted to find some Hawaiian-themed goodies for Gretchen's surprise bridal shower. I had ten days, but I didn't know how much trouble I was going to have finding what I had in mind, so I wanted to check out the local party store pronto.

"Thanks," Alice told Gretchen as she accepted the receipt, tucking it in her purse without even glancing at it. "Now I have bragging rights."

The wind chimes sounded. A tall green bean of a man with a mane of sandy brown hair and earnest brown eyes walked in. I knew him by sight; everyone did. He was Pennington Moreau, the intrepid adventurer, award-winning athlete, and on-air legal personality for Rocky Point's TV station, WXFS. Penn, as he was known, was as well regarded for his record-setting, multimillion-dollar, long-distance balloon rides, iron man triathlon wins, and high-stakes poker games as he was for his illuminating commentary. Penn had a gift for translating complex legal issues into common English, using engaging examples and self-deprecating humor. He used his twice-weekly two-minute segments to explain things like the city's responsibility to repair beach erosion after a brutal nor'easter ("Where people like me keep rebuilding, an example of hope trumping experience"); how a restaurant dishwasher had used his computer skills to set up shop selling fake IDs ("Using computer skills so sophisticated, it makes you wonder why he stayed washing dishes"); the government's right to regulate gambling in private homes ("Like last month's poker game where I lost my shirt"); and the long-term impact on building the new high school if voters turned down the proposed bond issue ("Ultimately, lower property values, even for those of us who keep adding real property by trucking in tons of sand to counteract the effects of beach erosion"). Although he had to be in his late forties, his loose-limbed gait, full head of hair, and unlined face made him appear younger.

"What on earth are you doing here, Penn?" Alice asked, leaning in for a butterfly kiss.

He kissed Alice's cheek. "I'm looking for you, gorgeous! Got a sec?"

"For you? Of course. Anytime." Alice pointed to the dolls on Sasha's desk. "Look what I just bought! Twenty-three beauties."

"Nice! Are they rare?"

"Rare enough," she said proudly.

"I like your style, Alice. Always have."

She smiled. "Do you know Josie?" she asked him, and when he said he hadn't had the pleasure, she introduced us.

"I enjoy your reports," I told him.

"Thanks," he said, grinning broadly. "Can I steal Alice for a sec?"

"We're done anyway," she said. She waved around the office. " 'Bye, all!"

Penn held the door for her, and she followed him out into the warm afternoon. Glancing at the thermometer fastened to the outside of the big window overlooking the parking lot, I saw it was seventy-five degrees, a glorious May day. I watched them walk to the center of the lot and stop. Penn said something, opening his arms and flipping his palms up—I have no choice, the gesture communicated. Alice shook her head, no, no. He spoke again, grasping her upper arms and shaking her a little, then dropping his hands and waiting for her reply. She looked away, toward the stone wall across the road, then smoothed her hair, though not one strand was out of place. She inhaled so deeply I could see her chest move. She pulled her shoulders back and raised her chin as she said something, pride stiffening her spine, it seemed. She reached a hand out to touch his arm, an appeal. He shook his head, brushed her arm aside, and strode off to his car, a cream-colored vintage Jaguar. She stood and watched. *Poor Alice,* I thought.

I said good-bye to everyone in the office and stepped outside. Penn was just pulling out of the lot, turning right, east, toward the church, toward the ocean. Alice watched him until his car was out of sight, then turned to face me. We stood, the silence lingering awkwardly between us. A muscle twitched in her neck. I guessed Penn had been the bearer of more bad news. If I were her, I wouldn't want to talk about it, at least not with a relative stranger like me.

"Bye-bye," I said aiming for a light tone. "I'll let you know when the appraisal's done." I turned away and hurried toward the last row of the parking lot, where I'd parked.

"Penn didn't want to blindside me," she said in a brittle monotone.

I stopped and looked at her. Her eyes burned into mine. Earlier she'd sounded philosophical. Now she sounded angry.

"He said he came to tell me in person because we're friends. Ha. Some friend. His segment tonight will explain what my impending indictment for fraud means to the alleged victims, and whether they have any recourse against me personally. They're giving him double time. Four whole minutes."

"Oh, Alice," I said. "I'm so sorry."

"Don't you agree it was thoughtful of him to come?" she asked sarcastically. "He didn't want to tell me on the phone, but he wanted me to know. So considerate! He even went to the trouble of tracking me down. Not so much trouble, of course. All he had to do was call my office. My assistant told him where he could find me. Still, he didn't have to do it. Penn's a peach, all right. A real peach. Damn him. Damn his eyes."

"Isn't there anything you can do to stop him?"

"No. He said he has a source at the attorney general's office. Apparently I'm about to be arrest—." She broke off as a crack reverberated nearby. "What was that?"

I recognized the sound. Gunfire. Someone was shooting at us.

"It's a gun!" I shouted as I dropped to the ground. "Get down, Alice!"

Another loud, sharp clap shattered the quiet. Then another. *Think,* I told myself. *Where are the shots coming from?* I knew that sound traveled and reverberated and bounced off solid objects, making it hard to trace under the best of circumstances and probably impossible now, but concentrating on finding the shooter was all I could do to try to save us. I peered into the closest slice of forest and saw only pines and brambles and forsythia bushes swaying in the light breeze. More shots were fired. I scooted to the front of my car and looked across the street, past the stone wall, into the dense growth that stretched from the road to the interstate almost a mile to the north. No glint of silver or unexpected movement caught my eye. I crawled around my car until the dirt path that led to the church came into view. Nothing. I looked back at Alice. She hadn't moved. She looked half shocked and half confused, as if she simply couldn't process what was happening.

"Get down!" I yelled again, patting the air for emphasis.

She didn't move. She wasn't looking at me, and I wasn't certain she heard me. It was as if she were a million miles away, frozen in some private memory.

"Alice!" I hollered as another shot rang out. "Get down! Duck!"

She grimaced and grunted. She rocked forward, falling against her car as she uttered a low guttural groan. As splotches of red spread over her chest and stomach, her eyes found mine, and she sank to the ground.

CHAPTER THREE

Alice!" I hollered, sick with fear, certain she was dead.

I leapt to my feet and dashed to where Alice lay on her back staring at the sky. Her gaze was fixed. Believing that miracles sometimes happen, I pressed my hands against her wounds. Blood oozed between my fingers, but the flow had stopped. Her heart wasn't pumping. I started CPR. As I worked, tears filled my eyes and spilled onto my cheeks.

"Josie?" Gretchen called from the doorway. "What's going on?"

"Call nine-one-one," I shouted over my shoulder. "There were shots. Alice's been hit. Stay inside and away from windows."

I heard the front door close.

Please, God, I prayed, *don't let her be dead.* I stayed on my knees, continuing the rhythmic pushing and breathing until my wrists began to throb and my chest began to ache. I prayed and pushed and breathed, and prayed some more.

An ambulance whipped into the parking lot, and a young man bolted out of the cab, shouting, "Are you hurt?"

I shook my head and fell back, my chest heaving, my wrist muscles tingling, my fingers numb. After a few seconds, I crawled out of his way. Another man, this one older, ran up carrying a black case. I hugged my knees to my chest, then shut my eyes, trying to catch my breath. I felt disconnected from time and place, hyperalert yet fuzzy, as if I were trapped in the dark confusion of a bad dream.

"Josie?" Gretchen whispered. I hadn't heard her approach. She touched my elbow, and I opened my eyes. "Are you all right? Can you stand up?"

I allowed her to help me up.

Two police vehicles, one a blue patrol car, the other a black SUV, roared into the lot, their lights flashing. ROCKY POINT POLICE DEPARTMENT was emblazoned on both, white text outlined in gold. Police Chief Ellis Hunter stepped out of the SUV, took in the scene at a glance, nodded at me, then jogged toward the paramedics as they lifted Alice onto a gurney I hadn't noticed them bring out of the ambulance. They wheeled her to the back of their vehicle, then joined Ellis in a loose huddle. *Alice is dead,* I thought, sickened by shock and sadness. If she'd been alive, the paramedics wouldn't be taking time to chat; they'd be rushing her to the hospital. I looked away, tears striping my cheeks. Gretchen stroked my arm.

"Thank you," I said without looking at her, grateful for her quiet support.

"It's okay," she said.

"No. It's not."

"You're right. It's not."

Ellis turned in my direction. He was tall, with regular features, weathered skin, knowing eyes, and a confident stride. He wore a lightweight tweed jacket and a brown tie. His scar, a jagged line near his right eye, looked bloodred under the midday sun. He'd been Rocky Point's police chief for about two years, ever since he retired as a New York City homicide detective. He explained that he'd taken the job to see if Norman Rockwell had it right about small towns. Ellis, who'd been dating my landlady, neighbor, and best bud, Zoë, for almost as long as he'd been here, was my friend, but he didn't look friendly as he walked toward me, his eyes boring into mine; he looked purposeful and stern.

"You're not injured?" he asked.

"No. Alice's dead, isn't she?"

"Yes. I'm sorry, Josie."

I clamped my eyes closed. "The shooter aimed at her, Ellis. No bullets even came close to me."

"How far away were you?"

"Far. Five car lengths. More."

"Did you know her well?" he asked.

"Sure. Did you?"

"No, not personally."

It took a second for his meaning to register. "Of course . . . you've been helping the attorney general investigate her."

"You should go inside and clean up," he said, deftly turning the subject, revealing nothing, as usual. "I'll join you in a few minutes." He nodded at Gretchen, telling her without words to escort me inside, to help me cope.

"Come on, Josie," Gretchen said, and I let myself be led away from the bloody, deadly scene.

Twenty minutes later, wearing a Prescott's T-shirt and the spare pants I keep in my office since my slacks always seem to get dirty crawling under furniture or traipsing through dusty attics, I sat on my yellow love seat. Ellis sat across from me in one of the wing chairs sipping coffee. I held a cup of tea, grateful for the warmth.

In response to his questions, I told him what little I knew about the shooting.

"How would you describe Alice's mood?" he asked.

"She seemed remarkably even-keeled about her legal troubles. Way more calm than I would have been."

"What did she say about the situation?"

"She was upset, thinking she was about to be arrested and that Penn was going to talk about it on air."

"How long have you known her?" he asked after I'd repeated as much of our conversation as I could recall.

"For years. She was a good customer. She bought five rare dolls at various auctions over the last six years. One from Frisco's in New York. That's my old firm. She had me bid on her behalf."

"How come?"

"Bidding with the big boys is a major league sport. It's easy to get caught up in the moment. You don't want to end up paying more than you have to, but you can't delay bidding or you'll miss out. It's tense when you're playing with real money."

Ellis nodded. "Sounds like she was a serious collector."

"That's a fair assessment," I said. "We appraised her dolls for insurance purposes about a year ago. The collection is comprised of twenty-five dolls and was valued at nearly four hundred thousand dollars."

He whistled, low and long.

"The most valuable one was the doll we acquired from Frisco's. A French Triste Bébé, which is a nineteenth-century doll with a sad expression. It's in near-perfect condition and included several pieces of original clothing and a human hair wig. We valued it at about thirty thousand dollars."

"Thirty thousand dollars for one doll."

"The doll and all the bits and pieces, and everything in excellent condition, yes." I closed my eyes for a moment, then opened them and looked out the window, past my old maple toward the church. "Alice gave us a deposit check today. She intended to buy all of Selma Farmington's dolls."

"How much will the collection sell for?"

"I won't know until the appraisal is complete. It looks like Selma chose her dolls because she loved them, not for the investment." I explained how chipped paint, broken limbs, cracks, breaks, mars, flawed repairs, missing garments, and uncertain provenance reduced value.

He jotted a note. "Why do you think Alice was killed?" he asked.

"I don't know."

"Why here? Today? On your property?"

I drank some tea, then looked at him. "If Penn was right and she was about to be arrested, maybe someone decided to kill her rather than risk the chance that she'd talk to get herself a deal."

"So maybe she had a partner?"

"I don't know, Ellis. I just can't believe the Ponzi scheme charges are true. Alice wasn't a fly-by-night sort of gal. She grew up around here. She was everyone's first call when you needed someone to lend her name to your charity or to donate money. She was, as my mom might have put it, good people."

"What do you know about her business?" he asked, changing the subject.

"Almost nothing. Did you see Wes's article in today's paper?"

"Sure. She denied everything very neatly."

Ellis was right—Alice flatly denied personal culpability—but he was wrong, too. She didn't deny that something was wrong. Wes quoted her as saying that she'd had no choice but to fire her chief operating officer, Lenny Einsohn. "If a Ponzi scheme was being run out of my office, Lenny has to be behind it. In a business that bears my name, even the tiniest whiff of impropriety is unacceptable. I wish Lenny all the best, but I need to think about my company's clients. I can't worry about one employee who either took his hand off the wheel or worse." From the timeline Wes had included in a sidebar, Lenny must have got whiplash, he'd been in such a hurry to sue Alice for character defamation and libel. Now there was a jumble of lawsuits and on-the-record allegations and off-the-record implications. It was a mess.

Wes quoted Ian Landers, too. I didn't know Ian to talk to, but I knew his wife, Martha. Ian was some kind of day trader; Martha was the manager of the best day spa in town and collected eighteenth-century British sterling silver salt spoons. She'd bought several spoons from me, and I'd spent many relaxing hours at her spa. Martha and I had tried to get together for lunch a couple of times, but it hadn't worked out. We were two busy people who'd wanted to explore whether our friendly acquaintanceship could blossom into genuine friendship, but so far, we hadn't found the time.

Ian told Wes that they'd lost most of their retirement savings investing with Alice's company and it was all Alice's fault—he and Martha, he explained, had been good friends with Alice, and she'd betrayed their trust. When Wes asked Alice to respond, she'd said that while she couldn't comment on individual clients, some people make risky investment decisions and then, when the risk doesn't pay off, cry foul. According to Wes, Ian called Alice a blight on the community that needed to be squashed like a bug. Ouch.

Ellis was looking at me, waiting for me to respond to his comment about Wes's article. He seemed to have all the time in the world.

"I don't have a clue about anything, Ellis, not a clue."

"You're not an ADM Financial client?"

"No."

"Why not?"

"My dad was a very conservative investor. He taught me to keep most of my savings in government-backed securities, I-Bonds and the like. That approach suits me, too."

Ellis nodded. He finished his coffee and placed his cup on the butler's table. "Did Alice mention any trouble she was having with anyone?"

"She called her daughter-in-law, Ms. Attila the Hun." I shook my head.

"You said she got the news she was about to be arrested from Pennington Moreau, the TV lawyer. Do you know him?"

"I met him for the first time today. I know his reports. I like them."

Ellis shifted position. "I hate to ask you to relive the shooting, Josie, but I need to take you through it one step at a time. Some new memory may come to you. Start when you stepped outside."

I felt my muscles tighten and raised and lowered my shoulders, hoping to ease the discomfort, then took a deep breath, closed my eyes, and thought back. Vivid memories came to me. As soon as I'd opened the outside door I'd smelled the moist sweet aroma of fresh-cut grass. Fluffy clouds dotted the baby blue sky. The sun warmed my skin.

"Okay," I said, opening my eyes. I slid my cup onto the butler's table and stared at a spot on the Oriental carpet, a beige dot near the gold fringe, and reported. I didn't remember anything new.

When I finished, I raised my eyes and glanced around. There was my rooster collection in the corner cabinet. There was my desk and the window that gave me the view of the old maple tree. I touched the damask fabric on the love seat. Everything was familiar, yet it all looked and felt different, as if I'd been away for a long, long time. It was discombobulating. I rubbed my arms as if I were cold.

"Thank you, Josie," Ellis said. He paused, then asked, "Are you going to keep the business open today?"

I glanced at my grandfather clock, a Daniel Chessman original. It was after three. "I don't know. When I'm upset, my inclination is always to work. Although I gotta say a hot bath and a Blue Martini sound pretty good right about now."

"Before you head home, I'm going to need you to come to the station and give a statement."

I leaned back. "I really cared about Alice, Ellis. No joke. If I could help you find her killer, I would, but I don't know anything else."

"It won't take long, Josie, but it's got to happen. I need the formal record. On our way, I'm going to ask Doc Volmer to give you a once-over, to check you out for shock and scrapes and bruises and the like."

I shook my head. "I don't need a doctor. I'm fine. I'm shook up and sad, but overall, I'm fine."

He nodded. "We can skip the doctor, although I don't recommend it, but we can't skip the statement. Sorry, Josie."

I recognized a losing battle when I saw one. Protocols were protocols and that was that.

"Okay," I said.

"I need to talk to your staff for a minute."

"Fred is at the design museum doing some research, and Eric is at the Farmingtons' packing up some things. Everyone else should be here."

I walked him downstairs and into the front office. As we passed through the warehouse I looked to the left, toward the spacious quarters that Hank, Prescott's Maine Coon cat, called home. I wanted a little cuddle, but that would have to wait. Per my insurance company's regulations, unless you were a bonded employee, you couldn't be anywhere inside my building unaccompanied, not even if you were a police chief on official business. I pushed open the heavy door that led from the warehouse into the main office.

"You're back," I said, spotting Fred, Prescott's second-in-command appraiser, seated at his desk. "Did you have trouble getting past the police line?"

"Not really. They had me park on the street and walked me in along the perimeter."

"Has someone filled you in?"

He nodded but didn't specify who or what. I looked around, gauging everyone's reaction. Cara sat with her hands laced together in a tight little knot. Her eyes were moist. Gretchen was rubbing the knuckles of her right hand with the fingers of her left. Her normally sparkling eyes were clouded. Sasha twirled a strand of her shoulder-length hair into a tight thin twist. Fred leaned back in his chair, sucking on the earpiece of his cool-kid square black glasses, attentive and observant. Everyone was watching me, waiting for me to speak.

"You all know Chief Hunter," I said. "He has a few questions."

Ellis asked who'd heard what, whether they'd seen anything, and if they had any information that might help the police identify the shooter. Except for Fred, who'd just returned, they'd all heard the shots. No one had seen anything. No one knew anything. Six minutes after Ellis began questioning them, he finished. He handed out business cards in case they thought of anything later, told us he'd instruct the officers stationed outside to allow us to drive our cars out of the lot, added that he'd meet me at the station house in twenty minutes, and left.

I stood by the window and watched him stride across the lot. Griff, a uniformed officer close to retirement, stood talking to a young woman with short brown hair wheeling a rolling black pilot case, a crime scene technician, I guessed. Another uniformed officer, a woman I'd never seen before, was stretching yellow and black tape around orange traffic cones, cordoning off the asphalt area where Alice had died. A tow truck idled off to the side, ready to remove her car.

I wanted to talk to Ty, Ty Alverez, my boyfriend, to hear his words of comfort, to feel his strength. Before I could, I knew I needed to say something to my staff about the murder. I wanted to go home, crawl under the covers, and wait for summer, but I couldn't. I had a responsibility, as Prescott's owner, as their boss. I made a mental note to call Eric, then took in a deep breath and looked at each of them in turn.

"Alice Michaels was more than a good customer," I began. "She was a friend. I know you are all aware that she's been under investigation for mismanaging her clients' money. I don't know anything about that. All I know is that her dealings with Prescott's have always been aboveboard. I tell you this because I want you to know what I told the police and what I'll tell any reporters who ask. That to my direct knowledge she was a proud member of the Rocky Point community and a loyal supporter of Prescott's. Period." I paused, pleased to see that Sasha had stopped twirling her hair and Gretchen had stopped worrying her hands. "If you have any factual information that can help the police catch her killer, it's your duty to share it with them. If you don't, if all you have is opinions, then probably you should keep them to yourself, but that's up to you. As to the media, they're going to be on this like white on rice, and it's solely your decision what, if anything, you tell them. If you talk to them, remember to stress that you do not speak for Prescott's. You may not talk to reporters on company time or on company phones. You may not e-mail reporters using company computers. Reporters are not allowed on Prescott's property without my permission. Any questions?"

No one spoke.

"Okay, then. Out of respect for the tragic death that just occurred, and to give us all time to process the event, Prescott's is officially closed for the day. If you need to take tomorrow off, that's fine. Cara, please set the phone to the standard night message. I have a couple of calls to make, then I'll lock up. Go home, everyone."

Fred, a New York City transplant who'd brought his big-city style to laid-back New Hampshire, slipped his glasses on and loosened his skinny black tie. "Do we have to go?" he asked. Fred, a night owl, often started his workday close to noon and stayed on into the evening. "It's better for me to work."

"Me, too," Gretchen said. "I mean, I liked Alice, too, but I have things to get ready for the tag sale setup."

I nodded. "Right—and Eric told me we have two temps coming in tomorrow morning to help. You're welcome to stay. Or not. Business can take a backseat for a day. Don't feel any pressure." I looked around. "I don't mean to dictate to anyone one way or the other. If you want to work, carry on. If you need some time to yourselves, feel free to call it a day—and to take tomorrow off. Personally, I'm going to make my calls and pack it in. I'll probably be in tomorrow, but I'm not making any promises."

I dashed up the stairs to call Ty at his weeklong strategy session in D.C., and I got lucky. Ty, a training manager for Homeland Security, was between meetings.

"I wish I could blink my eyes and be there for you," he said after I filled him in. "The way things are going, I won't be home until

Friday—I'd hoped we'd be done by Thursday, but no such luck. Will you be okay? All you have to do is say the word and I'm outta here."

"You're so wonderful, Ty . . . but I'm fine. I need to give my statement down at the station. Then I'm going home. God, I want a hot bath."

"You can't wash away what you saw."

"You're right, but it will help. It always does. I'm supposed to have dinner at Zoë's. That will help, too."

"I couldn't stand it if anything happened to you, Josie." His tone was low and urgent.

Tears sprang to my eyes. "Ditto. I love you, Ty."

"I love you, too, Josie. I'll call you later."

I decided to call Eric en route to the police station and was halfway down the spiral stairs when Cara's voice crackled over the intercom.

"Josie," she said, "Wes Smith on line one."

I considered ignoring his call, then thought better of it and trudged back to my desk. I knew what Wes wanted—information. I also knew that if I didn't give him some now, he wouldn't give me any later, and I knew that once the initial shock of witnessing Alice's murder had passed, I'd want as much as he would give me. Someone had killed a woman, a client, a friend, in my parking lot. My panicky upset had already begun to morph into simmering anger. Just below the still-roiling terror and horror lurked a more primal emotion—rage. No way was it okay to shoot someone on my property and get away with it. Wes, I knew, was part terrier and part bloodhound. I was amazed, and sometimes alarmed, at the facts he could dig up and the lies he could sniff out. It was a reasonable guess that he already had information to share.

CHAPTER FOUR

What did you see?" Wes asked, skipping hello, like always.

"I'm fine. Thanks for asking, Wes."

"I know you're fine, Josie. I picked that much up from my police scanner. So what did you see?"

"Nothing," I said, closing my eyes against the memories. I didn't want to revisit Alice's befuddled expression or remember how the patches of blood had blossomed across her chest.

"Josie!" he whined. "You had to see something!"

"I saw her shot, Wes. I didn't see who did it."

"Did you look?"

"Of course I looked!"

"And?" he prodded.

"What have you found out so far?" I asked, using a technique I'd learned from him years earlier: If you don't want to answer a question, ask one instead.

"The police say she was at your place to buy some dolls. What kind?"

"I'll tell you," I said, aware that Wes was using his gift as a reporter to draw me out, "but first you need to promise not to quote me."

"Josie!" he protested, sounding shocked.

"It's our usual arrangement, Wes. Take it or leave it."

Wes sighed, and I knew he hoped to convey his deep disappointment in having to agree to my patently unreasonable terms. I didn't comment.

"Okay," he said, stretching out the word to communicate his begrudging acceptance.

"The dolls are old, but not special."

"How much are they worth?"

"I'm guesstimating somewhere around fifty thousand dollars, but I don't know for sure. We haven't appraised them yet."

"Fifty big ones . . . for dolls?"

"That's not a lot of money for rare dolls. Alice's own collection is worth much more, around four hundred thousand."

Wes low-whistled. "Yowzi."

"So who inherits Alice's estate?"

"Why? What do you know?" he countered.

"Nothing. Just that she had some personal assets. Like her house, which is on the ocean." I swiveled to face my window. "It occurred to me that maybe her murder has nothing to do with the Ponzi scheme thing, that's all."

"Gotcha. Once we know who inherits, we can check his or her alibi and go from there. Good one, Josie!"

"It's so awful, Wes."

"Yeah," he said, sounding as if he were champing at the bit. "I'll check it out. What else?"

"Nothing," I said. "Or rather, nothing in particular. I shouldn't think there'll be a shortage of suspects, not when everyone seems so angry at her."

"Like who?"

"Like everyone you wrote about today."

"You mean Ian and Lenny. Who else?"

"All her other clients, I guess."

"The police think so, too. They're going to use the same forensic accountant for the murder investigation that the attorney general used for the fraud case." Wes paused for a moment. "Back to the shooting itself—how did Alice react once the bullets started flying?"

"She froze and looked confused, as if she couldn't understand what was happening. I yelled for her to duck, but she didn't. She just stood there."

"Juicy image, Josie. Thanks. What did you think of her? What was she like?"

I sighed and shook my head. *Juicy,* I thought. "She was direct, with a kind of sharp edge, and witty. Also, she was quick. Quick-talking.

Quick-walking. Quick to get what you were saying. Quick to react. I liked her, Wes, but she wasn't warm and fuzzy, if you know what I mean. If you were sick, she'd be more likely to tell you to stop whining and get out of bed than she would be to make you chicken soup."

"She sounds like a hard-ass."

"That's about right," I said, "but she was also funny and generous. You know how many charities she supported."

"So which was she mostly, good or bad?"

"You can't simplify people like that, Wes. They're too complicated."

Wes sighed again, signaling his impatience. "This is just between us, Josie. I won't quote you. Was she a good egg or a rotten one?"

I thought it over. "Good," I said. "I don't think she was a paragon, but no way was she rotten."

"You've been wrong about people before, Josie. Lots of times."

I swallowed hard. Wes was right. I wasn't infallible. Still, I was way better at summing up personalities and character flaws than most people. In my business, I had to be.

"Let me know when you find out who inherits, okay?" I asked, skipping a response that would only sound defensive.

Wes promised he would. "Catch ya later!" he said and hung up.

My neck and shoulder muscles had been so tense for so long, they felt like twisted bands of steel. I watched the maple leaves shimmy in the breeze and raised, then lowered my shoulders in a futile effort to ease the stiffness. I wished I could skip going to the police station, but I knew I couldn't. I had to call Eric, too. *Might as well get it over with,* I told myself and dialed his cell phone.

He answered on the second ring. It was four thirty-seven.

"How's it going?" I asked.

"Good. The dolls and tools are packed. I'm finishing up the glassware now."

"You've made great time," I said. I took a deep breath and jumped in. "Something's happened, Eric. I need to tell you about it." I kept my tone neutral and stuck to the facts as I reported Alice's murder and repeated my admonition about talking to the police and the press. He didn't respond. I could hear him breathing. I waited several seconds. "Are you okay, Eric?"

"I don't know what I'm supposed to do."

"It depends on how you feel. Prescott's is officially closed. Some people find that getting away on their own helps them process trage- dies like this. Other people prefer to work. Which means that if you want to continue packing up the glassware, that's fine. If you'd rather wait until tomorrow or even the next day to finish up, that's fine, too."

"I'll stay and work," he said without hesitating even for a second.

"Are you sure? You don't have to."

"Yes."

"Okay. I'm going to be leaving now. I don't know if anyone will be here when you get back. I expect I'll be in tomorrow, but maybe not. If you decide to take the day off, just let me know."

"Sure," he said. "If I'm the last one there, I'll make sure Hank is all squared away for the night."

What a great guy he is, I thought as I hung up the phone. What you see is what you get, and what you see is an uncomplicated, hard- working, all-around stand-up guy. I sighed, wishing everything in life were as simple to understand.

Downstairs, I made a beeline for Hank's area. He was curled up in his basket, asleep. I squatted beside him and stroked under his chin, his favorite place to be rubbed. Second favorite was his tummy.

"Hank," I cooed, "you're such a good boy. Are you a good boy, Hank? Yes, you are. What a good boy."

Hank's fur was mostly silver with charcoal and apricot highlights. His vet called the color chinchilla. Hank had lived at Prescott's for just over a year now, ever since Gretchen had spotted him wandering around outside. We hadn't been able to find his owner, so we'd adopted him. It had taken him about a minute to settle in. It had taken me about two minutes to fall in love with him.

"I'm leaving a little early, Hank. I'll see you tomorrow . . . okay?"

He turned his head just enough to lick my hand. His eyes stayed closed. I stood up, and he settled back in, curling into a perfect comma.

I took a deep breath, getting ready to face the police presence out- side, wondering how long it would take Wes to get the skinny on Al- ice's will.

• • •

The Rocky Point police station was located on Ocean Avenue, across from the beach. It had been designed to match the prevailing architectural style in the affluent New Hampshire seacoast town and looked more like a cottage than a police station, with shingles weathered to a soft dove gray and trim painted a muted Colonial blue.

Ian Landers stood in the lobby staring at the bulletin board where notices about church suppers vied for space with top-ten wanted lists. Even from the back, he looked as if he were fuming. He was tall and broad, and his shoulders were hunched forward in a fighter's stance. His arms hung by his sides, his fingers curled into half-fists, and his legs were spread just right for springing. He turned at the sound of the door latching shut. His eyes were ice blue and as cold as a glacier.

"Josie Prescott," he said, sneering, his tone daring me to deny it.

I fought the urge to look away, to move away. "And you're Ian Landers," I said, keeping my voice even.

"Alice Michaels died at your place."

"In the parking lot, yes."

"I wish I could have been there to watch."

I stared at him, unable to think of what to say.

"The police think I killed her," he continued. "I wish I'd thought of it."

Ellis stepped out of his office, and from his expression I could tell he'd overheard Ian's last comment and wasn't impressed. Ellis shut the door behind him with a snap and took several steps toward Ian, moving in too close for most people's comfort, challenging his dominance and independence. Ian took a step toward Ellis, signaling that there was no way he was backing down. Even though their interaction was nowhere near me, I stepped back instinctively as I looked from one to the other. I could feel the crackle of male energy in the room.

"What can I do for you, Chief?" Ian asked, using the same tone for the word "chief" that I might use for "cockroach."

"Follow me, Landers," Ellis said, his voice frigid. He turned to me, and as if he were an actor switching scenes, he was a different man.

Instead of looking at me with the stony eyes and severe expression he was showing Ian, he smiled. "Thanks for coming in, Josie. We'll be right with you."

I watched as Ellis led Ian down the hallway that led to Interrogation Room One. Ian's strut communicated that he felt both cocky and unperturbed.

"Josie?" a female voice called. I looked around. Detective Claire Brownley stood on the other side of the lobby. She smiled at me. "Come this way." As we walked, she added, "Chief Hunter wanted me to let you know this is simply a formality. You should be done in no time."

"Thank you," I said. I glanced back over my shoulder, but Ellis and Ian had turned the corner. *I'd love to be a fly on that wall,* I thought.

Detective Brownley was right. Forty minutes after she led me to Interrogation Room Three, she escorted me back to the lobby. I hadn't been able to add anything to my original story, and she didn't push too hard to try to make me.

As we passed Interrogation Room Two, I glanced in the long, skinny window fitted into the wall to the right of the door. The venetian blind slats were open, and I recognized Lenny Einsohn, Alice's recently fired chief operating officer. His brow was furrowed; he was biting his lower lip; his shoulders drooped; overall, he looked as if he were about to cry. I slowed down. A video camera was aimed at his face, the tiny red light indicating his statement was being recorded. I couldn't see who was conducting the interview. The last thing I noticed as I walked past was him shaking his head; no, no, no, he seemed to be saying. You have it wrong. No, no, no.

"Thanks again, Josie," Detective Brownley said when we reached the lobby.

"Glad to help," I replied, eager to be gone.

I felt myself relax, just a bit, as she disappeared down the hallway. The two Farmington sisters, Lorna and Jamie, sat close together on an oak bench that ran the length of one wall. Jamie, the older of the two, was about thirty. She was somewhat taller than me, with big bones and a sturdy build. Lorna, about twenty-five, was about the same height but slimmer. Lorna's eyes were red and puffy, and I wondered if she'd been crying about Alice, and if so, why.

Jamie stood to greet me. "Josie ... you must be beside yourself. What a relief to know you weren't hurt. We came as soon as we heard the news. We're devastated ... just shattered."

"I didn't know you and Alice were close."

"Oh, God, yes!" Jamie said. "She and our mom were best friends. We grew up thinking Randall was our brother."

"Randall ... that's Alice's son, right?"

"Yes."

"Please accept my condolences."

"Thank you," Jamie said. She glanced at Lorna, sitting with her eyes on the floor, wiping her cheeks with the side of her hand. "It's such a shock ... we just saw her the other day."

"She was so decisive," Lorna said. "I admired that."

"Alice was decisive, all right. She stopped by while we were going through that box of Civil War memorabilia. You remember, Josie, we told you about it—how we're direct descendants of Salmon Chase, President Lincoln's secretary of the treasury, and couldn't decide whether to keep it all or sell it all or what. Anyway, when Alice saw what we were up to, well, she took over. She looked through the box, told us to pick a letter to keep for posterity and sell the rest."

"It was good advice," Lorna said.

Jamie shrugged. "It was advice. I don't know if it was good or not." She met my eyes. "What do you think we should do?"

"Take your time and think it through."

She looked at Lorna. "Now *that's* good advice." She sent her eyes around the lobby and nearby corridors. "Have you seen Randall? Is he here?"

"Not that I know of," I said. "Actually, I wouldn't recognize him. We've never met."

"Darleen is here," Lorna said. "Randall's wife. She was walking into the station house as we drove into the lot, but by the time we got inside, she'd disappeared. Knowing Darleen, if she's here, Randall must be here, too."

"Likely, but not necessarily," Jamie said. "You know how much he travels on business." To me, she added, "Between you and me and the gatepost, what Lorna means is that Darleen keeps Randall on a pretty short leash." She shrugged. "To each his own, that's what I always say. Randall could be out of town, though—I know for sure he has clients throughout New England." Reacting to my perplexed expression, she added, "Alice bought a marketing communications company about ten years ago, and Randall runs it. They do writing and design and printing and I don't know what else. Oh, my ... I can't believe Alice's dead ... it's horrible, just despicable."

"Gruesome," Lorna said.

"Did you leave Eric at your place?" I asked.

"Yes. Actually, he's the one who told us what happened. He said he'd lock up and set the alarm."

"We didn't know what to do," Lorna said, "but we thought we ought to come in and offer to help. Not that we know anything. Still, she was our mother's best friend."

"I'm sure the police will be grateful for the cooperation," I said, feeling trapped, wishing I could escape. I took a step sideways toward the door. "I have to go. I'll be in touch. I'm really very sorry for your loss."

Outside, I crossed Ocean Avenue and clambered up a dune. The ocean was dead calm, the sun-specked water shimmering like sequins in the early evening sun. The tide was high, the water licking the ragged line of bottle green seaweed that stretched along the sand near the dunes, the high-water mark. Watching the water's rhythmic ebb and flow, I felt myself relax another notch. The sun was sinking into the horizon, and swirls of red stippled the solid blue sky. Tomorrow would be another warm and sunny day.

I didn't like that the Farmington sisters had asked Eric to close up their house. I was certain Eric would do fine, but I wasn't comfortable with it. Locking up other people's houses sounded simple, but it wasn't. From a liability point of view, you needed to confirm you'd completed all the steps of closing up. I knew him well enough to know that he would fret, worried that he would forget something or do something wrong.

I dug my cell phone out of my tote bag and called him. After six rings, voice mail picked up. I flipped the phone closed without leaving a message. It was six thirty-three. Probably, I thought, he was home and in the shower, washing away the workday's dust.

Wes called as I was pulling out of the parking lot. I slipped in my earpiece and punched the ACCEPT CALL button.

"I've got news," Wes said, his voice nearly pulsating with excitement. "Big news. Bonzo-big news."

Bonzo-big, I repeated silently. "What?" I asked.

"Two things. First, Brooke Michaels, Alice's granddaughter, inherits everything. Poor little rich girl, huh?"

"Why do you say that?" I asked.

"Because when I called the mother, Alice's daughter-in-law, Darleen, and asked for a comment, she was shocked. The bequest was news to her, and I can tell you she was none too happy. As far as I was concerned, I was the bearer of good news, but she sure acted like I was an ambulance chaser, if you know what I mean—ready to pounce on an innocent victim. Why, do you think?"

I paused, considering the options. "Maybe she expected that her husband would inherit everything."

"That's what I figure, too. Not that it matters given the legal snarl everything is in. Little eight-year-old Brooke will be lucky to get her inheritance in time to pay for college."

"That's true, isn't it? I mean, every investor will probably sue the estate to try to get their money back. God, Wes, what a nightmare." I thought for a moment. "Just because Alice's will was news to Darleen doesn't mean it was news to Randall. Maybe he learned of his mother's intentions and snapped. Or maybe Darleen was lying about being surprised. Do they have alibis?"

"I'll check." Faint scratching sounds alerted me that he was writing himself a note. "What about Alice's investors? Could one of them have killed her? Or maybe Lenny, her former employee?"

"For revenge?" I asked. "I mean, killing Alice won't help them get their money or job back."

"Revenge is a biggie, though," Wes said. "What other reasons can you think of?"

"Lots," I replied, thinking that sometimes, maybe often, things are less complicated than we expect them to be. "I mean, don't investigators look for people who hated the victim? Like a love relationship gone bad?"

"Good point," Wes said, "but she was long divorced. I mean, like twenty years, plus."

"Was she dating anyone?"

"At her age?"

I shook my head at Wes's myopic view of love. "You're never too old to love, Wes. If you don't know that now, you will."

"I guess. I'll ask around about who she might have been seeing. So how was it being interrogated?"

"I wasn't interrogated," I protested, irritated at Wes's incendiary language. "I was interviewed. There's a difference."

"How did it go?" he asked, unabashed.

"Fine. I couldn't tell them anything new."

"Who else was there?"

I told him, thinking it was happening again. Wes had a gift for getting me to confide in him, to trust him as if we were close allies. Which, as I thought of it, we were.

"Where's Randall?" I asked. "Do you know?"

"Yup," Wes said, chuckling again. "At his lawyer's, looking for ways to break the trust. My contact says his wife called for an emergency appointment and made him keep it."

"On the day his mother is murdered. That's unbelievable, Wes."

He chuckled. "I know. From what I hear their relationship is all about his doing as he's told."

"Ick. So what's your second piece of news?"

"The weapon used to kill Alice was probably a target pistol, like a Ruger. They found shell casings near the path that leads from your place to the church parking lot."

I gasped, shocked and horrified at the thought that a sniper had used my woods as a hiding place. A shiver ran up my back. I'd strolled along that path a hundred times. Two hundred.

"If it is a Ruger," Wes continued, "that's like the most common target pistol in the world, or at least one of them, which means it's unlikely to help them find the killer."

It will help them convict him once they know who he is, I thought.

"They're checking prints on the shell casings," he added.

"It's completely creepy, Wes." A click sounded, indicating a text message had just arrived. Ty, probably, I thought, wanting to know how I was doing. "I've got to go, Wes. I'm driving."

"Give me something, Josie," he whined. "About the interrogation or something."

"I wasn't interrogated," I repeated. Wes was hopeless. "I'm hanging up now."

"Josie!"

I hung up.

The text message wasn't from Ty. I didn't recognize the number and didn't want to try reading the message while I was driving. I pulled onto the sandy shoulder and set my blinkers. The text was from Cathy, the Rocky Point police civilian admin. CALL ME. URGENT.

I dialed her number, and she answered on the first ring.

"Thanks for calling so quickly, Josie," she said. "Chief Hunter asked me to call on his behalf. He's hoping you'll join him at a location on Garry Road. Do you know it?"

"Sure, it runs from Tripper to Oakmont," I replied, thinking that Garry wasn't far from the Farmington house.

"Chief Ellis asks that you go there now."

"Why?"

"He'll explain when you get there."

"All right," I said, feeling my heart begin to beat harder and faster. "What address?"

"You'll see his vehicle. It's a short street."

I wanted to ask more questions, to keep her talking, to get some answers, but I couldn't think of anything to say.

"Josie?" she asked.

"You can tell him I'll be there in about ten minutes."

Something was very, very wrong.

CHAPTER FIVE

E llis's SUV sat on the packed dirt shoulder ten feet behind my company's van. Three police vehicles, their overhead red lights pulsing and spinning, were lined up in front of it. As soon as I rolled to a stop behind his SUV, the two lead vehicles pulled out. One drove a hundred yards forward toward Tripper, pulled a hard left, and blocked the road. The other backed up a hundred yards toward Oakmont, the way I'd driven in, turned a hard right, and blocked access from that end. Ellis stood next to my van, waiting for me to approach. I stepped out and walked slowly toward him.

"Is this your van?" Ellis called.

"Yes," I said. I recognized that he was asking for some official record. There was no mystery that the van was mine. PRESCOTT'S ANTIQUES & AUCTIONS was printed in white and gold on a maroon background.

"Do you know why it's here?"

I glanced around. Garry Road was narrow, flanked on both sides by ancient hardwood forests. The sun was still bright, yet under the thick canopy it could have been twilight.

"No," I said. "Where's Eric?"

"Was he driving?"

"Where is he? Was there an accident?"

"When did you last hear from him?"

"Stop fencing with me, Ellis," I said. "Where is he?"

"I don't know. When did you last speak to him?"

"About four thirty. A little after. I called to tell him about Alice."

"He didn't call in after that?"

"Not that I know of. Maybe he called the office."

"Is anyone still at work? Can you check?"

I jogged back to my car and dug through my tote bag, finally finding my BlackBerry at the bottom, where it had somehow worked itself after I'd tossed it in. There were two missed calls. I held my breath, hoping they were from Eric. They weren't. Both were from Wes, no surprise. He would have heard about the van on his police scanner. I called the office, and Fred answered.

"Has Eric called in?" I asked without preamble.

"I don't think so . . . Let me check Cara's message book."

I heard rustling and footsteps, and then Fred said, "No. Is everything okay?"

"I'll fill you in later," I said and hung up. My throat closed, momentarily choking me. "He didn't call in. I tried calling him about half an hour ago on his cell. It rang, then went to voice mail." I took a breath, then turned to meet Ellis's eyes. "What's going on, Ellis?"

"One of our officers on routine patrol spotted the van off to the side of the road. The officer, assuming the van had broken down, stopped to see if he could help. No one was on scene, and the van was unlocked. He noted significant destruction, so he called it in."

"What do you mean, 'significant destruction'?" I asked, shivering as if I'd stepped into an unexpected blast of icy wind.

Ellis swung open the back doors, and before I looked inside, I met his eyes, trying to intuit what he wasn't revealing, but got no hint. I turned my gaze to take in the inside of the van. Destruction was right—the van floor was a jumble of splintered wood; shattered porcelain, bisque, and colored glass; shredded leather and papier-mâché; torn fabric; flattened doll torsos; and hanks of hair, presumably from the dolls' wigs. A blue sugar bowl was intact, lying in the gully between the two front seats. The lid, also unbroken, sat nearby. A wooden level was perched against the bowl. The crates were more or less intact, with several side panels ripped off but not smashed. Most of the glassware and tools appeared to be undamaged. It was the dolls that had taken the brunt of the attack. I reached for the door frame so I could hoist myself up, but Ellis stopped me.

"The crime scene team isn't here yet," he said.

"Where's Eric?"

"There's no sign of him. There's a cell phone on the center console. Would you know by sight if it's his?"

"No." I dialed Eric's number and heard the ring on my end. "Do you hear it?"

Ellis walked to the front of the van and leaned in. He nodded, his expression somber. I ended the call and clutched the unit to my chest, stricken at the nightmare images flooding my brain. Eric was somewhere without his phone.

"What's all that stuff on the floor?" he asked.

"It looks like the objects Eric packed up today. I see splintered slats from the wooden crates he would have used to pack things in, as if someone ripped into them willy-nilly. Those blue glass pieces are from the cobalt glassware collection." I pointed. "That's an old wooden plane, from the tools collection. Look at all the doll parts— the dolls sure got the worst of it. There's a head. That's a torso over there. Those bits are glass eyes. That white piece of cloth was probably torn from a doll dress. The clumps of hair are from dolls' wigs."

"I presume they were in one piece when he went to collect them?"

"Yes," I said. "It looks like someone tossed the glassware and tools aside but stomped the dolls. Why would somebody do that?"

"You tell me."

I shook my head. "I have no idea." I paused, then added, "Maybe the dolls were in the last crate they opened, and they were so disappointed that the crates weren't filled with gold coins or something, they took it out on the dolls and fled."

"You think it was a theft?" he asked.

"What else could it be?" I waved my hand dismissively. "Who cares? All I want to know is where Eric is."

Ellis scanned the woods and the road in both directions. When he looked at me again, I saw caring and concern, which only served to ratchet up my panic.

"It looks as if Eric is missing," he said.

I stared at him. *Eric is missing.* His words reverberated in my head. *Eric is missing.* I couldn't seem to process what that meant. A roar from what sounded like a motorcycle interrupted my thoughts. I turned toward Oakmont in time to see Wes's old car screech to a halt at the police barricade. He leapt out and would have dashed to join us if the police officer hadn't blocked his way.

"What's going on, Chief?" he shouted from behind the patrol car.

Eric is missing.

Ellis turned his back to him and didn't reply. "Follow me, Josie," he told me and walked toward the front of the van, farther away from Wes. "Let's go over what we know. Not what we think, but what we know."

I nodded, glad to have something specific to do. Ellis gestured toward the police officer standing by her vehicle. She was tall and blond. Her badge read F. MEADE. She jogged to join us.

"Take notes," Ellis instructed.

"Yes, sir," she said and extracted a small notepad and pen from her pocket.

Ellis raised a finger. "One: At a little after four thirty—we'll get the exact time from your phone record—Eric was at the Farmington house, packing up. Everything was fine. Right?"

I nodded. "Right. He told Jamie and Lorna that Alice was dead. They were upset, left him to close up, and headed straight to the police station."

"They're the Farmington sisters, right?"

"Yes." I explained the sisters' connection to the dolls and to Alice.

"When did you last speak to them?"

"Just now, at the station house." I repeated our conversation.

"Hold on a second, Josie." He lifted his collar and spoke into his microphone. "Cathy, are you there?" A staticky noise sounded, which he seemed to understand as words, because he continued talking. To me the sound was just a sound. "Are Jamie and Lorna Farmington there?" Another crackly noise. "Good. Let me talk to Claire." A pause, then a noise. "Claire, ask the Farmington sisters about Eric. He was at their house packing antiques, and Josie spoke to him around four thirty." A longer crackle. "All right, then. Let me know as soon as you get something." He turned back to me. "When you spoke to Eric, how much more work did he say he had to do?"

I thought back. "Not too much."

"How long would it take him?"

"I don't know exactly. Fifteen minutes, maybe half an hour."

"So that puts us a little after five at the latest. He didn't call in to the office. Is there anyone he would call?"

"Maybe his girlfriend," I said. "Grace."

"Grace what?"

"Abbott."

"Do you have her number?"

I nodded and scrolled through my phone log. "Should I call her?"

"I will. What's the number?"

I gave it to him. He punched it in, took two steps away, and said, "Ms. Abbott? This is Chief Hunter of the Rocky Point police. I have an out-of-the-blue question. Did Eric call as he was leaving the Farmington house this afternoon?" He shifted position. "I know it's odd . . . Please just answer . . . He did. All right, then. I'm going to ask you to come join me and Ms. Prescott, Eric's boss, for some conversation . . . Yes, I'll explain when you get here . . . Shall I send an officer to bring you . . . That's fine." He told her where we were and hung up. "She's with her brother. He'll drive her here."

"She's got to be upset. It's awful when you won't answer questions."

"I know." He shrugged. "It's better, though, that I don't waste time answering questions that won't move the investigation forward. She'll hear what's happening soon enough." He took in a breath and raised a second finger. "Two: So we have him in the van calling Grace just before five." Another finger went up. "Three: Garry Road is a natural cut-through from the Farmingtons' to your company." He glanced around. "It's also a great spot for an ambush."

"Why?" I asked, my heart tightening at the word. "Why would someone want to ambush Eric?"

He held up a fourth finger, then a fifth. "Four: Someone destroyed the dolls, and the tools and glassware seem incidental. Five: There's no apparent sign that anyone or anything was dragged through the woods anywhere near the van. I'm no tracker, but while I was waiting for you, I examined the ground cover and low-lying branches and twigs. Nothing is smashed or trampled."

"How about tire tracks?" I asked.

He held up his left thumb. "Six: There are no tire tracks. It's been dry, so I wouldn't expect deep gullies or anything like that, but there's nothing, so I'm guessing the attackers left their vehicle in the street, transferred Eric into it, and drove away."

An unmarked black SUV rolled to a stop near the police vehicle blocking the Tripper end of the street. The same woman I'd seen at my company's parking lot wheeling a pilot's case stepped out, saw Ellis, extracted her case from the back, and hurried toward us. I glanced over my shoulder. Wes hadn't moved. His eyes were narrowed, taking it all in.

"Can you video-record first thing?" he asked her as she approached. "I want Josie here to study it, to see if she can figure out what they were looking for, and if they found it."

"That's a great idea," I said, optimism spiking. "I can compare it to the recording I made during my initial walk-through. I have a video record of every object."

"Good," Ellis said.

"I'm on it," the tech said. She wheeled her case to the back of the van.

"What have you done so far?" I asked.

"We're canvassing for witnesses and beginning the forensic examination. I put in a call to the state police for a tracker." He glanced at his watch. "He should be here any minute."

A dark blue pickup truck pulled up beside Wes. Grace was in the passenger seat. Before the car fully stopped, she flung open the door, jumped to the street, and ran in my direction.

"That's Grace, Eric's girlfriend," I told Ellis.

Wes shouted something, which she ignored. The police officer, Daryl, I thought his name was, moved to intercept her but stepped aside when Ellis called to let her through. A man about her age, twenty-three, maybe a little older, got out from behind the wheel and stood for a moment, then ran to join us. He was tall and husky, with neatly trimmed dark brown hair, the same shade as Grace's. He also ignored Wes's questions.

"Where's Eric?" Grace asked.

I didn't want to break down in front of her, and her wide-eyed panic was contagious. I took a deep breath and told myself to stay calm.

"We don't know," I replied, pleased that my anxiety hadn't affected my voice.

"Ms. Abbott?" Ellis said. "I'm Chief Hunter." He paused as the tall man reached us. "You are?"

"Jim. Jim Abbott, Grace's brother. We heard a news flash about the van being jacked. What's going on?"

The two men shook hands, assessing one another. I held my breath, waiting for Ellis's answer.

"We don't know yet," he said. "The vehicle Eric was driving was found here with some of the contents, antiques, destroyed. There's no sign of Eric."

Grace took a step back, and her already white complexion lost what little color it had. She fumbled with her purse. "I'll call him."

"His phone is in the van," Ellis said.

Her eyes widened. "Was it that man?"

"What man?" Ellis asked.

"The one who tried to get into the Farmington house." She looked at me, then back to Ellis. "Eric called me when he was ready to leave and told me about it. It was right after the sisters left to go to the police station. This man rang the doorbell."

She stopped talking, and Ellis encouraged her to continue. "Who?"

"I don't know. Eric was a little annoyed at all the interruptions, the man, and having to lock up the house, because it made him late and we had plans." Rosy dots of color appeared on her cheeks, and she looked down for a moment. "Eric asked me to change our dinner reservation from seven to seven thirty. We were going out to celebrate my new job... I've been looking for so long... I just landed my dream job, teaching third grade."

"Oh, Grace—congratulations." I said. "What an accomplishment." To finish her degree and get her teaching license, Grace had attended night school for years while working full-time as a teacher's aide.

She smiled, small and wavering, but a smile nonetheless. "Thanks." She turned back to Ellis. "Eric apologized for being late."

"Did he say what the man wanted?"

"He told Eric he'd left something inside and would only be a sec." She turned to talk to me. "You know how much Eric hates confrontation, and that's what this felt like to him. Eric was a little upset. He said the guy tried to walk through him like he wasn't there, and Eric had to strong-arm him a little to keep him out. That's when the neighbor stopped by. Another interruption."

"What did the neighbor want?"

"To drop off a casserole for the sisters. Eric put it in the fridge."

"All set," the technician called from the back of the van. She hopped down and added, "I uploaded it, Chief, and e-mailed you the URL and password."

Ellis looked down at his BlackBerry, then up at me. "I'll forward it to you." He tapped something into his handheld, then asked, "How long do you think it will take you?"

I mentally reviewed the steps I'd need to go through. "At least an hour, probably more."

"Are you okay to drive?"

I nodded, then turned to Grace and her brother. Grace looked frightened and worried and sad all at once. Her brother just looked worried. "Will you be home later?"

"Yes," she replied. "Or at my brother's."

As I entered Jim's phone number into my cell, just to have it, the police officer I thought was named Daryl had Wes back his car out of the way. I felt everyone's eyes on me as I walked to my vehicle. Latching my seat belt, I felt my eyes fill and blinked the tears away. I wouldn't tell anyone what I was thinking, not even Ellis, not even Ty, but I couldn't stop the words from forming in my head. There was a chance, maybe a small one, maybe a big one, but there was a chance that Eric was dead.

CHAPTER SIX

red looked up as I walked into the main office, then leapt up, sending his chair skittering sideways. Something in my expression must have alerted him to trouble.

"What's wrong?" he asked.

"I'm glad you're here," I said. "Has everyone else left?"

"Yes," Fred said.

I took a last look at Griff, sitting in his idling police car, guarding the marked-off crime scene area, then plunked down at Gretchen's computer and took a deep breath. "Brace yourself—I have bad news." I told him what little I knew. "So . . . here's the deal . . . while the police do what they do, trying to find witnesses, looking at the forensics, and so on, they've asked us to help figure out what someone had against the antiques, and why they seemed to focus mostly on the dolls.

"I'll take the recording I made during my initial walk-through and print still shots of the dolls. We might need photos of each piece of glassware and every tool, but from what I saw, I don't think we will. Most of those objects were still in the crates. It was the dolls that took the worst hit. You take the tech's recording showing the debris in the van and print stills using a grid pattern to ensure we have every inch covered. When we tape them together, we'll have one image of the entire van floor. We'll each take half the doll photographs and use them to ID everything, all the doll body parts and accessories. That way we can see if anything is missing. Okay?"

He nodded. "I'm game."

I turned on Gretchen's computer, and while it booted up, I glanced at her Mickey Mouse clock. It was seven forty-five. It occurred to me that Penn Moreau's bit aired just about now. I used the remote to turn on the flat-screen TV mounted on a side wall. An ad for a new hybrid car was just ending.

I opened my e-mail program and forwarded Ellis's e-mail to Fred, then went to the FTP site where we store client videos. When I had the Farmington video up and running, I fast-forwarded to the doll section. I muted my audio descriptions and began framing individual images of each doll, both front and back, and sent them one at a time to our high-end color printer/copier.

"And now our Legal Eagle, Pennington Moreau, will discuss investor rights," the TV anchor said.

"Thanks, Mitch," Penn said. "There's never a good time to lose money, and everyone knows that investing carries risks, but losing money because an investment didn't pan out as you'd hoped is a different animal altogether than losing money because of fraud.

"A senior employee in the district attorney's office told me that Alice Michaels, the owner of ADM Financial Advisers, was about to be indicted for fraud. The allegations state that she'd been running a Ponzi scheme for at least the last decade. As you may know, a Ponzi scheme is a scam that pays returns to investors, not from profits, dividends, or interest earned, but from the monies they themselves paid into the company or from the monies other investors paid into the company.

"While individuals must take responsibility for their investment decisions, they can't be held responsible if they don't have the facts or if they were lied to. Sorting out who knew what and when and who told whom what and when is always complex. The situation got even more complicated today. Alice Michaels, who was a friend of mine, died. She was shot, murdered, in Prescott's Antiques and Auctions' parking lot. Alice had been at Prescott's to buy antique dolls for her stellar collection. So what does all of this mean to you, if you're one of the more than two hundred investors who lost money with ADM Financial Advisers?

"In all probability, if Alice had been found guilty of fraud, the court would have frozen both the company's assets and her personal assets. The judge would then appoint an administrator to vet investor claims and divvy up the proceeds in an attempt to make the victims whole, that is, to try to get people back to where they started.

"Her death complicates the issue, but that's all it does—complicate it. It doesn't eliminate her obligation to repay her investors—if she did, in fact, commit fraud. So what should you do now? Make certain the district attorney's office has your name and contact information. Call the number running along the bottom of the screen. You can bet they'll be burning the midnight oil to sort out this thorny situation as expeditiously as possible.

"I want to leave you with one last thought. The old saw that if something sounds too good to be true, it probably is, are words to live by. This is Pennington Moreau, the Legal Eagle, soaring high and signing off."

I clicked off the remote and finished printing the doll photos, then taped the front and back views so each doll was represented on one two-sided printout. I labeled each one with the doll's number from my listing. I divided the photos into two piles, the dolls I had brought back with me and the dolls that Eric had been sent to pack up. The dolls we had on-site were:

1. The Bébé Bru Jne Alice had held earlier in the day
2. A Bébé Teteur (a Bru with a mechanism that allows the doll to suck liquid from a baby bottle)
3. A Bébé Musique (a Bru with a mechanism that allows the doll to play music)
4. A Bébé Gourmand (a Bru with a mechanism that allows the doll to be fed)
5. The G.I. Joe prototype
6. The kachina
7. A Long-Faced Triste Bébé, made by Belton & Jumeau
8. A nineteenth-century European doll with a bisque head and leather body wearing a plaid jumper over a white eyelet blouse
9. A Dutch doll with a cloth torso and wooden legs wearing clogs
10. A Japanese kokeshi doll
11. A set of nineteenth-century Russian nesting dolls, painted with an Oriental motif

The dolls Eric had been sent to pack up were:

1. An Effanbee doll depicting George Washington, paired with #2
2. An Effanbee doll depicting Martha Washington, paired with #1
3. An early European papier-mâché doll, wearing a white cotton dress and red felt boots
4. A Barrois French fashion doll
5. A leather-bodied doll with a papier-mâché head
6. A Conta & Boehme parian doll
7. An early Kestner doll
8. A midcentury Kestner doll
9. A K*R Simon & Halbig doll
10. A German-made Armand Marseille doll, dressed after a Renoir portrait
11. A Heinrich Handwerck Simon & Halbig doll
12. A Belton shoulder head doll by Bahr & Proschild

"How are you doing?" I asked Fred as I tapped the sheets on the desk to square up the edges.

"It's a little tricky taping it together—the images overlap."

I nodded. "Let me help."

Fred had laid out the printouts on the floor and was piecing them together like a jigsaw puzzle. Once we got in the rhythm of matching known elements, accounting for the overlaps was easy, and the process moved quickly. Fifteen minutes after we started, we had produced a life-sized image of the van floor. I handed Fred shots one through six of the dolls Eric had been sent to pack up. I took the remaining photos myself.

My cell phone rang, and I grabbed it, silently intoning a quick prayer that it was Eric, that he'd broken free and was somewhere safe needing a ride. It wasn't. It was Zoë, my friend, landlady, and neighbor.

"Oh, God, Zoë," I said. "I completely forgot about dinner. We have a situation here. I can't explain now."

"I heard about Alice and Eric on the news. You must be flipping out. Are you okay?"

"More or less. I'll call you later, okay?"

"Sure—just know I'm here if you need me."

"Thanks, Zoë."

I hung up and noticed two texts, both from Wes. I wouldn't be surprised if he came pounding on the door.

I looked at the taped-together image of the van floor. I leaned back, resting on the heels of my hands and crossing my legs Indian-style.

"I'm thinking we should use Post-it flags to indicate which doll part is from which doll," I said. "We shouldn't write on the photo itself until we're certain we're right. So many of the dolls are similar in style, material, and color, identifying which body part comes from which doll isn't going to be easy. Even identifying the wigs and clothes is going to be tough. Look at this brunette wig, for example." I pointed to a fan-shaped straight bit of long dark brown hair partially hidden under the passenger's seat, then spread my collection of photos out as if I were melding a hand in a card game. "If you look at these dolls, you can see that three of the six have similar hair." I shrugged. "Oh, well. All we can do is the best we can."

Fred and I worked methodically, side by side. We crawled around the van photo to get as close to each image as possible. The process was tedious but not complicated and, to my relief, went much more quickly than I'd feared. Within half an hour, I'd eliminated all of my six dolls. Fred was almost done with his allotment as well.

"Look," I said, pointing to a bisque head. "The eyes are glass, glued on. They haven't been ripped off or destroyed." I raised my eyes to meet his gaze. "Which means whatever is going on, the attacker isn't looking for jewels. If he were, he'd have removed all the eyes to check if they're sapphires or emeralds."

"Good point," Fred said. He stretched out his legs. "Now what?" he asked. "Everything is accounted for."

"That doesn't make any sense. Why would someone destroy the dolls?"

"Beats me," Fred said, shaking his head.

I stared at the van floor image. Strips of pink and yellow Post-it flags crisscrossed over the debris. "So since it's clear this wasn't about stealing for profit, what was it about?"

"Anger. Destruction. Someone was completely pissed off at the dolls' former owner and took it out on the collection."

"Maybe," I said, trying to reason it through.

If this was some kind of payback or commentary on the Farmington family, wouldn't it be more satisfying to break the glassware, to hear the shattering? If someone had set out to destroy something, maybe the dolls, why wouldn't he simply have broken into the Farmington house and trashed them on the spot? Maybe he tried. Maybe the kidnapper was the same man Eric told Grace had tried to get into the house. Why not break in when the place was empty? Because the Farmingtons have an excellent security system. Why kidnap Eric? Because Eric saw him hijacking the van and could identify him. The scenario seemed obvious, but it didn't answer the key question—why would someone destroy only the dolls?

I stood up. "Sasha put the eleven dolls we have here in the safe, right?"

"Yup, in a bin."

"I'll go get them—maybe we can figure out what's going on if we have them in our hands."

"I'll do a video of the van floor so we'll have it on record if the police want the original."

"Good thinking," I said and pushed open the heavy door that led into the warehouse. I headed down the central aisle. The lighting was dim. Shelves of inventory stood on either side, casting long, spider-shaped shadows along the walkways. Midway down, I glanced to the left. Hank was in his basket. I wondered if he was still asleep or back asleep. I recalled an article I'd read years earlier stating that cats need roughly three times as much sleep as people. Observing Hank, I could believe it.

At the end of the aisle, I turned left toward the walk-in safe. Two steps before I reached it, I heard a soft rumbling and stopped short. I glanced at Hank, but he hadn't budged. The soft, steady, low sound was familiar, but I couldn't place it. A lawn mower? No. Some construction equipment? No. The loading dock garage-style door being raised? Yes.

I ran along the back wall to the access door, my boots clomping on the concrete floor. By the time I got there, the rumbling had stopped. I peered out the tempered glass miniwindow. The loading dock door was closed. I pressed my eyes against the glass and looked in every direction. No one was visible. I checked the bolts. The door was secure. Even if someone succeeded in accessing the loading dock, there was no way they could get into the warehouse. Still, it was creepy. I shrugged and shook my head, wondering if I could have imagined the sound. I hadn't.

"Oh, my God!" I said aloud.

I ran full speed to the front, wrenched open the office door, and dashed outside. Griff was sitting in his idling patrol car. He saw me charging at him, jumped out of his car, and ran to meet me.

"Someone was trying to break in through the loading dock door," I said. "They stopped, but they can't have gotten far. You should look for them. Now."

"How could they have opened the door?" Griff asked.

"Using a remote. Eric would have had it with him in the van."

Griff nodded and ran back to his car, grabbed his radio, and said something. He turned off the car and pocketed the key, then said, "Get inside and lock the door. Stay there."

I nodded and ran. Fred was standing by the window.

"I didn't know whether to stay here or follow you out," he said.

"You did the right thing." I locked the door and set the perimeter alarm as I told him about the mystery sound. "Someone opened the loading dock door using Eric's remote. I bet that when it was up about three feet he peeked in and saw that we have security cameras aimed at the opening. So he lowered the door and left the same way he came onto the property, probably through the woods."

"That's crazy—who'd try to break in with police all over the place?"

"A risk taker," I said. "We need to get a look at the cameras." I called our security company. The monitor on duty was a man named Vince. "There are two cameras on the loading dock platform, mounted in the top rear corners facing the loading dock door," I said. I described what I wanted, and he asked me to hold on.

"Will there be enough light?" Fred asked while I was on hold.

"Yes. When the door lifts, spotlights come on so there's enough light for us—and for the cameras—to work."

"I found what you're looking for," Vince said when he was back on the line. "Each camera takes a shot every three seconds. Whoever lifted the door aimed a flashlight inside, a big one, like a torch. The beam is so bright you can't make out anything about the person holding it. You'll see what I mean. I was on break then, but I looked up the notes. The guy on duty wrote that the door lowered twenty seconds after it began to lift and there was no intrusion."

I thanked him and repeated what he said to Fred.

My cell phone rang—it was Ellis checking in. He said Griff had called in that he hadn't spotted anyone in the woods.

"Forward me those e-mails from the security company, okay?" Ellis asked. "The computer guys are adept at isolating images."

"Okay," I agreed.

Vince sent fourteen shots, seven from each camera, all showing the same thing: the inside of the loading dock door, the concrete floor, and a black-clad human shape visible in the space under the partially raised door—and a large circle of blindingly bright light.

From all my years working with Photoshop pros whose job it was to showcase the best of an antique without in any way misrepresenting it, I knew they could enhance a glint of gold on an ormolu clock or add a luminous quality to the rich reds in mahogany furniture. Yet they could only work with what was visible. I couldn't discern a single thing in these photos that might be useful, not a hint of a monogram that might help identify a club or organization, not a color variation that might reveal a patterned fabric, not a hint of flesh. I didn't think there was a chance the police expert would be able to bring anything useful to light.

Someone, probably Eric's kidnapper, had been at my business. He'd tried to break into my warehouse. And he'd made a clean escape.

CHAPTER SEVEN

T here are only two remotes," I said to Fred, thinking it through. "I have one, and Eric has one. Which means this wasn't a run-of-the-mill break-in. I bet he was after the other dolls."

"Then whoever it is knows the collection includes additional dolls."

I met his eyes. "Or he forced Eric to tell him."

Fred's lips thinned. "What can we do?"

"Examine the rest of the dolls."

Using hair-thin needle probes designed for the purpose, Fred and I pierced each limb, section of torso, and head, seeking out resistance. Our probes penetrated the cloth and leather easily, without causing any damage and without running into any obstacles. We angled our probes up into the bisque and papier-mâché heads through the neck openings. All the heads were hollow, no surprise. Hollow-headed dolls were lighter weight and easier to sew or glue to torsos.

"The heads would be perfect places to store contraband," I said. "It's possible we're looking for something as small as a jewel glued to an inside edge."

Hollow-headed dolls had been used for smuggling for centuries. I'd recently read about a Civil War–era doll named Nina who, it seemed, had come from Europe with her papier-mâché head filled with morphine and quinine, an effort orchestrated by Southern sympathizers to get medical supplies past the Union blockade and into the hands of sick Confederate soldiers.

One by one, Fred and I examined all the dolls, gently shaking the wooden one, listening for the telltale rattle of contraband or hidden treasure; separating the nesting dolls, ensuring there were no unusual thick or rolled edges that could secrete a document of some sort; and removing the Dutch doll's clogs to see if her feet had plugs or seals that might reveal a hidden space running the length of her wooden legs.

I leaned back, disappointed and frustrated. "I'm thinking we need to X-ray them."

The doorbell sounded, and I looked up, startled. Ellis stood under the overhang holding a pizza box. I searched his eyes for clues about whether he had news. As always, his expression revealed nothing.

"Anything?" I asked, braced to hear the worst.

He shook his head. "The tracker says there's no evidence that Eric was taken out through the woods, but we didn't think he had been, so it's not really news."

"Are you saying he was taken away in a car?"

"Or a truck. Or a van." He placed the box on the guest table. "We drove the perimeter of the woods circling your property and didn't find any sign of whoever it was who opened the loading dock door."

"No surprise. I don't think they'll find out anything from the photos, either."

Ellis shot me a look. "Time for a pizza break," he said.

"I'm not hungry," I said. "Did you find out anything about the man Eric told Grace about? The one who wanted in?"

"No, not yet."

"How about the neighbor with the casserole?" I asked.

"She remembered the incident but can't tell us much. She didn't recognize him and can't really describe him."

I frowned. "Why not?"

"A lack of interest in strangers combined with bad eyes. We found another witness, a woman driving along Garry who saw a white car parked in front of your van. Unfortunately, she didn't notice anything else. It seems her baby was screaming nonstop and she was completely frazzled."

"Another dead end. It's so frustrating!"

"I'm going to reheat the pizza," Ellis said. "You've got to eat. Me, too."

I shut my eyes and heard the microwave whir to life.

A minute later, Ellis said, "Here."

I opened my eyes as he slid a paper plate in front of me. "Thanks," I said.

Steam rose from the pizza, plain cheese. I took a bite, and as I chewed I thought about dolls and hiding places. When I was done with the slice, he offered another, but I declined. Instead, I filled him in.

"I have an idea," I told him. "It seems obvious that since only the dolls, not the other collections, were destroyed, it's dolls the would-be thief was after. Fred and I have just tried everything we have available to discover whether some contraband is hidden inside any of them. We didn't find anything, but that doesn't mean there isn't anything to find. We need to commandeer a medical office so we can X-ray them."

"Interesting," Ellis said. "Will it work, do you think?"

"I know it will. Last fall, a woman brought in a mahogany writing box that had been in her family for generations. It had all sorts of hidden compartments. Her grandfather had told her that he'd seen a huge emerald and gold brooch in one of the secret cubbies when he was a kid, but he couldn't for the life of him remember which one or how it was accessed. We examined that box inch by inch and found two additional hiding places she'd never seen before, but they all were empty. Finally we went to a medical testing facility over in Portsmouth and had it X-rayed, and guess what? No brooch. Either Granddad remembered wrong, or someone found it and pocketed it. The point is, the owner of the facility was very helpful. He thought it was fun. I'm sure he'd open up for us so we could X-ray the dolls now. Tonight."

"I'm convinced," Ellis said. "Let's do it."

I turned to Fred. "Would you look up the number for that X-ray place we went to last year? I'm sure they have an emergency number."

Ellis finished his slice and brushed crumbs from his fingers. "Let me," he said. "I can claim police business."

"Good idea," I agreed.

Two minutes later, Dale Reich, the doctor owner of Portsmouth Diagnostic Imaging, agreed to meet us at his facility in half an hour.

When Ellis and I reached the facility, we found the lights on and Dale Reich leaning against the stone portico, waiting for us. Dr. Reich was about ten years older than me and short for a man. He was almost completely bald, with blue eyes and an appealing habit of nodding as he listened.

His building shared a parking lot with a strip mall on Route One not far from Portsmouth Circle. As we pulled up, I scanned the empty lot and the row of shops. Everything else was closed. Nancy's Nails. Fritz's, a Swiss restaurant Ty and I ate at sometimes. Franklin Insurance. Ellis parked near the front and reached in the back for the bin containing the dolls. Dale straightened up as we approached.

"I've got everything fired up and ready," Dale said.

Ellis thanked him for opening up so late and with no notice.

"Anything to help get Eric back. Any news?"

I shook my head. He made a sad clucking noise as he held open the door.

Ellis and I followed him down a short hallway. We turned left into a small examination room. A table sat in the center, and an off-white multiarmed behemoth of an X-ray machine loomed overhead. Off to one side, a glass partition separated the control panel from the rest of the room. There were three framed van Gogh prints on the walls.

"Before we get started," Ellis said, "I need your assurance that our visit here is confidential. It's not overreaching to tell you that Eric's life might depend on you keeping quiet."

"I'm a doctor," Dale said. "Keeping confidences is second nature to me."

"Thank you," Ellis said. He nodded at me, and I opened the bin.

I carefully unwrapped each doll. First up was one of the Brus. I positioned her on the table, Dale lined up the swinging arm of the X-ray machine, and then we all stepped behind the protective divider.

"We probably don't need front and back images," Dale said as he turned a dial. "The X-ray penetrates all the way through, but just in case someone inserted a barrier of some sort, we might as well err on the side of taking extra shots."

Dale pushed a button, and when the click came, indicating the machine had taken the picture, I stepped out and rearranged the doll. One by one, each doll's front and back were X-rayed. After we were done, Dale took us into his office and turned his computer monitor so we could all see it.

"We just switched to an all-digital system," he explained. "No more film."

He clicked through, staring with educated eyes at one image after another. When he got to the X-ray of the back view of a nineteenth-century European doll, the one wearing the plaid jumper, he leaned forward, his attention riveted. He right-clicked his mouse to enlarge the image.

Dale took a thin metal pointer from his desk and tapped her head. "Look here," he said.

Ellis and I stepped closer. A half-inch-thick wad of paper curled around the inside of her head.

"That looks like money," Ellis said.

"That's what I think," Dale said.

Ellis handed me a pair of plastic gloves, and I felt a stab of guilt.

"Fred and I didn't use gloves before," I confessed.

"You had no reason to," Ellis said. "Now we do."

I nodded, relieved, and snapped them on. I extracted the doll from the bin, spread the protective flannel across Dale's desk to serve as a work surface, and moved her under the desk lamp.

Her head was stitched on. Without chemical analysis and carbon dating, there was no way to tell when the head had been attached to the neck, but I could look for clues. The thread color matched the blouse, white, but closer to linen in hue, maybe because it had yellowed from age, or possibly because someone who had stitched her up recently had matched the color well.

"Can you tell anything about it from the stitching?" Ellis asked.

"Not in terms of when it was sewn, but I can say that whoever set these stitches was patient and meticulous and had the right tools. It's not easy sewing leather, yet the stitches are small and neat and flaw-lessly aligned." I looked up. "I hate to cut the thread, but I think we have to."

"Do it," Ellis said.

Dale handed me a pair of surgical scissors he found after rustling through his desk drawer. I snipped the thread.

Ellis pulled a small flashlight from his side pocket and aimed it into the hollow head. Unfamiliar-looking currency had been laid flat around the inside of the doll's head. Using tweezers Dale provided, I worked slowly, gently lifting the currency away from the head. I laid the pile on the flannel and studied the top one.

"Do either of you recognize it?" I asked.

Dale shook his head.

Ellis said, "No."

Engraved decorative scrolls and a pleasant-looking man wearing a formal suit adorned the front. The number 63518 was stamped in red at the top. On the reverse side a central circle with a fancy green bor-der contained the words "This note is a Legal Tender for all debts public and private except duties on imports and interest on the public debt; and is receivable in payment of all loans made to the United States." On either side of the circle the numeral 1 and the word "ONE" were printed. Most of the remaining surface was covered by a green curly flourish. From even an arm's length away, the decorative scrollwork was so ornate it appeared to be solid green. A scalloped, star-studded white chain wended its way through the green embel-lishment.

"It looks to be the same shade of green that's on currency now," Ellis commented.

"Greenbacks," Dale said. "Isn't that what they call money?"

"We need a numismatist," I said.

"Do you know someone?" Ellis asked, looking at me.

"Yes," I said. I called New York City information and asked for Barry Simpson's number, but the operator couldn't help me. There were more than a hundred Barry Simpsons, and I didn't know where he lived and couldn't recall his business's name. There was no listing for a numismatist shop named Simpson's. "I need to get to my office."

Ellis transferred the currency to an evidence bag as I packed up the doll and head. Ellis took the bin and went for the car while I thanked Dale again for his help.

Ellis's dash clock read 9:51. I leaned back in the seat, exhausted. I'd been on the move since six thirty in the morning, and I was cooked.

"We need to X-ray the doll parts that were left in the van," I said.

"Yeah. I'll get the techs on it."

A big pickup truck was parked near Griff's patrol car. Two men wearing blue overalls were stacking the orange cones the police had placed earlier in the day in the back of the truck.

"You're removing things already?" I asked.

"Yeah. The crime scene folks gave the all clear, so there's no reason to stay."

I sighed and shook my head. "I'm so focused on Eric I haven't even asked if you have news about Alice. Do you?"

"We're pursuing several viable leads," he said, which could mean anything or nothing at all.

I led the way inside. Fred sat behind his computer. He leaned back and pushed up his glasses, asking a question with his eyes.

"Wait 'til you see what we found," I told him.

When I showed him the currency, the right side of his mouth shot up, a cocky expression of shared delight.

"I don't recognize it," he said. "Do you?"

"No."

"Now what?"

"Now I call Barry Simpson, numismatist to the stars."

CHAPTER EIGHT

I knew Barry Simpson from my days working in New York City at Frisco's, the venerable New York City antiques auction house where I'd gotten my start. He knew more about coins and bills than anyone else I'd ever met or heard of, and he had a spotless reputation. Barry could and would tell me the whole truth and nothing but the truth, which is more than you could say for a lot of people. I looked up his phone number, but all I had was the number of his shop, which was called Madison Avenue Coins. The phone went to an answering machine. I thought for a moment. *Shelley!* If anyone would know how to reach him after hours, it would be her.

Shelley and I had started at Frisco's the same summer, freshly minted college grads thrilled to have made the cut. Shelley is one of those people everyone warms to. She listens well, smiles a lot, and never has a bad word to say about anyone or anything. Even after I blew the whistle on my boss's price-fixing scheme and became a pariah at the company, hounded by the press, shunned by my colleagues, and eventually chased out by a weenie of an acting director, Shelley stayed neutral. Lots of other so-called friends said they admired what I'd done, but their words were empty. They stopped returning my calls, and invitations to parties dried up. Shelley was different. She was one of the few people I'd been able to count on not to act as if I had a contagious and dread disease. We were mostly professional friends, but our affection for one another ran deeper than that. I liked her through and through.

"While you're tracking this guy down," Ellis said, "I'll get CSI over here to check out the currency and tell them to X-ray the other dolls." He turned to Fred. "In the meantime, you and I can count the money." Ellis pulled two pairs of plastic gloves from his side pocket and handed one to Fred.

I would probably wake Shelley up from her disco nap. Shelley liked clubbing as much as she liked her job, so she'd developed a system of sleeping in shifts, which allowed her to party 'til three and still work at her turbo-charged best the next day. Her first sleep shift ran from seven to ten thirty or eleven in the evening; the second shift ran from four or five in the morning until eight thirty or so. I was sorry to disturb her, but with Eric's life potentially hanging in the balance, I didn't hesitate to make the call.

Shelley answered on the eighth ring, sounding groggy and irritated.

"Shelley," I said, "it's Josie. From New Hampshire."

"Jeez, Josie, where's the fire?"

"I'm really sorry to bother you, Shelley, but it's an emergency. I need to reach Barry Simpson, you know, the numismatist—I mean I need to reach him now. Do you have his home number?"

"You're kidding, right? I was having a dream, Josie, a good one. A tall, dark, extremely handsome stranger was involved."

I couldn't help smiling. "I'm sorry, Shelley. You can go back to sleep as soon as we're done. I'm sure he'll reappear."

"Hold on," she said with a sigh.

I heard rustlings and could picture her padding across her bedroom to retrieve her laptop.

"When are you coming to New York?" she asked a moment later. "I found a great new place for line dancing."

"Nothing's on the schedule yet. One of these days, Shelley, you've got to face the fact that there's life outside Manhattan and come up for a visit. You'd love our local country music hangout. Live music and dancing every weekend."

"Uh-huh," she said, dismissing the idea of leaving New York City out of hand. "Do you have a pen?"

She called out Barry's number, starting with a 201 area code, which meant Barry either lived in New Jersey or had a cell phone he'd acquired there.

"You're the best!" I said. "Go back to sleep."

"Don't give it a thought—I never really woke up. See ya, Joze!" She hung up.

"A hundred, right?" Ellis asked Fred as he straightened the pile's edges. The stack looked to be about a half inch high.

"Yup," Fred said.

"Which might mean megabucks or it might mean nothing worth mentioning," I said. "We should scan one in, so I can e-mail it to Barry."

Fred used the scanner located next to Gretchen's desk; then I attached the image to an e-mail and dialed Barry's number.

When a male voice answered, I said, "Barry? I hope you remember me . . . Josie Prescott. I used to work at Frisco's."

"Sure, I remember you. You moved up north somewhere, right? How you doing, Josie? What's it been? Five years?"

"Closer to eight, believe it or not. Yeah, I opened my own business in New Hampshire, and it's going very well. God, Barry, do you remember those ancient Roman coins?"

"Do I ever. In pristine condition. A hundred thou a pop. Not bad for a day's work."

"I'll say. Listen . . . I'm sorry to bother you at home and so late, but I have a kind of situation here and I'm hoping you'll do me a favor. Can I e-mail you scans of the front and back of a bill?"

"Sure," he said and rattled off his personal e-mail address. "What is it?"

As I typed in his address and hit SEND, I said, "An American 1862 one-dollar bill."

"Confederate or Union?"

"It just says 'United States.'"

"Let me get to my computer," he said. "Got it. Give me a sec."

"Okay. Barry, I'm going to put you on speaker, okay? I have some other folks here who need to hear what you say."

"Sure."

I held on for what felt like minutes but was probably only seconds.

"Of course, I'll need to authenticate it," Barry said, "but this sure looks like the real deal. Where'd you get it?"

"I'll tell you later. For now, give me a one-minute overview."

"This is Union currency, issued to support the Civil War. It's way rarer than Confederate money, because fewer bills were printed. Best guess is that there's only between three and five thousand extant. If this is genuine, it's an example of the first ever federally issued one-dollar bill. Think on that . . . the first ever. That's Salmon Chase on the front. He was secretary of the treasury under Lincoln and is considered the man who bankrolled the Civil War. In as good condition as this appears to be, which is to say uncirculated, it's worth two thousand dollars, maybe more."

"What would it do to the value if a hundred bills in this condition hit the market all at once?"

"Tell me it's true."

"It's true, but not for publication."

"I don't know. I'd need to gauge buyer response. We wouldn't want to flood the market, that's for sure, so I'd keep the total number available on the q.t."

I understood his point. If Barry offered one of these bills for sale and got thousands of offers, the value of all one hundred would hold their value or increase in value. If he offered one for sale and got fewer than a hundred requests, that wouldn't bode well. If he went ahead and put the other ninety-nine on the market, the value would probably drop. Supply and demand.

"Want to FedEx me a few so I can begin the process of authenticating them?" he asked.

"Yes, but I can't. Not yet. Soon, I hope."

Barry went pit bull on me, and it took me a full two minutes to get off the phone. He'd gotten a whiff of an unprecedented find of rare currency, and he wasn't letting go without a fight. I understood. In his shoes, I'd act the same.

I felt Fred's and Ellis's eyes on me.

As soon as I hung up, I said, "Two thousand dollars times a hundred . . . two hundred thousand dollars."

Fred leaned back, lacing his hands behind his head, his eyes firing up with excitement. Fred was an antiques snob, and rare currency with a Civil War pedigree impressed him. When I finished we sat silently for a moment, thinking. I pictured the destruction in the van. Someone had stomped the dolls, a quick way to open them up and see if anything was hidden inside. Someone had known the currency was hidden in a doll, but not which one. I felt my fingers curl into claws. If we could find that person, we'd find Eric.

The wind chimes tinkled as the CSI technician who'd video-recorded the inside of the van stepped into the office. As Ellis started to greet her, my cell phone rang, and I reached for it so quickly it skittered off the desk. I caught it just before it hit the floor. It was Ty. I pushed into the warehouse for privacy.

"I'm reeling," I said after I filled him in. "I'm sick with worry about Eric. I can't even imagine how Grace must feel. I'll call her later, just to touch base."

"You know you're doing everything you can, Josie."

"I know. Still."

"Yeah."

I sighed. "How are you? Talk to me about your day."

"There's nothing to report. We're beefing up training protocols, interesting stuff, but with all the interdepartmental cooperation I need to arrange, I'm stuck in extra meetings."

"I understand," I said, disappointed that he wouldn't be able to scoot out early but not surprised. "I miss you."

"Me, too. More than you can imagine."

After we finished talking, I stood for more than a minute, staring at nothing, thinking, wishing, and praying. By the time I got back to the office, the CSI technician had left. Fred handed me the receipt she'd given him. She'd taken the doll, the doll's head, and the currency.

"They're halfway through the X-rays," Ellis said, his eyes on his BlackBerry display. "Nothing so far."

"Obviously Jamie and Lorna don't know about the money," I said, "or they never would have sold me the doll."

"Or they knew about the money and it was an oversight," Ellis said.

"A two-hundred-thousand-dollar oversight?" Fred asked.

"It happens," I said.

"Is the currency ours?" Fred asked. "I mean, the Farmingtons didn't consign the dolls to us, they sold them outright, so we own everything free and clear, right?"

"Probably not. When I worked at Frisco's I once found a ruby the size of my thumb taped to the bottom of a drawer in an oak secretary—a desk," I added for Ellis's benefit. "That was a moment, let me tell you! We'd bought the desk from an older couple getting ready to retire to Florida about a month earlier."

"You got a bonus from the company?" Ellis asked.

"No way. Along with everyone at work, though, I assumed the ruby was ours, just as Fred assumed we own the currency. In order to discover the ruby's provenance, Frisco's jewelry appraiser asked the sellers for information about it—that's how they learned we had it. They said they'd forgotten the ruby was there, and when Frisco's wouldn't give it back, they sued for its return. I followed the case both because it was interesting and because I didn't know what to think. I could see both sides of the issue. We claimed it was a case of finders keepers, which actually has legal precedent. Shipwrecks, for instance. After a certain period of time, the ship is deemed to be abandoned, and anyone who finds it can file a claim and salvage it— and keep anything they find in it. In this case, the seller's lawyer argued that the ruby had to be returned because of something called 'unjust enrichment,' which says the court shouldn't allow someone to benefit when they've done nothing to deserve it. Since neither of us intended to include the jewel in the purchase/sale contract, the ruby was outside the scope of the deal. Our unexpected windfall was a direct result of their unexpected loss. Patently, that's not fair."

"Frisco's settled for an unnamed amount, right?" Ellis asked, his tone as sarcastic as his expression was cynical.

"No, actually. Frisco's returned the ruby. I think the powers that be thought it was the right thing to do. Some of my colleagues took a more jaded view. They thought we returned it because the lawsuit would take forever and generate a ton of bad publicity, a big powerful corporation trying to pull a fast one on an older retired couple."

"So are you going to give the currency back?"

"Of course." I was surprised he had to ask. He knew me well

enough to know that I never tried to hedge. I called it the I-want-to-sleep-at-night theory of ethics.

He smiled. "No wonder you're such a business success. People are hungry for honesty."

"Thanks," I said, embarrassed. I glanced at Fred. "What do you think, Fred?"

"I think I have the best job in the world."

I laughed, surprised and embarrassed and pleased. "What a nice thing to say!"

"It's true. Too many people spend too much time in gray areas. I'm like you—I think most things are black and white, with no gray, and it's great to work for a company with that kind of principles."

"I agree with you both," Ellis said. "Back to the issue at hand. How hard would it be to sell this currency?"

"Not hard at all," I replied. "If you want to stay below the radar, you'd have to sell at a discount, but that's easy. There are about a million numismatist fairs and shows, worldwide. All you'd have to do is take some of the bills to a show, cruise the dealers, and sell them without other dealers seeing what you're up to, an arrangement dealers are happy to go along with. You want privacy so you can sell to more than one dealer without any hint you're flooding the market. The dealers want privacy because they want to keep their competition in the dark about their sources. You've heard me say that it's way harder to buy good product than it is to sell it, so dealers, me included, guard our suppliers like Fort Knox."

"How can they do that in an open show?"

"No prob. I'll give you a for instance. Let's say a guy shows up in your booth saying he has some Union currency to sell. The dealer tells him to meet him outside or in a hallway or in a stairwell in two minutes. The dealer's goal is to complete the transaction out of the view of everyone, get the guy's name and number so he can follow up and buy the rest of his inventory, if he has more, later, and get him gone. Look at the numbers: The seller will only get about a third to half the retail value—call it a thousand dollars a bill for a round number—but so what? If there are forty dealers at each show, and you sell five bills per dealer to ten percent of the dealers, that's what? Five bills times a thousand dollars per bill is five thousand dollars per transaction. Times four dealers per show equals twenty thousand dollars. Using this scenario, you're selling twenty bills per show. If you pace yourself and only go to one show every few months, inside of a year, maybe less, you'll have sold all the currency and you'll have a hundred thousand dollars in your jeans. I always give receipts and have sellers sign a bill of sale, but it's not a stretch to think that some dealers may be more lax. It happens all the time. There's a good chance you can get cash with no tax to pay and no record of the sales."

"Would experienced dealers really pay a thousand dollars for something without appraising it first?"

"Sure. The trick is for the seller to tell a good story. 'I found these five bills in the attic when my folks died and I went to clean out the house. I'd always known that my great-great-great-grandfather fought for the Union during the Civil War, and look what I found next to his discharge papers. I did a little research online and saw there's only a few thousand of them known to exist. From what I can tell they're worth about two thousand dollars each. Are you interested in buying them?' Then the dealer looks at them under a loupe, seeking out known marks, stamps, or imperfections, which he probably has in his head because this is a well-known, rare currency. If the bills pass his examination, he tells you that sure, he's interested, but as a dealer he can't pay two thousand dollars, which is full retail. You look disappointed. He explains about retail versus wholesale, and you nod. You don't like it, but you understand his point. The dealer offers seven hundred dollars, and you say no and offer thirteen hundred. Eventually you'll settle at a thousand per bill, and he hands you cash. Maybe he even gets you to sign a bill of sale, which is okay with you because you're using a fake name anyway. The whole transaction takes about five minutes."

"I can see that working with a ten-dollar item, but not a thousand-dollar anything. Wouldn't the dealer worry the bills were fake?"

"That's why he looks with a loupe. It's not carbon dating, but it's good enough so you'll catch obvious flaws, like printing that's out of alignment, mushy lines, uneven coloration, that sort of thing. Also, experienced numismatists know what the paper should feel like by touch."

"All this is happening in a stairwell?"

"Yup. Or out in the parking lot. Or in the men's room."

Ellis shook his head. "All I can say is it's a hell of a way to earn a living." His BlackBerry vibrated. He pushed a button, read a text, then said, "Nothing showed up on X-ray. There's a mishmash of prints on the currency, but nothing popped in any of the law enforcement databases she checked. There's no possibility of a DNA match."

"Can we get the money back? For when the ransom note comes in?"

He nodded and tapped a reply into his unit. "Done. She should be here in about ten minutes."

"At least we know why the dolls were destroyed," I said and sighed. "We need to talk to Jamie and Lorna. It's possible that they have an idea about who knew something was hidden in the doll."

Ellis nodded. "I left a message on their cell phones a little while ago."

"How come they haven't called back?" I asked, my worry meter whirring onto high. I knew myself: Until Eric was home safe and sound, I would fret if people weren't where I expected them to be and if, when contacted, they didn't respond right away.

"Lorna told me she only uses hers for emergencies, so I doubt she'll check it anytime soon. Jamie will call back as soon as she gets the message."

"Can't we just go there?" I asked. "Or call the house number?"

"I had a car drive by their house, but they're not home. They're probably at some friend's house. As to calling the house, they had their mother's landline turned off after she died." He smiled at me. "I'm not worried about it, and you shouldn't be, either. I'll let you know the minute I hear from them." Ellis stood up and stretched. "As soon as the tech shows up, I think we should call it a day, Josie."

"I guess." I pointed to the taped-together image. "Is it all right if we roll up the photo?"

"Yes. Don't throw it away, though, in case we need to refer to it again."

"I'll do it," Fred offered. "I'll wait for the tech if you want and put the currency in the safe. I just keep thinking word is going to come any minute that Eric is okay."

"Me, too," I said, sighing again. I told him I'd take care of getting Hank settled for the night, then turned to Ellis and said good night.

"I'll see you home," Ellis said. "I'm going to Zoë's anyway."

"Okay," I said. "Give me five minutes."

When I reached Hank's corner he hurried to meet me. He rubbed my leg and mewed. He wanted to play.

"Can you fetch this mouse, Hank?" I asked.

I tossed the little felt mouse toward the back wall, and Hank took off like a bullet. He pranced back with the mouse in his mouth, its gray tail dangling to one side, and dropped it at my feet. Maine Coons, we'd learned, fetch. Hank looked proud, even cocky.

"You're a very clever boy, aren't you, Hank?"

I threw the mouse again, and again he galloped toward it, scooped it up in his mouth, and brought it back. After a dozen more tosses, he grew weary. He stretched his top half, then his bottom half, then stepped into his basket. I told him he was a good boy, changed his water, topped off his food, putting out an extra bowl of each in case we all decided to stay home tomorrow, and told him I'd probably see him in the morning. Back in the front office, I confirmed I had turned off Gretchen's computer and scanner, then told Fred good night.

I was glad to get outside, into fresh air. The evening was balmy and humid. It felt like it might rain. I arched my back, trying to ease the iron-hard tension. Ellis was in his SUV waiting near the exit for me to join him. All signs of police presence were gone. I walked to Ellis's SUV. He rolled down his window as I approached.

"Why hasn't there been a ransom note?" I asked.

"There will be."

"You seem very certain."

"I am."

"Maybe he left by choice," I said. "It happens."

"Rarely."

"Maybe Eric flipped and attacked the dolls."

"Do you believe that?" he asked.

"No. I think he was kidnapped."

"Me, too."

"So why hasn't there been a ransom note?" I asked again.

"They're getting Eric situated. It's not so easy to kidnap a grown man in broad daylight and transport him somewhere without being seen. They might be driving around, waiting until the middle of the night to hide him away."

"Do you think he's still alive?" I asked, looking past the stone wall into the thicket of dark woods, not wanting to see the uncertainty I was sure would appear in his eyes.

"Yes."

I looked back at him. "Why?"

"Because there's no percentage in killing him."

I nodded. "Thanks, Ellis."

"For what?"

"For being kind."

He smiled. "Don't let it get around."

"Too late."

CHAPTER NINE

Within minutes of getting onto the interstate, my fingers began to throb—I had the steering wheel in a death grip. I sighed, a deep one, and said aloud, "Relax, Josie. Relax." I glanced in the rearview mirror and felt inordinately relieved to see Ellis's headlights.

I pulled into my driveway, and Ellis pulled into Zoë's. If I'd stretched out an arm, I could have touched the passenger-side door. Her porch light was on. I leaned over the dash to look up at my bedroom window. The little golden light I always kept burning because I hated entering dark houses alone shone brightly.

"You going to be okay?" he asked.

"Yes. I'm just beat." I tried to smile. "Tomorrow's another day, right?"

I mounted my porch steps and stretched. The air had thickened, and the moisture felt fresh and clean. I opened my front door, turned, and waved to Ellis. He was on Zoë's porch, watching me. He didn't open Zoë's door until I had closed mine. Inside, I shot the bolt and had taken one step toward the kitchen when my home phone rang. I grabbed it, hoping it was some news about Eric. It wasn't. It was Wes calling for a quote. I leaned back against the wall, deflated.

"Tell me about the dolls," he said. "Why would someone want to destroy them?"

"I don't know," I replied.

"Why would Eric disappear?" Wes asked.

"I don't know that either."

He sighed. "Do you have a list of the dolls that were destroyed? And pictures? I can publish them and ask our readers for ideas about how the dolls might be involved. It might help, Josie."

He was right. It might. "Let me think about it," I said. "I need to be careful, Wes. I don't want to make a bad situation worse."

"How could it make anything worse?" he asked.

"I don't know. That's why I want to think about it. I'm hanging up now. I'll call you back in a few minutes."

"Wait!" he shouted, and I did. "You asked me to find out whether Darleen and Randall had alibis for when Alice was killed. They didn't. Darleen was supposed to be chaperoning a field trip with her daughter's class but canceled at the last minute. She told the cops it was because with all the publicity surrounding Alice, she didn't want the grief. Randall says he was walking on the beach, alone, that he was upset about his mom's death, but he can't prove it. He can't even provide any details. He said he was in his own world and simply didn't notice where he parked or which section of beach he was on or when he got there or anything."

"From your tone, I can tell that you don't believe him, Wes, but it could be true. I can see how grief might befuddle memory."

"Yeah, especially when you've gone AWOL. Darleen told the cops that Randall was at the funeral parlor, making Alice's burial arrangements. Turns out, that's what Darleen told him to do, but he didn't do it. Instead, he went to the beach. I bet he was in trouble when he got home."

"Poor Randall," I said.

"You think? He comes off wussy to me."

"Yeah . . . still . . . I think it's sad. It sounds as if he's never been his own man, even a little bit. I mean, we're talking about a walk on the beach as a rebellious act, Wes. That's sad."

I could practically hear Wes shrugging. "Whatever. The bottom line is that the police think he's wide open." He paused, then added, "You also asked me to find out who Alice might be dating. No one knows if or who. She had lots of different escorts to charity and club events. Often she went alone, too. As to investors out for blood, the one name that keeps coming up is Ian Landers."

"I saw him at the police station," I said. "He was plenty mad. Nasty mad."

"He's wide open, too. He says he was jogging near the library, but so far no one remembers seeing him."

"How about weapons? Do either of them own guns?"

"Not registered," Wes said, "but you know how that goes. Anyone can get a gun."

"True. Thank you, Wes." My voice cracked as my throat closed. I took in air. "I've got to go, Wes. I'll call you back soon." I hung up, then lifted the receiver again and dialed Ellis's cell phone. I apologized for disturbing him, repeated Wes's suggestion, and asked his opinion. "I'm thinking it might be a good idea, Ellis. If I let Wes quote me begging for help in finding Eric, it will create the impression that we have no idea what's going on—which, of course, we don't. That might reassure the kidnapper, don't you think?"

"I do. I like it, Josie. I can't see any downside."

"Good. I'll do it now."

I dashed into the den, flipping on lights as I ran, and booted up my home computer. Once it was ready, I remoted into my work computer and e-mailed myself the two doll inventories, the one listing the dolls I'd taken away and the one listing the dolls that had been destroyed in the van. I also uploaded the still shots Fred and I had created earlier to an FTP site. I combined the two inventories into one and paused, thinking. I nodded and said aloud, "Why not?"

I brought up the original video recording and fast-forwarded until I came to the three dolls the Farmington sisters had decided to keep, Chatty Cathys from the 1960s. I captured each one as a photograph and uploaded them to the FTP site. I sent the inventory to Wes along with instructions on how to access the photographs.

"Whew," I said aloud as I dialed Wes's number. It was after midnight. "Wes, it's Josie. I decided you were right. Any help is welcome."

"That's great, Josie!" he said after I explained what I'd sent him. "Now give me a quote."

" 'None of us at Prescott's has any idea if these dolls are somehow involved with Eric's disappearance. If anyone does have information, please notify the police. All we want is Eric's safe return. I know the police would say that no idea is too off-the-wall and no fact is too minor to be worth reporting.' How's that?"

"Good, good," he said. I heard him scribbling notes. "Had Alice Michaels bought the collection?"

"No. She left a deposit as a right of first refusal."

"So her estate still has a claim?"

"I'm not a lawyer, but since we hadn't deposited the check before she died, I can't imagine how it could," I said.

"Do you think her murder is somehow related to the dolls?"

"I don't know."

"How about Eric's disappearance? Do you think the murder is somehow connected to it?"

"I have no idea, Wes," I said, feeling like a broken record. My voice cracked again. There was so much I didn't know. I felt worn down and worn out. "I wish I did."

"You haven't gotten a ransom note, have you?"

"No," I said.

"Do you think he was kidnapped?"

"Yes . . . I mean, what else could it be?"

"Maybe he just disappeared. You know, maybe he's one of those guys who goes out for a pack of cigarettes and never comes home. They feel overwhelmed with whatever responsibilities they've gotten themselves into, trapped, you know? Isn't it possible Eric just vamoosed of his own free will? You know what I mean. Eric's quiet. Respectable. Nice. That's how they always describe the guy, the people left behind, I mean, when he turns up twenty-seven years later with a new family and a house and everything."

"You should write a made-for-TV movie, Wes."

"If it's a kidnapping, why hasn't someone, you or his family, received a ransom note?"

"We will," I said, repeating Ellis's words, wishing I shared his confidence. I didn't think Wes's analysis was right, but something in my gut made me wonder.

"When you do," Wes said, "I'm your first call, right?"

"You know I can't promise that, Wes."

"Josie!"

"I'm tired, Wes. I'm hanging up."

With Wes sputtering in protest, I cradled the phone. I glanced at the big clock mounted over the refrigerator. It was after one. I turned out the light and stood in an oblong of silver moonlight. "Here's to silver light in the dark of night," I whispered. I called Grace.

"I don't have any news," I said, not wanting to raise her hopes, even for a second. "I'm sorry to call so late, but it's the first chance I've had. I didn't want to go to bed without talking to you."

"It's okay," she said. "I wasn't asleep. I doubt I'll sleep at all."

"Yeah." I paused. "How are you holding up?"

"It's hard." She paused. "I called Eric's mom."

I bit my lip. *I should have done that,* I thought. Maybe not, not if I couldn't be supportive, and since Eric's mother was a sour old woman with a chip on her shoulder the size of Alaska, it was unlikely I could have offered what she would have demanded.

"She must be beside herself," I said.

Grace didn't reply right away. I could hear her crying. I hoped Grace was expressing her upset about Eric, not reliving an altercation during which his mother had shown her evil side, but that, I knew, was past praying for.

"What happened?" I asked.

"I don't want to repeat what she said," Grace managed, gulping. She lowered her voice to a near-whisper. "It was hateful."

I felt my throat close. Grace was a gentle soul, and thinking of her having to endure that shrew's spiteful tongue made me want to cry, too.

"I'm so sorry, Grace. I should have called her myself."

"No," she said. "It's better that I did."

I sighed, unable to think what to say.

"I'm sorry to be tearful," she whispered. "It's just that I'm so scared."

"Me, too." I closed my eyes for a moment, then opened them and took in a deep breath. "I spoke to Wes Smith, a reporter for the *Seacoast Star.* I gave him some information and pictures. I checked with the police first. They agree that asking the public for help can't hurt, and maybe it will help."

"That's a great idea, Josie!" she said, suddenly buoyant.

"We can only hope that it works. I figure that someone knows something."

We talked a little longer; then I headed upstairs to start my bath. I didn't for a minute believe that Eric had left of his own volition. Eric had been kidnapped.

Eric, I said silently as I trudged up the steps, *hold on.*

After a steamy-hot bath, a bowl of reheated homemade minestrone soup, a Blue Martini, and a good-night call to Ty, I fell into bed more relaxed than I would have thought possible an hour earlier.

I expected to toss and turn all night, but I didn't. I slept like a rock until six fifty in the morning. I would have slept even longer, but my cell phone buzzed, jerking me awake. Rolling toward the bedside table where I'd left it, I tangled myself in the sheets. I jerked my arm loose and grabbed the phone. The icon indicating that a new text message had arrived flashed, and I punched the button to display it.

"Oh, wow," I said aloud.

I was reading a ransom note.

CHAPTER TEN

I pulled on my jeans and a sweater and ran through the drizzle that had come up overnight to Zoë's. I took the porch steps two at a time and leaned on the buzzer.

"You're here bright and early," Zoë said as she swung the door wide. She was model tall and willow thin with sleek black hair and big brown eyes. She wore slim-cut black jeans and a fitted brick red collared blouse. She looked as if she'd just walked off the pages of *Vogue*.

"I need to see Ellis," I said.

"He's in the shower—he'll be down soon."

"Run up and tell him it's me, and that I have news, will you?"

"I hate to bother him while he's—" Zoë said, then noticed something in my eyes and stopped. "Sure, Josie. No problem. Go on into the kitchen and pour yourself a cup of coffee."

"Okay," I said.

I went into the kitchen, but I didn't get coffee. I paced from the kitchen door to the refrigerator and back again often enough to create a rut in the hardwood floor. I could hear the kids grumbling upstairs as they got ready for school.

Ellis entered, dressed for work in a brown tweed sports coat, brown slacks, off-white shirt, and green tie. His hair was damp.

"What news?" he asked.

I handed him my phone. He held my gaze for a moment, then lowered his eyes to the screen. The text message read:

**WE HAVE ERIC. PACK UP ALL FARMINGTON
DOLLS. INSTRUCTIONS LATER TODAY.
NO COPS OR HE DIES.**

He pushed the button to bring up the details of the text, then held the unit so I could read it. The text had come from a 603 area code— New Hampshire. I didn't recognize the number.

I shook my head. "The message says Eric is alive."

"Which may be true," Ellis said quietly, confirming my unspoken fear.

Ellis placed my phone on the counter and hit a speed dial button on his own.

"Claire," he said, "I need you to do something without telling anyone about it." He rattled off the number and told her to trace it.

"Now what?" I asked.

"We wait for confirmation that the phone the kidnapper used is a disposable unit, the kind you buy at a big-box store for cash."

I nodded, understanding. "Untraceable. How long will it take her?"

"Not long. Minutes, maybe."

"Meanwhile, I can pack up the dolls," I said.

"We need to discuss whether you should do what they say."

"Of course I should do what they say!"

"No matter what your gut tells you, Josie, you need to force yourself to think objectively. I'm sorry to be blunt, but Eric might already be dead, in which case we need to consider how best to catch his killer."

I knew Ellis might be right about Eric, but I couldn't bear thinking that Eric might be dead. I wouldn't. "We have to proceed on the assumption that he's alive."

"I agree, but we have to build in contingency plans. Like marking the money."

"Will they be able to tell?"

"No."

"Are you sure? Even if they look?"

"Right. Even if they look."

"Okay—except it's not my money. It's Jamie and Lorna's money."

Before responding, he reached for the coffeepot and poured himself a cup. The kids came clomping down the stairs, and I heard Zoë tell them to put on their rain slickers and galoshes. Ellis hoisted the pot in my direction, silently offering me a cup. I nodded. He took a mug from the cupboard, poured, and slid it along the counter toward me.

"I'll meet with them to explain the situation," he said.

"I should be there to explain about the money."

He nodded. "I'd appreciate the help. Let's assume they'll agree to let us use the currency. The next thing we have to talk about is whether to call in the FBI."

"No way! You read the note. It's bad enough I told you."

"Don't be so quick to dismiss it, Josie. The FBI are the experts here."

"Doesn't it make sense that I simply do as I'm told? I hand over the dolls and they hand over Eric."

"If they keep their end of the bargain."

I shut my eyes for a moment, then opened them and searched his face for signs of hope. I couldn't find any. He looked the same as always, businesslike, attentive, calm. Words escaped me.

"Another way to think about it," he said, "is that the only reason not to call them in is if you think they'll screw something up."

I looked out Zoë's kitchen window, taking a deep breath and then another, thinking it through. I knew I lacked both information and experience, a potentially deadly combination. I couldn't let my ignorance put Eric's life in jeopardy.

"I don't know what to do," I said. "How can I possibly decide? If the FBI can help us, of course I want their input, but you read the note—the kidnappers told me not to call the police. Maybe they've tapped my phone. Oh, God, Ellis—it didn't even occur to me... what if the kidnapper is watching my house at this very minute? What if he saw me come over here and recognizes your SUV? He'll assume that I've already spoken to you."

He nodded thoughtfully. "It's possible, in the way that anything is possible, but it's not likely. If anything, I think they'll keep an eye, and maybe an ear, on your office. That's where the dolls are, and that's where they would figure you'd be leaving from."

I took a minute to think some more. "Doesn't contacting the FBI feel like too big a risk?"

"No. I can call them from my office on a secure line and tell them our plans off the record. We can take advantage of their expertise without committing ourselves. I can solicit their opinion, then, if we want, we can call it a day."

I bit my lip. I wanted to do the right thing, the smart thing. I finished my coffee, and as I placed the mug in the sink I saw that my hand was trembling. "Maybe I should discuss it with Grace or Eric's mom."

"No. Or rather, of course you can seek whatever counsel you think is appropriate, but from where I sit, you need to think long and hard before you tell anyone anything. Loose lips sink ships, and all that." He paused. "You're frowning, but think about it, Josie. Eric isn't married and he isn't a minor. They have no right to know and no specialized knowledge that would help us. Don't get me wrong—of course I've assigned someone to be their police point person. We've been in touch with them since the beginning, and we'll continue to be in touch. That's different from consulting them on a decision of this magnitude." He paused again and shook his head empathetically. "The bottom line is that this is your decision, Josie. The note came to you. You own the dolls. This is all on you."

"I don't want to, and you can't make me!" Jake shouted from the hall.

"Don't try me, Jake Winterelli!" Zoë shouted back. "Put on your raincoat and do it now!"

I leaned against the counter, feeling weak and weighed down, and wishing I was helping Zoë get the kids into rain gear, not navigating a life-and-death decision.

"What would the FBI do?" I asked.

"Add a recording device to your phone, plant GPS chips in your car and in the dolls, mark the bills, and, once we know where the exchange will take place, plant agents all around, whether that means pretending they're homeless people in a dark alley or customers in a restaurant or whatever. If the location is isolated, they'll put snipers in trees or hide them behind rocks, that sort of thing."

My big fear was that the kidnapper would learn that we'd consulted the FBI. No matter what Ellis might say about professional discretion, I suspected that word would get out, that the media, and thus the kidnapper, would hear of it in about a minute and a half. I only had to look to Wes's far-reaching web of sources to know that in a criminal investigation, as in life, the only secrets that were safe were the ones you never revealed.

"That's too many people in the loop," I said. "Word would leak out, and that's a risk I'm not willing to take. You can use local resources to do everything you just listed. Local resources under your command, and thus under your control. We don't need the FBI."

"It's true that I can access all the technology and manpower we need. Don't misunderstand, Josie, God knows I'm not lobbying on the FBI's behalf—I just want you to make a fully informed decision. Here's the thing . . . in addition to resources, the FBI is known for their criminal profiling expertise. That's a capability we don't have locally, and it's one I can't access without calling them in."

"Okay, then. It's decided. No FBI. Since we don't need criminal profiling expertise, we won't call them in. This isn't some random snatch, Ellis, or a serial killer or a psychopath or anything like that. This is a kidnapping for ransom. This is about money. Plus, we already know a fair amount about Eric's kidnapper. We know he's aware that there's something valuable, and not breakable, hidden in one or more of the Farmington dolls. We also know that he has no idea which doll or dolls he's looking for. In the van, he stomped all the dolls, a quick way to reveal contraband—if you're not worried the bounty will shatter. What we need to do is look at Selma's best friends—" I broke off and felt my mouth fall open. "Oh, wow . . . I don't know why this didn't occur to me before, Ellis. According to Selma's daughters, Selma's best friend was Alice. If Selma told Alice what the secret was, it explains why Alice was so determined to acquire the collection."

Ellis nodded slowly, taking it in. "Alice didn't kidnap Eric."

"True, but maybe she told someone about it. It's possible the kidnapper is someone Alice confided in. Like her son, Randall. Or like her valued employee, Lenny. Or her good buddy, Ian. Back in the day, before the trouble started. You know, one of those fun conversations about goofy hiding places."

"Interesting idea," Ellis said. "What do you know about her relationship with any of those three?"

"About Randall, only what I've read in the paper and heard around town." I told him about Lenny's efforts to sell his antiques and reminded him of Ian's belligerent attitude at the police station.

"Who else might Alice have confided in?"

"I don't know."

"Who else might Selma have confided in?"

"Her daughters."

"Who else?"

"I don't know." I sighed. I took a deep breath. "All I know is that Eric is alive. Until I have a good reason to think otherwise, I'm going to do what I believe offers the best chance of keeping him alive, and that's to follow the kidnapper's instructions to the letter." I nodded, pleased I'd made a decision. "Which means I need to get to my office and start packing the dolls."

"Okay. It's your call. That said, since you've enlisted my help, I'm going to need you to follow my lead. You need to do exactly as I tell you. I know you're smart and determined and brave, but you're an amateur. You're not trained. You need to trust me and my expertise. Are you okay with that?"

"Yes," I said, thinking that it was mostly true. I trusted him completely—but I trusted myself, too.

"Okay, then. When we're done talking, I'll leave first and go about my business, staying away from you and your company for the rest of the day. We'll need to arrange for your car to go into the shop this morning so we can install the tracking devices, and I'll need you to okay a phone tap. I'll e-mail you instructions about both and attach the forms you'll need to sign." He rubbed his nose, thinking. "Also, I'll send a female officer to install the tracking devices in the dolls. She'll go in empty-handed and leave carrying a Prescott's bag, so anyone watching will just think she's a regular customer."

"Good. That all sounds good," I said, meaning it. I thought for a moment. "Is there any way you can have her bring me one of those untraceable phones? I could use it just to call you, and no one would know I have it, so no one would think to tap it."

He smiled. "Smart thinking, Josie. I'll take care of it."

"Come on, kids, let's go," Zoë instructed from the hallway.

She poked her head into the kitchen and blew Ellis a kiss. He smiled at her, his eyes softening. She turned toward me.

"If you need me for anything, Josie, I'll be back in about fifteen minutes. I'm just running the kids over to school."

"Thanks, Zoë," I said. "Sorry to take over your house like this."

She smiled and touched her hand to her chest, her heart. "Mi casa es tu casa."

We listened to them file out; then Ellis glanced at his watch. The time display on the microwave read 7:20.

"We need to establish a communication policy," he said. "If the kidnapper calls on your cell phone or landline before we get the tap installed, take copious notes, listening for an accent or a dialect, paying attention to his tone of voice and background noises, and writing down as close to his exact words as you can. Then go into your warehouse and call me immediately from the new disposable cell phone."

"Why my warehouse?" I asked.

"Technology is such that it's possible your home or work phones have been tapped by the bad guys without your knowing it. While it's possible to pick up cell phone conversations using triangulation, it's not easy if there are obstructions. Inside your warehouse, with those concrete walls, there's no way they can do it. I may not know the ins and outs of criminal profiling, but when it comes to this sort of thing, technology's effect on law enforcement, I keep up."

"Will the cell phone work there?"

"It should. Until then, if we're talking on your current phone, be circumspect. Also, copy any text messages you get into the new phone and send them on immediately, from the warehouse." He rubbed his nose, thinking. "When I speak to the Farmington sisters, I'll explain that I need to talk to them privately, that I can't talk to them on the phone, and they can't come to the police station. I should imagine they'll be mighty curious, but that can't be helped. Which means we need to figure out how we can consult them without raising any red flags. Could you meet them at a colleague's? Another dealer?"

I shook my head. "Too much potential for gossip."

"Your bank?"

"Too open, with too many people observing comings and goings." I paused, considering and rejecting options. "I know—Blackmore's Jewelers. I'm sure Mr. Blackmore would let us use his back office. You can get there first, maybe even enter through the back door."

He nodded. "I like it. When I get to the office I'll call Mr. Blackmore and set it up. Assuming he okays it, I'll send you an e-mail with 'Yes' and the time in the subject line."

"Sounds good," I said. "Thank you, Ellis. Everything you've said makes sense."

He shifted position. "I know you know this, but I need to remind you. Don't tell anyone that you've received a ransom message. Not your staff. Not Grace. Not anyone."

"Except Ty."

"Except Ty."

"I should respond to the text, right?"

He handed over my phone. "Yes. What are you going to say?"

I hit REPLY and tapped in: O K

I showed it to Ellis, and he nodded. "Simple. To the point. Responsive."

"Here goes nothing," I said. I hit SEND and watched the check mark appear. The message had been sent.

I walked alongside Ellis to the front door and told him good-bye. After he left, I stood off to one side, peeking through the side windows, seeking out a sign that someone was nearby, watching.

I couldn't see the street except where the driveways opened onto the road; the rest of the view was blocked by a thick privacy hedge that ran the length of the property. I walked back into the kitchen, scanned the meadow, then shrugged and walked home through the thickening mist. If someone was out there watching, he was well hidden.

Upstairs in my bedroom, I started the shower, leaving my phone on the edge of the sink. If another communication came in from the kidnapper, I didn't want to miss it.

Ellis called as I was toweling off.

"That message I mentioned," he said. "I just got a call back. Her cell phone battery was low, so she'd turned off her phone and didn't turn it on again until it was done charging. She called as soon as she got the message. She's agreed to stand by. You remember what I said I'd do?"

"Yes," I said. "You'll send an e-mail."

"Right. Hold tight, okay?"

I told him I would and hurried into the bedroom. As I got dressed I felt a surge of confidence. We had a plan, a good one, and I was ready to act.

CHAPTER ELEVEN

As soon as I rounded the corner after leaving the interstate en route to my office, I saw a caravan of media trucks and vans, some with satellite hookups. Six of them had parked along the grassy shoulder on either side of my company's entrance. Three others had parked in my lot. Reporters were milling about, including one from my New York days: Bertie. Bertie worked for *New York Monthly,* and I despised her.

During those tumultuous months, while I was waiting for my boss's trial to begin, she'd lied to try to get me to confide in her, and when her efforts failed, she painted my whistleblowing as a Machiavellian ploy to advance my own career. Now, here she was again, standing in my parking lot chatting with a network TV reporter. I sailed on by and turned into the church parking lot. I drove around the back, rolling to a stop by the back door, out of sight of the street.

I was shaking, as impotent anger mixed with an unfamiliar kind of fear. The rage-fueled terror snaking through my veins turned my blood to ice and caused my teeth to chatter as if I had a dangerously high fever. I spun the heat dial to high, hoping the warmth would quiet the fear as it warmed me, leaned my head against the steering wheel, and closed my eyes. I recalled the long lonely months I'd spent in limbo. Bertie had made bad times worse. I'd tried to reason with her. I'd begged for privacy. I'd refused to answer her questions. Nothing had worked to slow her down. She'd been as relentless and merciless as a killer bee. Now she was back. I needed to talk to Ellis.

I couldn't call him, not out in the open. I sat up and looked west, toward my place. I could see the path curving into the forest, and I was tempted to try to sneak into my building, but I knew better. Once I popped out the other end, I'd have to cross the parking lot. Bertie and the other reporters would see me easily, and I'd be dead meat.

I knew Ted Bauer, the preacher, started his day early—his wife, Maggie, a tag sale regular, was a nurse. Their routine had her dropping him off at the church en route to her 7:00 A.M. shift at Rocky Point Hospital, so the fact that the parking lot was empty didn't mean Ted wasn't there. I stepped out of my car and shivered, this time from the dank cold rain. With a glance over my shoulder to be certain no one had followed me, I hurried to the door and rang the bell. I heard melodious chimes sound.

Ted swung the door wide. "Josie," he said. He stepped back so I could enter. "Come in, come in. Maggie and I were shocked and so sorry to hear about what happened—both about Alice and Eric. Do you have any news?"

We stood in a square entryway. The floor was old linoleum, white with green flecks. The off-white walls were scuffed from years of traffic. I knew that the corridor in front of me led to a row of administrative offices. The church's commercial-grade kitchen was on the left.

"Not yet, thank you, Ted." I smiled, or tried to. "I know this sounds bizarre, but may I use your phone?"

His face registered surprise, but only for a moment. "Of course. Come this way." He set off down the hallway. "Can I get you a cup of coffee first?"

"Thank you, no."

"I saw the reporters when Maggie and I drove up. Looks like you're getting some national exposure."

"A kidnapping following a murder is certain to appeal to people's worst instincts. I guess the media is just doing its job, but I hate it, Ted. I hate everything about it."

He tut-tutted as he waved me into his office, a comforting, empathetic sound.

"I have some work to do in the basement. Stay as long as you want. Louise should be in soon. If I'm not back and she's not here when you're ready to go, feel free to let yourself out. The back door locks automatically when you close it."

"Thanks, Ted. I appreciate your hospitality."

I was glad he was leaving me alone. I was glad his secretary, Louise, wasn't in. I didn't want to be fussed over, not even by people I cared for and respected like them.

The overhead light fixture had an ocher-colored globe and cast a warm yellow glow throughout the room, an appealing contrast to the gray dreariness outside. A red-and-blue-patterned Oriental rug covered most of the hardwood floor. Ted's desk was huge, a walnut beauty with beadwork detailing. Built-in bookshelves lined two walls and were packed with periodicals, files, books, and miscellaneous knickknacks. I sat in Ted's oversized leather chair, dialed Ellis's cell phone, and swiveled to face the window. Rivulets of water ran down the glass. The drizzle had turned into a light but steady rain.

"Ellis," I said when he answered, "I'm glad I got you. I'm holed up in the church down the road from my place calling on their landline. My parking lot, along with a chunk of the roadside, has been taken over by the media. I was going to ask you to send someone to keep them off private property, but then I got worried. If the kidnapper is watching and sees police around, no matter why, he might freak out. How would you feel about making an on-air statement to the media? You could say you're there to keep the press off private property and slip in, maybe in response to one of the questions the reporters are certain to ask, that you haven't had any contact with me. What do you think? Would that work to reassure him?"

"There's no way of telling, Josie, but it's a solid idea. I like it. I'll leave here in about a minute."

I thanked him, hung up, and sat for a moment watching the rain. I wanted to give Ellis time to clear the press before I ventured back. I guesstimated that twenty minutes should be enough. While debating whether to find my way to the kitchen to snare a cup of the coffee Ted had offered, I checked my work voice mail. I had one message. It was Jamie asking me to call. I used the landline to return the call.

"Thanks for getting back to me so quickly, Josie," Jamie said. "I have a question ... you probably don't know the answer, but you might. Chief Hunter called earlier and asked Lorna and me to meet him at Blackmore's at eleven. Isn't that strange? Then I read the *Seacoast Star* article about the dolls ... I thought you might know if there's some connection."

There was nothing I could tell her, not on the phone.

"I don't know," I said.

"We heard about Eric. It's just shocking ... terrible. Do you have any news?"

"No," I said, closing my eyes for a moment, "not yet." I opened my eyes.

"Why did you give all those photos to that reporter?"

"The police thought it might produce a lead or two."

"Has it?" she asked.

"I don't know."

She said something sympathetic about Eric, and I said something polite in response, and she ended the call. I placed the receiver in its cradle and noticed that Ted's computer, a laptop, was on. I figured he wouldn't mind if I did a quick check of the *Seacoast Star*'s Web site. I wanted to see what Wes had written about the dolls.

The doll photos and one-line descriptions ran down the left side, next to a short report saying Pennington Moreau was the big loser playing blackjack on an evening cruise to nowhere out of Portsmouth, a crushing defeat since earlier in the evening, he'd won more than anyone else in the history of the ship. Wes's article was on the right. The headline read WHAT'S SPECIAL ABOUT THESE DOLLS? Wes reported that someone close to the investigation—me, I suspected—had revealed that something related to the dolls had led to Eric's kidnapping. He then solicited the public's help in figuring out what it was. He also asked if anyone had any information that might suggest a connection between the dolls and Alice's murder.

I exited the browser, took a blank sheet from Ted's memo cube and wrote, "Thanks, Ted. See you soon," and placed it on his chair. Louise popped her head in as I was approaching the door to leave. I hadn't heard her arrive.

"Ted told me you were here, Josie," Louise said, "and maybe in some trouble. Is there anything I can do to help?"

Louise Dietz was about Cara's age, but she looked more earth mother than grandmother. She wore her long gray hair in a single braid; her earrings and bracelets were designed with leather, beads, and feathers; and she wore a brown organic cotton skirt, bone-colored loose knit sweater, and Birkenstocks. She and I had shared many a cup of tea over the years.

"Thanks, Louise. I'm okay. Better since I know I can sneak in here and be safe."

"Good. I'm glad you're using us as a sanctuary."

I thanked her again and left the same way I came in.

In my car, I tuned to the local radio station and heard Ellis telling the reporters to stay off private property. Someone asked where I was, and he said he had no idea, that he hadn't spoken to me, that one of my employees had reported the trespassing.

Reporters started swarming when I was fifty feet from the parking lot entrance. Wes, standing off to the side, was smart enough and experienced enough to know that the more aggressive the approach, the less likely it would be to work with me. I recognized Bertie, the network TV reporter who'd been chatting with her earlier, an on-air reporter from the Manchester TV station, and a journalist from a Boston paper. The others were all strangers to me.

I slowed to a crawl but didn't stop, and as I drove, I kept my eyes on the road, not them. The police officer I thought was named Daryl stepped into the traffic lane and said something to them, scanning the crowd as he spoke. The horde parted, and I drove through. Ellis was nowhere in sight. Ian was, though. He was leaning against my front door with his arms crossed watching the action. I parked by the front door and stepped out of my car amid the jumbled roar of reporters' questions.

"Hi, Ian," I called, ignoring them.

"They're really something, aren't they?"

"That's one way of putting it," I said. I unlocked the door, deactivated the alarm, and invited him in. I glanced at Gretchen's clock. It was eight fifty-five. "I'll get some coffee started. In the meantime, what can I do for you?"

"Have you seen this morning's *Seacoast Star*?"

"Just the online version. Why?"

"Wes Smith's article said the dolls might be connected to Alice's murder. What do you know about that?"

I shrugged and poured water into the coffeepot, glad for an excuse to keep my eyes away from his icy glare. "Nothing," I said.

"You must know something, Josie. You sold them to Alice Michaels."

"No, I didn't," I said, switching on the machine. "She left a deposit giving her the right of first refusal."

He snorted. "Another fine entry in the unholy history book recounting tales of feckless leaders avoiding responsibility."

I met his eyes and pulled my shoulders toward one another, arching my back, trying to ease the sudden stab of tension.

"If you're making a point," I said, letting my tone match his, "I don't get it. If you're accusing me of something, or just being rude for fun, get out."

"Oh, no, not so quick. I'm making a point, all right. No disrespect, Josie, but since Alice's schemes have begun to unravel, I've learned a lot about how she did business. Deals wrapped around other deals until you don't know and can't find out who owns anything. Just because a deal hasn't been completed doesn't mean it didn't get made."

"First, I didn't sell the dolls to Alice. Second, Alice died before her check was deposited, which means no transaction of any kind occurred."

He took in a deep breath, and I could tell he was trying to control himself, to sound rational, not enraged, to speak, not rant. "Maybe. Maybe not. I'm no lawyer, and I'm not saying you're trying to pull a fast one, but the fact remains that all of Alice's assets are up for scrutiny. She stole over a million dollars from me. A million dollars, Josie. Those dolls need to be included in the list of her possessions."

"I'm sorry you lost money," I said, not knowing what else to say, "but Alice didn't buy the Farmington dolls from me."

"Yeah, you've said that. A couple of times. You can say it until you're blue in the face, and it won't make it true. I'm not taking my losses lying down. This is not a popularity contest. Those dolls need to be turned over to the district attorney, independently appraised, and sold to benefit Alice's victims, me included. If you want to do the right thing, which I gather you don't, that's exactly what you'll do. If you want to get square, let me take them now. I'll see they get to the attorney general."

I couldn't imagine that he actually expected me to turn the doll collection over to him, yet he sounded serious. I knew he wasn't stupid, but he sure was acting dumb. He stared at me with his hands on his hips, his gaze icecap frigid, probably hoping to intimidate me. He didn't know me well enough to know that I don't intimidate. I just get mad.

"Last time, Ian. I never sold the dolls to Alice. If there's nothing else, I think you ought to leave."

"That's your story and you're sticking to it," he said, sneering.

"If you're trying to be offensive, you're succeeding. Go. Now."

He raised his chin. "If the shoe fits . . ."

The chimes jingled. Gretchen smiled brightly as she stepped inside.

"Wow!" Gretchen said. "That's quite a gauntlet! I had trouble getting past the . . ."

The words petered out and her smile faded as she realized that some kind of altercation was under way. She looked at Ian, then back at me.

Ian's sneer deepened. His eyes remained fixed on mine. "Maybe I'll talk to some of those reporters and tell them what you said."

"Feel free," I snapped. "Just make sure you get it right. Otherwise you'll be defending yourself against a charge of slander. Now that Gretchen's here, I have a witness to your threat and my statement. Here's what you can quote: I never sold Alice Michaels the Farmington dolls. Period." I strode to the door and pushed it open, holding it ajar. "For the last time—leave."

He held my gaze for three seconds, then marched out.

"Holy cow!" Gretchen said, her eyes big, watching him stomp to his car. "What was that about?"

"I'm not sure." I rubbed my arms. "To tell you the truth, he was a little scary."

"What did he want?"

Good question, I thought. I ran through our conversation. If I eliminated all the fancy trimmings, what it came down to was simple.

"He wanted the doll collection," I said.

CHAPTER TWELVE

Ten minutes later, as I placed the Belton & Jumeau Bébé on the worktable that ran along the back wall, Cara's voice crackled over the PA system. A woman named Dawn LeBlanc wondered if I had a few minutes to talk about a birthday gift for her mom. I hoped Dawn was Ellis's police officer come to install the GPS devices, but I doubted it. I knew most of the police officers on the Rocky Point force by name from when Ty had been the police chief, and I didn't recognize hers.

"I'll be right there," I said over the intercom.

"Hi," Dawn LeBlanc said, smiling broadly and extending her hand for a shake as soon as I stepped into the font office. "Ellis suggested I stop by. He told me he was certain you'd be able to help me find the perfect birthday gift for my mom. I love her to death, but she sure is hard to buy for!"

Dawn was one heck of an actress. She was short and stocky, with shaggy brown hair, dark brown eyes, and a sprinkling of freckles on her cheeks and nose. She wore low-rise blue jeans and a leather jacket open to show a pink and turquoise plaid T-shirt. She looked more like a college student than a cop. Her smile was big, and her eyes twinkled with fun. I had to keep reminding myself to act as if her words were true.

"Welcome! We'll find something she'll love. Follow me."

I led the way into the warehouse. Fifteen paces in, I stopped walking. "You said Ellis sent you?"

She took a look around. "Are we alone?" she whispered.

"Yes. Everyone else is in the front."

She extracted a brown leather card holder from an inside pocket and flipped it open to display her badge. She was a detective with the Portsmouth Police Department.

"Portsmouth?"

"Rocky Point has a fairly small department. Just in case the bad guys are watching and might know Rocky Point's personnel, Chief Hunter thought it was prudent to use someone from another department. I'm on temporary duty, assigned to Rocky Point." She touched her hair. "It's a wig. Even my husband wouldn't recognize me."

"Smart," I said, smiling. "I appreciate your help." I turned down the center aisle toward the worktable. "The dolls are over here. So how does this work?"

"The first thing I have to do is figure out the best way to insert the GPS tracking disks in the dolls. The disks are small, but looking at these dolls, I'm reminded that 'small' is a relative term." She reached into a side pocket and came out with a plastic bag filled about halfway with shiny silver metal disks, each about the size of my thumbnail.

"With so many devices, how can you keep track?"

"Each one has a unique ID number. I note which device is placed where."

I nodded. "That part's all right, but look at them—I don't see how this can possibly work. They're too big. Too conspicuous. Let's say the kidnapper refuses to turn over Eric until he examines all the dolls. Last time he had a bunch of dolls, he stomped them to smithereens. If he does that this time around, he'll either destroy the GPS devices or he'll discover them. If he discovers them, he'll be so pissed off, he'll probably kill Eric out of spite. If he destroys them, we risked Eric's life for no reason."

Dawn scanned the row of dolls and reached for one, the kachina, then paused and asked, "May I touch it?"

"Yes. Just be gentle."

She picked it up and turned it over, then upside down, then placed it back on the table.

"I understand your point, but I think you're looking at it backward. If we don't install them, it would be like sending you into a hornet's nest without a face mask. It's not if you'll get stung, it's how many times, and how severe the damage will be. We have to know where you are. With all respect, we have to assume that you're going to need backup. Without these devices, you'll be on your own."

"You'll know where I am. We're putting those things, or something like them, in my car."

"We have to know where the dolls are, too."

"Why?"

She stared at me for a moment. "What if he transfers you and the dolls into another vehicle?"

Prickly shivers ran up my spine, then down again. What she said was terrifying, but what she left out was even scarier. What if he killed me? I shook my head. What the kidnapper might or might not do was out of my control. I needed to focus on what was in my control, on what I could do to rescue Eric, and nothing else.

"How about putting one somewhere it probably won't be found . . . I don't know . . . how about inside my boot? It's unlikely the kidnapper would make me run around barefoot."

"Good idea. We can place another one in your purse. There's a chance they'll take it from you, but maybe not. I can't okay skipping the dolls without permission from the higher-ups, though."

"I'll call Ellis," I said.

"Here," Dawn said, handing me a cell phone. "Use this. I was asked to give it to you."

I thanked her and dialed. Ellis answered so quickly, it was as if he'd been waiting for the call. I explained my objection to inserting the GPS devices in the dolls.

When I was done he said, "Interesting," and asked to speak to Officer LeBlanc.

"Yes," she said. "No . . . Yes . . . Yes . . . All right."

She flipped the phone closed and handed it back to me.

"Chief Hunter is okay with our not placing the GPS devices in the dolls, but he wants me to look at the packaging." She looked around, her eyes moving first to the oversized roll of bubble wrap mounted on the wall, then to the clear plastic tub with the dark green top where the dolls had been stored in the safe, and finally to the dolls themselves.

"How do you plan on transporting them?" she asked.

"Individually wrapped in flannel, then packed in this tub. Last time, the kidnapper destroyed the crate as well as the dolls, so he might do the same with this tub. I think it's too risky."

"You're probably right. Let me take a look at one. Maybe I can find a way to sneak a device in there so it will survive an attack."

I watched as she studied it. The tub was nothing special. We bought them by the truckload. It was built for strength and durability, not beauty. There was no soft lining. There was no place to secrete a thumbnail-sized metal disk. She removed the lid and looked inside. She shook her head.

"It's too exposed," she said, "so that's a wash." She looked at my feet. "Let's take a look at your boots."

I brought her upstairs and sat on the love seat while she worked. She notated two disks' numbers, then tore a short length of superstrong clear plastic shipping tape. She secured one disk under the tongue of my right boot. She slid the other one into the toe section of the left boot and affixed the tape.

I put the boots back on, wiggled my toes, and nodded. "This will work. I can barely feel them."

"Good. What about your purse?"

"I don't carry a purse. I carry a tote bag." I stood up. "I'm thinking I can slip one of those bad boys in the zippered compartment and place a second one in my change purse. What do you think?"

"Sounds good."

She wrote down their numbers while I walked across to my desk for the bag. "Can I leave them loose or do they need to be taped down?"

"Loose is fine," she said. She handed me the disks. "Here you go." She watched me drop them into place, then asked, "Will you be wearing a coat?"

"No, probably not. Even though it's raining, it's not all that cold out."

"Do you carry an umbrella?"

"Sometimes I do. Sometimes I just get wet. For this, I'll probably just get wet."

The new cell phone buzzed.

"It's Ellis," I told Dawn. "He said only to use it in the warehouse.

I'll run downstairs. You come, too, okay? In case he wants to talk to you."

I hurried down the spiral steps, pushing the ACCEPT CALL button as my foot hit concrete. Dawn was two steps behind me.

"How's it going?" Ellis asked.

"Good. We're done." I described where Dawn had placed the GPS disks and why, then told him that Jamie had called me to ask me why I'd given Wes the information about the dolls.

"Interesting," he said, which told me nothing about his reaction. He asked for the details of our conversation, then changed the subject. "How are you feeling about things? Any second-guessing your decisions? Any questions?"

"No. I'm okay."

"If that changes, get in touch. Don't brood. I just sent you an e-mail about meeting Jamie and Lorna at eleven. You can leave, drop your car off on the way. Let me give you the name of the service station. Do you have a pen?"

I got one at a worktable and jotted the name and number down. I knew the location. It was close to Blackmore's. I glanced at a wall clock. It was just after ten. He didn't need to talk to Dawn, so we ended the call.

"So what am I getting my mother for her birthday?" Dawn asked as we walked toward the front office.

"How about a silver soup ladle?"

"How much?"

"Seventy-five dollars, nineteenth century, newly replated."

"Sounds fair. She'd love it. For real, actually."

I smiled, a small one. "After this is over, come back and we'll pick out something really special for her, a thank-you for her daughter's efforts. For now, it's the ladle."

I took it from the shelf as I walked her out and handed it to Gretchen for processing and wrapping.

Dawn thanked me so everyone would hear, and I watched her walk to her car, seemingly impervious to the reporters' hollered questions.

I turned back to my staff. Cara was typing something into her computer. Gretchen was using an adding machine with her right hand as her left index finger ran down a column of figures. Sasha was just finishing a call. Fred was reading an auction catalogue from my former company, Frisco's, featuring objects related to magic. We'd learned that in the antiques witchcraft world, the two terms were often used interchangeably.

"What are you all doing here?" I asked, smiling. "I expected you to take the day off."

"Once we know what we're dealing with," Fred said, "you may need help."

Sasha nodded.

"I couldn't stay away," Cara said. "It wouldn't be right."

"I keep hoping we'll hear something," Gretchen said.

Feeling their eyes on my face, my throat closed, but only for a moment. I wanted to fill them in, to reassure them that they were in the loop, but I couldn't reveal our plans and I didn't want to lie. Everything I could do to help find Eric was being done. The campaign was under way. What I needed to do now was act natural.

"I'm as anxious as anyone," I said, choosing my words carefully. "As soon as I can tell you anything, I will. In the meantime, update me. What are you working on?"

Gretchen told me she was reconciling last week's tag sale receipts and waiting for the temps to come in to help with this week's setup; Sasha reported she was working on the doll appraisals; Cara said she was entering names for our mailing list; and Fred said he was reading about a shaman spirit trap similar to the one we planned to include in the witchcraft auction. Our shaman spirit trap was Burmese in origin, carved out of local hardwood, and comprised of two wooden halves. Eighteenth-century shamans, or medicine men, had used the six-inch box to trap and transport supernatural spirits.

"They're describing it as folk art," he said. "That's an interesting take on it."

"I agree. I like it. Any valuation yet?"

"Yeah. Less than we'd hoped. Probably around a hundred dollars."

I shrugged. "Oh, well . . . some collector will be thrilled!"

Without providing details, I told Cara I'd be back in a while and left.

CHAPTER THIRTEEN

hree reporters tagged along as I drove to the service station, each in a separate vehicle. One of them was Bertie. Wes was nowhere to be seen. I didn't try to lose them. When I pulled into the station and rolled to a stop at an open bay, they parked in the lot. They followed me inside, squeezing into the small office to watch me fill out the service order.

"Josie," Bertie said warmly. "How are you doing during this dreadful time?"

"Hi, Tim," I said, using the name embroidered on the service station employee's dark green jumpsuit, ignoring her. "I just need an oil change."

"We'll take care of it," Tim said. "Give us half an hour or so."

"Thanks. I'll be waiting at Blackmore's Jewelers."

Blackmore's was only two blocks from the station, but a northeast wind had come up, driving the rain sideways and lowering the temperature enough to make me wish I'd worn a jacket. The reporters trailed along, calling out questions. I pretended they weren't there.

Wes called as I approached Market Square. I answered and told him I couldn't talk to him and wouldn't be able to for a while.

"Why?" he asked.

"I'm hanging up now, Wes. You know you can trust me to tell you everything I can as soon as I can."

I punched the OFF button, leaving him arguing with the air.

Inside the shop, I shivered, damp and chilled from the walk. I waved to Nate Blackmore.

Nate, the owner's grandson and Prescott's go-to guy for jewelry appraisals, was about thirty. He was as tall and handsome as his grandfather, with manners just as polished. Blackmore's, which had been in its current location for more than ninety years, was, hands down, the finest jewelry store on the seacoast, and it looked the part. From the cherrywood paneling to the Vivaldi sonata playing softly in the background, the shop exuded refinement.

Nate waved back and started toward me, then stopped as the three reporters entered the shop.

"May I help you?" he asked, looking from one to the next.

"I just have a quick question for Josie," one man said.

"Sorry," I replied, turning my back. "'No comment' is my only answer today."

"What about Eric?" the man asked. "Do you think he's dead?"

"How about Alice Michaels, Josie?" Bertie asked. "Any thoughts on why she was killed on your property? Do you think it was a warning to you?"

"Okay, that's it," Nate said. "This is private property. Out. Now."

They went, but not quickly, and not without shouting out additional provocative and offensive questions. Once they were gone and the shop was quiet, I exhaled and looked around. A matronly woman looked shocked. A young sales clerk seemed stunned. I smiled.

"Sorry about that, everyone." I turned to Nate. "Thank you."

He shook his head. "It's awful, isn't it?"

"On so many different levels."

"Follow me," he said. He started toward the back. "Can I bring you anything? You look like you could use something warm to drink."

"That would be great. I'm so not dressed for this weather."

"Don't blame yourself—you can't dress for this weather. No one can. You know what they say about spring in New Hampshire . . . if you don't like the weather, wait five minutes."

"Totally true," I said and glanced at my BlackBerry, hoping a text from the kidnappers had arrived. No word yet.

Nate opened the heavy door, and I slipped into the back office. Morton Blackmore sat behind his oversized mahogany desk. Ellis sat in one of four guest chairs lined up on the other side of it. Both men stood as I entered.

"There's a restroom over there," Mr. Blackmore said after greeting me, "if you want to dry off a bit."

I took him up on the offer, and by the time I returned, a steaming cup of tea was waiting for me. Before I'd taken a sip, Nate opened the door and the Farmington sisters walked in. Lorna looked worried. Jamie looked wary.

"Thank you for coming in," Ellis said. "This is Mr. Blackmore. He owns the shop and has agreed to let us meet here." He completed the introductions, the polite convention and elegant surroundings creating a odd counterpoint to the potentially deadly scenario unfolding outside the shop. Mr. Blackmore offered refreshments, which were declined.

"Ladies," Mr. Blackmore said, "Chief . . . if you'll excuse me."

"Please . . . have seats," Ellis said as soon as the door clicked closed.

He stayed standing until the sisters sat down. They perched on the front edges of their seats. Lorna twisted her purse strap into a tight screw. Jamie kept her eyes on Ellis's face.

"I arranged this meeting," Ellis continued, "because I need to talk to you without anyone knowing about it. In case someone is watching, I couldn't come to you and I couldn't ask you to come to the station house. I don't know that anyone is following any of us, but we're dealing with a life-and-death situation, so I'm taking no chances. When I say no one can know about this meeting—I mean no one. I asked Josie to join us for her antiques expertise. Are you okay with committing to keeping this conversation strictly private?"

Lorna looked at her sister. Jamie kept her eyes on Ellis. "Yes, that's all right. We can do that."

"Thank you," he said to Jamie. He turned to Lorna. "Ms. Farmington? Are you all right with that commitment?"

Lorna jumped as if she'd been touched by a live wire. "Yes."

"Thank you." He took in a breath. "You know that Josie's employee Eric has been kidnapped." They nodded. "Josie has received a ransom note from the kidnapper. He wants the dolls she bought from you that are currently in her possession. That's okay. She has no problem giving them up. Where it gets complicated is why they want the dolls."

"I read that they destroyed the ones in the van," Jamie said.

"Right." He nodded in my direction. "Josie, will you explain, please?"

"We searched the dolls and found that one contained rare and valuable Civil War currency."

Jamie shot a glance at Lorna. Lorna's mouth was hanging open.

"Rare Civil War currency?" Jamie repeated, her intonation making it a question.

I recounted what Barry had told me about the origin and potential value of the find.

"It doesn't make any sense," she said.

"Why not?" I asked.

She glanced at her sister again, but Lorna didn't notice. Her eyes were me. It was educational to watch her while Jamie talked. So far, I hadn't noticed any inconsistencies between Lorna's nonverbal communications and Jamie's words.

"The currency is in three Chatty Cathys," Jamie said. "We told you that we wanted to keep them for sentimental reasons. The truth is that our mom told us that's where she hid the money."

"Chatty Cathys?" Ellis asked, all at sea.

"Chatty Cathy is a brand of doll," I explained to him, "that was manufactured by Mattel starting in 1959. They're no longer available, but at the time, they created quite a stir because they spoke. They could say eleven phrases." Ellis still looked bewildered, so I added, "The dolls had miniphonographs in their chests. You pulled a ring in the doll's back that set the phonograph spinning and it spoke one of the phrases randomly." I turned to Jamie. "They're highly collectible but not particularly valuable. First-edition blondes go for around three fifty, maybe four hundred dollars. First-edition African American dolls with pigtails are the most scarce and thus the most valuable, selling for as much as twelve hundred each." I turned to Jamie. "Someone removed the phonograph, right, and placed the currency in the now-empty chest cavity?"

"Exactly."

I nodded. "What's especially clever about that is that the dolls are often mute. The pull ring snaps off or the string it's attached to breaks.

Rubber gaskets wear out. Anyone noticing that your dolls couldn't speak wouldn't think anything about it."

"How much currency do you have?" Ellis asked Jamie.

"Nine hundred dollars, three hundred in each doll," Jamie replied. She turned to me. "How much did you find? Do you know what it's worth? Mom thought it probably had some value."

"We found a hundred bills, giving you a thousand, total." I paused to do the math. "Your mom was right. The currency may be worth as much as two million dollars at full retail, which would net you somewhere between six hundred thousand and as much as a million dollars, wholesale."

The sisters exchanged glances, and Lorna raised her hand to her mouth.

"I hope you're right," Jamie said, "but I still don't understand. Mom only told us about the Chatty Cathys. She never told us about another doll."

"Maybe she forgot, or maybe she didn't know about it. Did she tell you how she came to place the money in the Chatty Cathys?"

Jamie nodded. "It happened when my dad died. Our mom got nervous having the currency lying around, and she never trusted banks much, so she refused to put it in a safe deposit box. Mom told us that the bills had originally been hidden in dolls, but that *her* mother had removed them when World War II broke out, thinking that hiding the money in dolls was too risky if they ever needed to make a quick getaway." She shook her head and glanced at Lorna. "There's a high-strung gene that runs through some of the women in our family. Lorna's got it. I don't. Grandma and Mom both had it. I know it was a horrible time in our nation's history and everyone was on edge and scared, but from all reports, Grandma was convinced we were about to be overrun by enemy forces, so she was prepared to make a run for it. It must have been very hard on her. In any event, she must have missed emptying the cache in one of the dolls, and Mom never knew it."

"That's logical," I told her.

"Which other doll had the money in it?" Jamie asked.

"A nineteenth-century European one."

Jamie glanced at Lorna, then back at me. "Maybe there's more in some of the others."

"We X-rayed them all. There isn't."

Jamie shook her head. "I'm so taken aback." She paused for a moment. "I don't mean to be crude . . . but I assume you'll be returning the currency."

"Of course. There's no question the money wasn't part of our deal."

"Thank you."

"Do you know how the currency came into your family's possession?"

"Yes. We were always told that it came directly from our great-great-however-many-greats-grandfather Salmon Chase. We have a letter from President Lincoln discussing the currency. I don't recall that he mentioned a specific amount, but I haven't read it in years."

"That makes sense," I said. "That letter sounds amazing. Depending on the content and the context, it and the others may be even more valuable than the currency. But that's a conversation for another day." I leaned forward. "The police think, and I agree with them, that the kidnapper knew the currency was hidden in the dolls but didn't know which one or ones. Maybe he planned on taking the dolls with him but got spooked when someone drove by. Breaking them apart was a quick way to see if he could find the money."

Lorna covered her mouth.

"Which brings us to the point," Ellis said. "We want to mark the bills. We have to assume the kidnapper will check to make certain the money is intact before releasing Eric. Leaving the currency in place offers the best chance of the exchange going smoothly."

"You mean just let the money go?" Jamie asked, shocked.

"We would hope and expect to recover it all within minutes of the transfer."

Jamie shook her head. "That's too risky."

"Jamie," Lorna said on the verge of tears.

Jamie swiveled to face her sister. "No," she told her. She turned back to Ellis. "My sister is the rescue-the-wounded-bird type. I'm the practical one."

"But a man's life—" I said, breaking off as Ellis squeezed my shoulder, signaling that I should keep quiet.

"Let's come back to that in a moment," he said. "I have another question. Who knows about the currency?"

"No one."

"Someone must," Ellis stated. "Someone who's going to a lot of trouble to get it."

Jamie pressed her lips together. "The only person besides us who knew about it was Alice, but she's dead."

Ellis crossed his legs, balancing his ankle on his knee. "Your mom told you she'd confided in Alice?"

Lorna shook her head.

"Not exactly," Jamie said. "One day, while Mom and Alice were, well, I guess you'd say playing with the dolls, Alice discovered one of the caches. My mother had gone into the kitchen to make tea. When she came back with the tray, she found Alice counting the currency. Alice had found the trick latch that opened up Chatty Cathy's chest piece and removed the money Mom had hidden inside the cavity." Jamie took a deep breath. "Mom wasn't concerned. Alice and she were old friends ... best friends ... a friend Mom had safely confided in for years. Plus, Alice was rich. There was no reason to think there was any risk that she'd steal the money. As far as we know, Mom's instincts were right. Obviously Alice didn't kidnap Eric."

"You knew Alice well," Ellis said. "If you had to guess, who do you think she might have told?"

"I couldn't venture a guess," Jamie said smoothly, but my eyes were on Lorna's face.

Lorna's eyes had opened wide, and her mouth formed a little circle. Maybe Jamie wouldn't venture a guess, but I was willing to bet that Lorna had plenty of ideas.

"What do you think, Lorna?" I asked, jumping in. I smiled, hoping to rob my question of significance, trying to ease Lorna into talking more openly.

Lorna sent a panicky glance at her sister. Her hands grasped the twisted purse strap so hard her knuckles turned white. "I don't know."

"I know you don't," Ellis asked, leaning back, apparently relaxed and unconcerned, "but what do you think? Unsubstantiated guesses are welcome."

"Just that Alice and her son were very close."

"Randall," Ellis said. "You're close to him, too, aren't you?"

Lorna nodded. "We both are. Were. Randall's a wonderful man."

"What about Darleen, his wife?" I asked.

"I don't know her well," Lorna said in a different tone. Describing Randall as wonderful had sounded sincere; saying she didn't know Darleen well had sounded polite. Her purse strap snapped. "Oh! I broke it. I'm sorry, Jamie."

"It's all right, Lorna," Jamie said, patting her hand. "The cobbler will be able to fix it."

"Might Alice have confided in anyone besides Randall?" Ellis asked.

Lorna shook her head. "I don't know."

Ellis turned to Jamie. "Do you have any ideas? As I said, any thoughts are welcome. Gossip included."

"I couldn't venture a guess." Jamie turned to Lorna. "Our families were close when we were growing up, but Lorna and I have lived in Tomball, outside of Houston, for almost ten years now. Other than Christmas cards and dinner during an occasional visit, we haven't been in touch with any of the Michaels since then."

"Because of Darleen?" he asked.

Jamie snorted. "Let's just say his marriage didn't motivate us to stay in touch."

"Thank you," Ellis said. "Back to marking the money. The marks are invisible and won't affect the value of the currency."

"What if the kidnapper escapes?" Jamie asked. "Then our money is gone."

"We can make copies," I said, forcing myself to stay focused on the task at hand and directing my comment to Ellis. I didn't trust myself to look at Jamie. Letting her see my contempt wouldn't help my case and might hurt it. We still needed her cooperation—I hoped she'd let me use the Chatty Cathys. The kidnapper might not know which dolls contained the money, but he might have heard that three Chatty

Cathy dolls were part of the collection. Everything had to appear as he expected it to appear, Chatty Cathys included. "I have a super high-end color copier at my place."

"Good enough to fool someone who might know what the real stuff looks like?"

I nodded. "Yes. The paper will be the issue. I'll call Barry and get some suggestions." I glanced at my cell phone. It was eleven thirty-five. "If we have time. The kidnapper said he'll send the instructions later today, which might mean anytime from soon to midnight. Can we use your Chatty Cathy dolls?" I asked Jamie, forcing myself to smile. "I won't have time to track others down."

"Why do you need them?" Jamie asked. "The kidnapper demanded the dolls Josie bought from us, isn't that right? That sale didn't include the Chatty Cathys."

"You're right," I agreed, carefully keeping my tone neutral. "We're dealing with three distinct batches of dolls. The first batch includes the ones Eric had in the van. The second batch includes the ones I have in my safe. The third batch is the Chatty Cathy dolls in your possession. I included the Chatty Cathys in the *Seacoast Star* article listing to cover all bases. At this point, we have to assume the kidnapper thinks they're actually in the second batch."

"Maybe that's why he tried to break in," Lorna said, her eyes showing panic. "To steal the Chatty Cathy dolls." She looked at Ellis. "You asked us about that man who tried to get past Eric."

Ellis nodded. "Yes, but if that's the kidnapper, he probably was after all the dolls. At that point, it's unlikely he knew that Eric had packed them up. Still, it raises a good question. You might reconsider keeping that much currency at home."

Jamie nodded. "We will."

"I'd recommend sending the currency out for appraisal after I make the copies," I said. "We should confirm what we have, and in my opinion, we should do it sooner, rather than later. There may be something about these bills in particular that we don't know, and knowing it might lead us to the kidnapper. It's a long shot, but it can't do any harm, and sometimes long shots pay off."

"Like what?" Jamie asked.

"Like association or provenance." She looked bewildered. "Association refers to connections between an object and important or interesting historical figures or events. Provenance refers to an unbroken record of ownership. For instance, if President Lincoln personally presented these bills to Secretary Chase, that association adds value to the currency. On the other hand, if there's some marking on the bills that indicates they're part of a stash that was stolen during a robbery two years, ago, well, obviously, we don't have a clean provenance."

Jamie nodded thoughtfully. "You can tell just by looking at them?"

"Sometimes. Occasionally there are clues in or on the object itself; often discoveries occur through related research. Prescott's can't appraise the currency. For something this specialized, we need an expert."

"That's a good idea. Yes, please, send all one thousand bills for appraisal. And yes, you may have the Chatty Cathy dolls. I'll leave the money inside for now, all right?"

"Absolutely," I said.

"You understand the dolls might be destroyed," Ellis said.

Jamie nodded. "Yes. They're nothing special, just old, broken dolls from the sixties."

While she and Ellis discussed how to smuggle the dolls out of her house without alerting anyone who might be watching, I called Barry and reached him at his Madison Avenue shop. I could picture it. His storefront totaled about fifteen feet. The slip of a space was wedged between an equally narrow cigar shop and a larger men's haberdashery. Barry's window displays were always dramatic. One I recalled having seen some years earlier featured a single gold coin resting on a burgundy velvet cloth. Inside, a solitary display case, filled with miscellaneous coins and bills and related curiosities, divided the long room into two sections. Anyone was welcome in the front, but the rear section was accessible by invitation only.

"I need some help," I said. "Say I wanted to produce counterfeits of the bills I asked you about earlier. What kind of paper should I use?"

"Josie, Josie, Josie. You starting a sideline? Business a little slow?"

"Ha, ha," I said. "You know me better than that. This is for a kind of emergency situation we have going on up here."

"Is this about the kidnapping I heard about on the news?" Barry asked.

"I can't answer that."

"Understood," he said. He paused. "Will an expert be assessing the counterfeits?"

"No, I don't think so, but I don't know."

"I don't think it matters. Most experts handle so much money they can tell by feel if it's overtly wrong, but these bills were printed on thin rag paper, a specific cotton-linen mix that almost no one is familiar with. So you're probably okay. At a minimum, though, you need a similar rag paper. It's only available at specialty stores, not office supply stores, but you should be able to get your hands on it pronto. Give me a sec and I'll look up if there are any stores close to you."

"Thanks, Barry," I said, relieved. I heard him tapping into his computer.

"Kingsbridge Paper Supply in Elliot, Maine. That's their main factory, and they have a sales showroom on-site. They'd give you a sample, but not a supply. How much paper do you need? To print all one hundred?"

"One thousand."

He whistled. I could almost hear him begin to salivate. "When this is over and your employee is back safe and sound, you've got to give me a crack at the deal."

"The money isn't mine, but you know there's no one else I'd recommend, Barry. We'll be sending you the currency today for appraisal."

"What can you tell me about it?"

"According to the current owners, they're direct descendants of Salmon Chase. As you know, his signature is on this currency. They have letters from Chase to President Lincoln and from President Lincoln to Chase, so we can treat their assertion with a high degree of confidence."

"I'll want to see the letters," he said.

"If they want a written appraisal, I'll make sure you get a look at them. Right now, we just want to know about authenticity and assumptive value. Because the currency was found in four distinct locations, I'll package it as four units, one containing a hundred bills, the other three containing three hundred bills each."

He asked some logistical questions, when we needed the info and whom he was billing. I answered his questions, then asked, "Is there anything else I need to know to produce credible counterfeits?"

He thought for a minute before answering. "Back then, they printed them four to a sheet and hand-cut and hand-trimmed them. How do you plan to cut them?"

"You tell me."

"Use a paper cutter with a sharp blade. For touch-ups, use an X-Acto knife."

"I can do all that."

"Let me call Kingsbridge," Barry offered.

"Have them messenger it to the Congregational Church," I said. "I don't want a paper company truck coming to my location." I scrolled through my phone log and gave him Ted's number and the church's address.

Barry said he'd get right back to me, and by the time I'd talked to Ted's secretary, Louise, asking her to accept delivery of the paper for me and to let me know as soon as it arrived, referring to it only as a package, he was calling back. The paper was already en route.

After Jamie and Lorna left—they were going to pack the dolls in a rolling suitcase and deliver it to the service station where my car was being loaded with tracking devices—Ellis asked, "Are you okay?"

"Except for Jamie's refusal to let us use the money, yes."

"Yeah. I'll send Dawn back to help you print and trim the bills."

"That will be a big help." I glanced at my phone. "So long as the kidnapper holds off until we're ready."

During the half hour it took for Jamie to drive to her mother's home, pack the Chatty Cathy dolls, and deliver them to the service station, I ate two lemon cookies. While I sat quietly, thinking and nibbling, Ellis made a series of phone calls, getting updates, asking for details, guarded, as usual. I was sitting right next to him, but I learned nothing.

I was reaching for another cookie when his phone rang.

"Good," he said. He hung up and turned to me. "Are you ready to go? Jamie just dropped off the suitcase."

I leapt up. "Absolutely."

Louise called as I was turning onto the interstate to tell me the package had arrived. I told her I would be there in ten minutes. I kept my eyes on my rearview mirror as I drove but got no hint that anyone but the minicaravan of reporters was following me.

This time I needed to lose them. The church was my private refuge, and I wasn't willing to compromise it. I took the back roads but couldn't shake them. I turned onto the interstate again. I tried speeding up and slowing down. They stayed with me as if their lives depended on it, and as I thought of it, I realized that maybe their livelihoods did. It wasn't going to be easy to deliver the ransom without company. I slipped in my earpiece and called Louise at the church.

"I hate to ask," I said, "especially in this nasty weather, but I'm wondering if you can deliver the package to my company without telling anyone what you're doing. I've got reporters following me, and it's vital that no one knows what I'm up to."

"Of course, Josie," she said. "I'll do it now."

"Thanks so much, Louise. It's important it stay dry. Wrap it up well, okay?"

"Will do. Will you be there?"

"I'm en route now, but I don't know whether you'll beat me there or not. It's best that you leave it regardless. Maybe you could put it in some plain box or container and simply put my name on it."

She agreed, and I thanked her again.

I stopped trying any fancy moves to lose the reporters and drove straight back to Prescott's. As I was navigating the last turn before reaching our parking lot, Gretchen called.

"Darleen and Randall Michaels are here," she said. "They're hoping to talk to you."

I knew the shades of Gretchen's voice well enough to know that she was not happy.

"What's wrong?" I asked.

"Uh-huh," she replied.

"You can't talk. So I will. Is it Darleen who's the problem?"

"Yes."

"Wow . . . I can tell from your tone that you're annoyed. Is she really that bad?"

"Absolutely," Gretchen said with conviction.

"I'm braced. I'll be there in five minutes."

"Great! I'll let them know."

Apparently Alice wasn't alone in thinking Darleen deserved the title Ms. Attila the Hun.

CHAPTER FOURTEEN

I ran through the steady rain to my company's front door, dragging the suitcase behind me and clutching my tote bag to my chest to shield it as best I could. I'd found an umbrella in my car, a good thing, but even so, I was glad to reach the overhang. I shook off the umbrella and opened the door, but before stepping inside, I paused and looked back. Several reporters, including Wes and Bertie, stood watching me. Some, like Bertie, stood under umbrellas; others, like Wes, stood under dripping trees. All of them looked irritated and impatient.

"When you have a minute," a woman said from inside the office.

Her tone got my hackles up. She sounded as if she were speaking to a lazy child. I stepped inside, shut the door, said a general hello to my staff, then smiled and nodded at the woman who'd spoken to me and the man sitting beside her.

"This is Darleen Michaels and her husband, Randall Michaels," Gretchen said, "and this is Josie Prescott."

Darleen sat with her hands folded and her elbows resting on the table. She wore a dark gray dress, maybe a sign of mourning, maybe a reflection of her mood. Her supershort, spiky hair was dyed platinum blond. Her eyes were dark brown and unforgiving. I glanced at Randall. He was tall and slender, with rounded shoulders. His hair was sandy brown and cut short. His brown eyes were flecked with gold. I only saw them once, when he raised them momentarily to my cheek as we were introduced. He lowered them right away and kept them down.

"Nice to meet you," I said. "I'll be with you in a sec." I slid my umbrella into the Chinese blue-and-white-patterned stand we kept by the door for that purpose, then wheeled the Farmingtons' suitcase to the center of the room. "Fred, will you take this to the back work-table?"

Fred stood and grabbed it. "You bet. Want me to empty it?"

"No, thanks. Just leave it there." He headed off.

I turned to Darleen and Randall. "Come on upstairs. Can we get you anything? Coffee? Tea? Lemonade?"

"We're fine," Darleen replied sharply.

"How about you, Randall?" I asked, irritated at her domineering attitude.

"Darleen?" he asked.

"A quick one, if you want."

"Thanks," he told her. To me he said, "I'd love a coffee. Thank you."

He sounded almost friendly, but there was nothing friendly about Darleen. The muscles in her jaw grew rigid as he spoke. Evidently she didn't like his expressing an opinion at odds with hers, even about something as insignificant as coffee, even though he'd checked with her first. Or maybe I was reading too much into it. For all I knew, Randall asked for coffee so they'd have to sit a while and visit, so Darleen would have to slow down, calm down. I knew from experience that sitting and chatting could sometimes be an antidote to distress. Asking Gretchen to bring his coffee upstairs, I escorted them to my office. I took one of the yellow wing chairs. Darleen perched on the matching love seat, her body language conveying that she didn't intend to stay long. Randall sat next to his wife, farther back, a small rebellion, perhaps.

"I'm so sorry for your loss," I told them. "I enjoyed knowing Alice. Very much. And I've long admired all she's done for Rocky Point."

"Thank you," Randall said, his eyes on the carpet. "It's hard to fathom that she's gone."

"I know what you mean. She's there. Then she's not. It was like that for me, too, when my dad died. Have you made funeral plans yet?"

He shook his head, shot Darleen a glance, then raised his eyes to my cheeks. "No, not yet."

"Please let me know when you decide what to do."

"We will. My mom admired you very much. She was impressed with your knowledge and integrity."

Darleen jiggled her bracelet, then, moments later, began tapping her foot. Sometimes chitchat calmed people down; other times it stirred them up. I kept my eyes on Randall's face, willing him to look me in the eye. It didn't work. He never glanced higher than my cheeks.

"That's really nice to hear," I said. "Thank you for making it a point to tell me." I turned to Darleen. "What can I do for you?"

"We need your help," she said, her tone clipped. "We have reason to think the attorney general is about to get a court order that will freeze all of my mother-in-law's assets. It's completely unjustified and unreasonable, and of course we'll fight it. In the meantime, we need to get prepared. After her house, one of her most valuable nonfinancial assets is her doll collection. You appraised it about a year ago."

"Right. For insurance purposes."

"We want you to update the appraisal. If the attorney general confiscates it, he'll get an appraisal from someone we know nothing about and we'll have no power to argue their determination of value. This way, at least we'll have a benchmark. The issue is this: Alice left everything to our daughter, Brooke. It may seem insensitive that we're doing this now, with Alice just dead, but we have to protect Brooke's inheritance as best we can. The vultures are circling. There's no time to delay."

I heard Gretchen's heels click-clacking up the stairs. I was glad for the diversion. I wanted a moment to think about how to handle this uncomfortable request. I didn't want to be in the middle between angry investors trying to recover lost funds and a lionesslike mother trying to protect her daughter's inheritance. Gretchen, her expressive eyes signaling she was aware of tension in the room, placed the tray on the butler's table and left. She'd brought a pot of coffee and three cups.

"Darleen? Gretchen brought extra cups. Would you like to reconsider?" I asked as I poured Randall's coffee from the tall Lenox pot.

"No," she said, crossing her legs, keeping her eyes on mine. "Is there a reason you're hesitating? We're not asking you to do anything illegal or unethical. We want a fair and impartial appraisal, that's all."

I nodded. "I'll be glad to help."

"Good. Thank you. Can you do it right away?"

"Yes. We have the appraisal information from last year, so that will speed up the process."

"We have the dolls in the car along with the documentation. There are twenty-six of them. We also brought along a jewelry box. It's a recent acquisition. Alice said it was just about the most valuable piece she owned."

"More so than the dolls?"

"That's what she said."

"Interesting," I said. Having already agreed to appraise the dolls, I didn't hesitate. "We'll be glad to appraise it, too. I'll ask Gretchen to prepare the paperwork."

I was reaching for the phone to call down to Gretchen when the intercom rang. Cara wanted to let me know that Dawn LeBlanc had arrived with a question about her mother's birthday gift and Louise from the church had dropped off a box for me. I told her we'd be right down and asked her to transfer me to Gretchen.

"Gretchen," I said, "we're going to appraise Alice's doll collection, the same one as last year, plus any new acquisitions she made. Pull the records so you can prepare the paperwork. Also, there's a jewelry box we're going to look at, too."

"I'm on it!" she said.

I hung up and smiled at Randall. "I offer you coffee, then don't give you time to drink it. Feel free to bring your cup with you."

He thanked me but left his cup on the tray. I walked them to the front office and turned them over to Sasha and Gretchen, then picked up the box Louise had delivered from Cara's desk and invited Dawn and Fred to accompany me.

As I stepped into the warehouse, I heard Darleen griping about having to fill out new paperwork, saying any delay might lead to disaster.

•　　•　　•

"Fred," I said as soon as we were in the warehouse, "I'm enlisting your help. I'm not going to explain. I just need you to do as I ask. All right?"

"Sure," he said, doing a good job of keeping his astonishment under wraps.

"Don't let anyone into the warehouse until I give an all clear. I have no clue what excuse you can use, but you need to think of a good one. Any ideas?"

"How long for?" he asked.

"Less than an hour, at a guess. Certainly less than two."

He stared at me for a moment, then grinned. "I'll tell Cara and Sasha you're working on a surprise for Gretchen's bridal shower. I'll tell Gretchen you're working on a surprise for Eric's homecoming."

"Perfect."

"Can I help? I mean, I could whisper around, then come in and help."

I thought for a moment. "Yes," I said. "We can use the help."

He looked pleased. "I'll be back in a flash."

"Meet us at the photocopier."

He returned to the office, and Dawn and I started toward the back.

"You're sure that was smart?" she asked.

"Yes. I trust him completely. Also, he worked with me on identifying the smashed dolls and looking for contraband last night, so he knows something is up."

"Fair enough," she said.

We walked for several seconds without speaking, our footsteps the only sound until I heard a soft mew followed by a pitter-patter. Hank padded up and mewed again.

"Hi, Hank," I said, looking down. "I can't play right now. I'm busy."

He trotted along beside me, certain, it seemed, that I'd change my mind.

"When I drove to Blackmore's," I said to Dawn, "the reporters were on me like bad breath. No way am I going to be able to drive to a ransom drop without a conga line of them trailing behind me. I don't know how to shake them loose."

"Yeah, that's not good," she said. "Let me call Chief Hunter while you retrieve the money."

I opened the safe and extracted the evidence bag containing the hundred bills I had in my possession. By the time I got back, she was off the phone.

"He'll take care of it," she told me. "When the time comes, you focus on getting wherever you're going safely and let him worry about the media. Just be sure and keep him posted so he'll know which route you'll be taking." She turned toward the dolls. "What can I do to help?"

"We need to photocopy this money," I said, pointing, "onto this paper." I held up the box. "Then trim it neatly. Follow me."

I led the way to the alcove near Hank's area where the super-duper color photocopier had its own alcove. We used it for weekly tag sale signage, auction flyers we posted around town, and auction catalogue mock-ups. I Windexed the glass, drying it carefully to avoid streaks, then laid out four bills on the glass surface. I ran off a single copy, then placed it in the paper drawer upside down. I turned over the currency, trying to position it so it lined up with the other side.

"Here's hoping the alignment is right," I said as I pushed the START button.

It wasn't even close. The back side of the currency was off by upwards of an eighth of an inch. I tried again, using the copier's built-in ruler as a guide.

"This is better," I said, "but it's not good enough. Do you see what I mean? The left border is narrower than the right."

Five tries later, I got it, or at least I got it as close as possible using trial and error.

"In the printing business, they call this a 'make-ready.'" I held it up. "It's far easier to replicate a single sheet than it is to replicate bits and pieces." I examined it closely. "Now we can copy the lot. Once they're done, we'll use the paper cutter to separate them one sheet at a time." I showed her how to line up the paper on the paper cutter so it was perfectly square.

"The secret to clean cuts is to use force," I said, demonstrating. "If you go too slowly or too lightly, the cutting arm drags through the paper."

"Got it. I'm pretty handy, so I think I'll be fine."

Fred joined us as Dawn was inserting the first sheet.

"Any problems?" I asked him.

He shook his head. "Nope. All set."

"Good. You can work with Dawn to cut and trim the bills."

I repeated Barry's suggestion for how to prepare the bills, watched Dawn cut one sheet with crisp precision, then hurried to the work-table.

I found the European doll whose head we'd detached and tacked it back on. My goal wasn't to achieve stitches of restoration quality; I simply wanted to ensure that the kidnapper wouldn't see anything awry. When I was done I held the doll up and nodded. It would do.

I lifted the Chatty Cathy dolls out of the suitcase.

Each of the three soft vinyl dolls was tucked in a clean white pillowcase, two blondes and a brunette. I placed one of the blondes on the work surface. She wore an ice blue dress with a white eyelet, short-sleeved bolero-style top, off-white anklet socks, and black Mary Janes. Her hair was styled in a pageboy. Her blue eyes were open wide. I removed her clothes, revealing the speaker built into her chest. The pull ring lay flat against her back. I pulled the string and it moved smoothly, but, as expected, she was mute. On her front side, her upper torso had been fabricated as a separate unit and was connected to her bottom half with what appeared to be some kind of sealant. Neither the design nor the construction allowed access to the miniphonograph that gave her voice.

I should have asked Jamie how to open her, I thought, deciding to give it a try on my own before calling her. I slid my finger along the seam seeking some sign of an opening, a gap perhaps, or a lever. The seal was unbroken. I turned her over and noticed another seam, this one hidden by her hips. I pushed and prodded, easing my fingernail into the crevice. Halfway around, I ran into an obstacle, a hard plastic latch. I tapped it, and Chatty Cathy's back raised up silently and smoothly. I was staring into her chest cavity. I opened all three dolls and extracted the bills. My count matched Jamie's information: Their inheritance now included one thousand bills. If Barry's estimate held, I was looking at two million dollars' worth of rare currency. I placed each doll's currency in a separate envelope and the hundred bills in another.

"We're done," Fred called, and I ran to join them.

All three of us examined each counterfeit bill to ensure it had been properly trimmed, then counted out stacks of twenty and rolled them into tight cylinders, fastening each one with a rubber band.

"We can take it from here," I told Fred. "Thank you. Check back in fifteen minutes or so, okay?"

"Will do," he said.

I stood, listening to his footsteps recede, and then Dawn and I slipped the rolls of bills inside the dolls' chests, stacking them like logs. As I wrapped each doll in flannel, I felt my anxiety grow.

"Why hasn't the kidnapper contacted me again?" I asked Dawn.

"He's getting his ducks in a row," she said. "He'll call when he's ready."

"I'm going a little nuts waiting."

"That's normal." She held up the kachina doll. "What's this?"

I explained its history, adding, "It's horrible to think that some-one may stomp it to bits. Not only is it beautiful, but it's historically and culturally significant, too. But we have no choice."

"I'm with you," Dawn said. "When given a choice of a man's life or an object, the object loses every time. Or should."

"Yeah. Not everyone agrees, though. Lots of people have died trying to preserve objects worth pennies. Value is relative." As I reached for another length of bubble wrap, I saw that my hand was trembling. "Look at me. I'm a mess." I closed my eyes and gripped the countertop to steady myself. "God, I hope we're doing every-thing we can to help Eric." I opened my eyes and looked at her straight on. "Do you think I'm making a mistake? Should I call the FBI? Tell me the truth. It's not too late to change my mind."

Dawn shook her head. "I'm sorry, but I can't advise you, Josie."

I straightened up. "Yeah . . . I know. No one can."

I finished wrapping the last doll and placed it in the plastic tub. I lowered the top and latched it; then Dawn and I double wrapped it in heavy plastic to protect it from the rain.

"Now if I can only keep it together long enough to deliver the ransom." I laughed, embarrassed. "I'm a quivering mass of jelly."

"You'd never know it. You seem darn poised to me."

"Thanks. It's all an illusion." I smoothed the last piece of tape. "That's it. We're done. Thanks for the help, Dawn. Thanks for listening. I'm fine. I'll be fine."

"You're welcome. I know you'll be fine. You'll be great. What else can I do?"

"Nothing. Neither can I. All we can do now is wait."

She said good-bye, and we walked to the front office. Keeping to the story, she thanked me for letting her check out a couple of other gift options for her mom.

"You were right in the first place, Josie," Dawn said. "She's going to love that ladle."

She ran through the still-steady rain to her car. I watched as reporters watched her. I didn't see Bertie or Wes. I wondered if any of them would follow her.

I caught Fred's eye and nodded, giving him a thumbs-up, then selected a large padded envelope from the stock in our storage cabinet and headed back into the warehouse.

"Cara," I said from the door, "I'll be in the back."

One step in, I heard Fred say to Sasha, "All clear."

Thanks, Fred, I said silently.

I wanted to pack up the currency and get it into Barry's hands as quickly as possible, but I needed a moment's respite. I'd confessed that I'd felt a little rocky to Dawn, but she didn't know the half of it. I needed a moment to regroup, to regain my equilibrium. I headed straight to Hank.

He was eating, so I stopped on the concrete just shy of his rug, not wanting to disturb him. He crunched purposefully. After a few bites and chomps and swallows he turned to his water bowl and lapped for several seconds, then, as if he could sense my presence, looked over his shoulder, saw me, and mewed. He scampered to me, mewing all the way, asking for a hug.

"Hi, Hank," I said, scooping him up. "Do you want a little cuddle?" He nuzzled my neck.

"I'm upset, Hank. I'm really, really upset."

He licked my ear, one lick, then tucked his head under my chin again.

"I know . . . I know . . . You're right . . . I'm doing all I can."

Hank settled in and began purring.

I held him close and petted him, long strokes along his back and short ones running from his tummy to under his chin. Down his back and up his chest. Down and up. Down and up.

"What a good boy you are, Hank. You're *such* a good boy."

His purring grew louder. After a minute, maybe two, I said, "I could stand here and pet you all day, baby boy, but I've got to go." I kissed the top of his head and placed him on the rug. He stretched, then sauntered back to his food bowl and picked up where he left off, and I walked to the table where I'd left the money with the comforting sounds of his crunching in the air.

I packed up the four envelopes containing the currency and brought the envelope back to the office. I asked Gretchen to call for a courier pickup and to e-mail the receipt for nine hundred bills to the Farmington sisters.

"Did you just find them?" she asked, as curious as Hank once he got a whiff of a new toy.

"I'll tell you about it later," I said. "Right now, consider it confidential information."

"All right," she said, her eyes communicating her concern.

I called Barry myself to tell him to expect delivery in the morning, then went back to my office to wait for word from the kidnapper. My part was done. All I was supposed to do now was wait. I wasn't a good waiter. I couldn't work. I couldn't think. I couldn't read or watch TV. All I could do was watch the rain patter against the window. I tried to think of something to do, anything. I called Grace.

"I've almost called a dozen times," she said. "I knew if you had news you'd tell me."

I bit my lip. "I'll tell you everything I can," I said.

"That sounds like you know something, but you won't tell me."

"No, I don't." *I wish,* I thought. "How's Eric's mom? Have you spoken to her since last night?"

"Yes. She's upset, as you might imagine. She wanted to call you but decided not to. She told me that she doesn't trust herself to talk to anyone, not when she feels like this." She cleared her throat. "Chief Hunter tells me he's certain there'll be a ransom note. Do you know why he would—"

My cell phone vibrated, wiggling across the desk, a text message. I pushed the READ button. It was a text from the kidnapper.

"Grace," I said, "excuse me for interrupting—I need to go. I'll call you later." I hung up.

The kidnapper asked, **DOLLS READY?**

My eyes filled, I was so relieved to hear from him.

I typed: **YES. ERIC OK?**

I hit SEND and stared at the screen waiting for his reply. None came. After several minutes, I realized there would be no immediate response. More waiting. More anxiety. More fear. I transcribed the message and my reply into the disposable phone Ellis had given me, then added, **WHY HASN'T HE REPLIED?**

I hurried into the warehouse to send the message, then called him directly.

"Did you get it yet?" I asked. "The text? I just sent it."

"I see it. Good news."

"Why is it good? We don't know anything more than we did before he sent it."

"Communication is always good. As long as he's talking and sees that you're cooperating, he has no reason to worry. Remember that he has to be feeling anxious, too."

I nodded, struck by Ellis's unexpected perspective. "That's funny to think about, isn't it? It hadn't occurred to me, but I bet this is his first time kidnapping someone. I mean, it's not the kind of thing you do week in and week out."

"Very true."

"But he didn't tell me about Eric," I said.

"He will."

"What would you think of my making him send me a photo of Eric holding today's *Seacoast Star* before I agree to the meet?"

"It's a risk, Josie. We don't know how twitchy he is. Your demanding anything may send him over the edge."

"Is this the kind of thing the FBI might be able to advise us about?"

"Yes."

"Can you ask them without committing us to bringing them in?"

"I know someone I can call."

"Thank you, Ellis. Will you ask them now?"

"Yes. Hang in there, Josie."

I paced, waiting for Ellis to call back, waiting for the kidnapper to reply. Hank was eating again, and when he was done I gave him a bottom pat. He nuzzled my hand and raised his chin. I took the hint and gave him a nice underchin rub. He was getting the massage, yet I found myself relaxing.

"Good boy," I said. "I don't know when I'll be leaving, Hank, so I'll refresh your food and water now, okay?"

Ellis called as I was adding crunchy bits to Hank's food bowl.

"My contact's answer is the same as mine. We don't know how he'll react to a demand. That said, my contact thinks, and I concur, that the kidnapper has to expect you to want proof Eric is alive before handing over the ransom."

"I'm going to do it," I said. "I think it's a reasonable request, and if the kidnapper is a rational person, he will, too. If he's not rational, well, we're in big trouble anyway." I paused for a moment. "Please thank your FBI person for me."

"I will. Are you doing all right?"

"No. I'm pacing. I can't work."

"Understood," he said. "I suspect you won't hear anything for the next few hours."

"Why?"

"Because if I were trying to pick up a tub full of dolls without attracting a lot of attention, I'd wait until after dark."

"That makes complete sense." I sighed. "But that's hours away."

"I know you, Josie. You should try to work."

Ellis was right. Throughout my adult life, whenever I've been depressed or worried, I've counted on work to help me cope. Doing nothing only exacerbates my anxiety. I trudged back to my desk and picked up Fred's draft for the catalogue of witchcraft objects. If anything could captivate my mind, reading catalogue copy could.

The auction was unusual and would, I was certain, attract a fair amount of publicity. One of our best finds was a sixteenth-century book, Reginald Scot's *Conjuring Tricks from the Discoverie of Witchcraft*. Scot published the book to debunk claims that witches had magical powers by revealing magicians' tricks.

"I'm hot on the trail of connecting this witchcraft book to James Boswell," Fred wrote in a parenthetical note to me.

I couldn't help smiling. James Boswell was well respected in his own right, but he was better known as Samuel Johnson's friend and biographer. If Fred could nail down the book's provenance, the value would skyrocket, going from our current estimate of twenty-five hundred dollars to perhaps as much as twenty-five thousand.

"It has an owner's signature reading 'James Boswel,'" Fred's note continued, "and I have a source who says Boswell spelled his name with one *L* for two years while he was in law school. If it's true, I figure it's like that girl Becky I dated in college. For about a month she wrote her name as Beckee, just to be different, I guess. After a while she got tired of correcting everyone, so she went back to good old-fashioned Becky."

I smiled at the thought of a young man in the eighteenth century wanting to show his individuality in a conventional world. *The more things change,* I thought, *the more they stay the same.* I could easily believe that Boswell had, while studying law, become intrigued with magic and witchcraft. Lots of college kids do.

Cara called up to tell me that everyone was leaving for the night. I glanced at my computer monitor. It was two minutes after five. I'd been absorbed for nearly three hours. *Thank you, Ellis,* I thought. I asked Cara to lock the front door, explaining I would be staying awhile longer and would set the night alarm when I left. I resumed my reading.

Ty called about seven.

"I'm done in," he said, "and feeling a little sorry for myself. I just got back to my room with my dinner, a turkey sub. I miss your cooking."

His mentioning food made me realize I hadn't eaten in forever. I had no appetite, but I knew I needed food.

"I miss cooking for you," I said, "and you've just reminded me to eat."

"Good. Go get something now and we can eat together."

"I can't. I'm waiting for word from the kidnapper."

"I want to hear what's going on . . . give me one minute, okay? I'll call you right back."

He hung up, and I stared at the phone.

"Mysterious," I said aloud.

Two minutes later, Ty called back.

"I called Zoë. She's en route with food for you."

"Ty! I can't believe you did that. What about her kids?"

"She'll bring them with her. You know, Josie, it's okay to let people help you."

"Thank you, Ty," I said quietly.

"You're welcome. I wish I was there to bring you food myself."

"Me, too."

"For now, fill me in."

"Let me call you back," I said and hung up. I walked into the warehouse so I could talk openly. I tapped in Ty's number on the phone Dawn had given me earlier.

As I recounted what had happened and what I'd done, I felt my bristly anxiety return. "What do you think?" I asked him. "Have I forgotten anything?"

"Not that I can think of. It sounds like everything is under control."

"I hope you're right," I said, sighing. The front doorbell rang, its low chimes resonating throughout the open space. "That's probably Zoë."

We agreed to talk later, and I ran into the main office. Zoë's car was idling at the front door. I waved to the kids. Jake waved back, but Emma didn't see me. She was playing with the stuffed monkey she'd rescued from the trash heap Zoë had created while cleaning out the attic. Emma had named her Mary-Rose.

"Do you want company?" Zoë asked, handing me a mini-Playmate. "The kids can bunk down here with no problem. I brought their sleeping bags."

"Thanks so much for this, Zoë. I'm okay alone. To my amazement, I'm actually getting some work done."

"If you change your mind, let me know. We'll come rushing back."

I hugged her. "Thank you." I stood in the doorway watching as she drove away.

A reporter I didn't recognize ran in front of her car and held up his hand like a traffic cop, trying to stop her from driving away. She tapped the horn and accelerated, and he jumped out of the way. Zoë wasn't the least bit shy.

Zoë's care package included a tuna salad sandwich, a plastic container filled with green and red grapes, three chocolate chip cookies, and a can of ginger ale. A feast.

I ate at my desk and didn't look up from reading until my cell phone buzzed, startling me. It was eight o'clock. I had a text message. Finally, my instructions had arrived.

CHAPTER FIFTEEN

he ransom instruction seemed so improbable, I reread it twice to be certain I had it right.

**PUT DOLLS IN TRUNK. DRIVE TO THE
ROUND THE CLOCK DINER. SIT AT THE
COUNTER AND ORDER SOMETHING. WAIT
FOR A MESSAGE. GO NOW.**

The Round the Clock Diner was about as unlikely a choice as I could imagine. It was open twenty-four hours a day and busy all the time.

"Okay, then," I said. I swung my tote bag over my shoulder and flew down the stairs to call Ellis.

"I'm to go to the Round the Clock Diner. Now. With the dolls in the trunk."

"Good. Turn left out of your lot and head to I-95. Don't worry about the reporters. Don't worry about anything. Dawn will be at the diner before you. Act like you don't know her. There'll be other officers around, too. If you happen to recognize anyone, don't show it."

"Got it. I'm on my way."

"Don't drive too fast. Stay calm."

Now that the exchange was under way, I felt utterly composed. I was ready. I'm good under pressure, always have been. It's in the swirling uncertainty before a crisis and the chaotic period afterward, when I second-guess myself, that I fall apart. During the crisis itself, I'm fine. Serenity infused my veins like a drug, slowing my racing pulse and sharpening my wits. I call the phenomenon crisis-calm.

I picked up the bin and placed it in my trunk, setting the night alarm as I left. Two minutes after Ellis and I hung up, I drove out of my lot. The rain had slowed to nothing, but the air was thick with mist. It felt colder, too. It had hovered around seventy-five all day, a veritable heat wave for May, but now it felt closer to the low sixties. It wouldn't be fully dark for another half hour, but it might as well have been. The cloud cover was thick, hiding the last glimmers of twilight. A column of reporters fell into place behind me. I noted that Wes wasn't there. Bertie was first in line.

Around the second curve, I hit the brakes. A roadblock loomed in front me. A mobile digital sign sat on the shoulder, its message flashing in red: SOBRIETY CHECKPOINT. PLEASE DRIVE SAFELY. Four spotlights, two on each side of the road, their lights aimed to the sky, illuminated the road. A single orange cone sat on the white dividing line about twenty feet from the barricade. Two uniformed police officers, one male, one female, stood at the barricade, waiting.

I rolled to a stop and lowered my window.

"How you doing, ma'am?" the male officer asked.

He was about fifty and overweight. His badge read PORTSMOUTH POLICE DEPARTMENT. His name was Officer M. Toomey. A glint of silver caught my eye, and I looked to the right. His partner had moved to the passenger side of my car, standing next to the rear door, and I'd seen a reflection from her belt buckle.

"Fine, thanks," I said.

"Please turn off your engine and step out of the car."

"Okay."

"I'm going to ask you to take a field sobriety test."

"Sure."

"Please follow me." We walked around the barricade. "Please walk from here to the orange cone, placing one foot in front of another and staying on the white line."

I was certain reporters were video-recording my performance. I could imagine how the video would look on television, what a reporter might imply in his report.

"Josie Prescott, whose employee was kidnapped, snatched out of her company's van, and whose customer, Alice Michaels, was brutally shot and killed in her parking lot, was stopped at a sobriety checkpoint last night. She was given a field sobriety test, a procedure typically reserved for cases where the police suspect drunk driving. And now to the weather."

I didn't care. Let them imply I was a fall-down drunk. All I cared about was rescuing Eric.

I walked the line with no problem. He asked me to touch my nose, asked the date and the day of the week, then thanked me for my cooperation and told me I could go.

They moved the barricade just enough for my car to squeeze through, then replaced it. When the next vehicle in line, Bertie's white rental, reached the barricade, the two police officers approached it, one on each side, just as they had with me.

The road curved to the right. I glanced in the rearview mirror and saw only darkness at road level behind me and the conical white light from the standing spotlights illuminating the sky above me.

"Thank you, Ellis," I whispered.

The Round the Clock diner was housed in a long aluminum structure on the east side of Route One, not far from Portsmouth Circle. As I waited by the IT IS OUR PLEASURE TO SEAT YOU sign, I scanned the restaurant. It was about half full, mostly couples, but there were families, singles, and groups, too. A waitress in a pink uniform led two men who'd arrived just ahead of me to a table.

"Hey, Ger," a big man in a booth by the window called to one of the newcomers. "Did you hear the news of the day? Doug here is going to build himself a kayak."

The man called Ger cackled. "Makes sense. That canoe he built worked out so well."

All of them laughed at the inside joke, and as I glanced around, I had the thought that shared jokes were a kind of glue in relationships. I wondered what kind of jokes Eric and Grace shared. I breathed in through my nose and out through my mouth, wishing I could stop thinking.

The Round the Clock was seriously retro. Hubcaps were mounted on walls as art alongside posters of James Dean, Marlon Brando, and

Marilyn Monroe. There were old-fashioned minijukeboxes at each booth. Four people sat on black leatherette and chrome spinning stools at a pink Formica counter. A sign mounted on the wall read HOME OF THE ORIGINAL HUBCAP HAMBURGER.

"How ya doing?" the waitress asked, smiling as she approached. She had chin-length brassy-blond hair and dark blue eyes. She wore a frilly white apron over her pink dress and sturdy white tie-up shoes. Her outfit was very 1950s chic. Her nameplate read ALLIE.

"Good," I said, because that's what you say when strangers ask. "May I sit at the counter?"

"You bet. Help yourself to any stool you want."

"Allie, darlin', more coffee when you get a chance," a man three tables away called out.

"Coming right now, Lar," Allie replied.

Laughter popped up at the table to the right, then faded away, then popped up again. Doug who was building himself a kayak slid out of the booth, chuckling. A woman in a nearby booth began dancing from the waist up to "Under the Boardwalk" as she flipped through the jukebox options. Dawn sat at a table facing the front door, sipping a tall Coke from a straw that bent. I didn't see anyone else I knew. Jovial banter wafted over me, as heartening as the smell of baking bread. I slid onto a stool near the end of the counter. No one sat on either side of me.

Another waitress came up and smiled, sliding a laminated menu in front of me. Her name tag read CYNDI.

"This sure is a happy place," I remarked.

"Wait 'til you taste the food, hon. You'll see why."

"I look forward to it, but for now I'll just have coffee."

I'd taken three sips when someone tapped my shoulder. I swiveled to see who it was. It was a boy, a young man, about eighteen, I guessed. He was a stranger.

"Is your name Josie?" he asked.

"Yes."

"Here." He handed me a bulky padded envelope and started to turn away.

"Wait a minute!" I called. "What's going on?"

"I dunno. Some guy asked me to run this in to you."

"What guy?"

He shrugged. "Just a guy. I was coming in with a friend when he called out from his car. Said he forgot to give it to you."

"What did he look like?"

He looked at me like I was crazy. "I dunno. A guy."

"How old was he?"

"I'm not so good with guessing ages," he said. "Look, I've got to go."

"What kind of car was he driving?"

"A white Impala. About five years old."

"Did you get the plate number?"

"No. What's going on, lady?"

"Please . . . bear with me, okay? What's your name?"

"Marc Johnson. Marc with a *c,* for Marcus."

"Do you live around here?"

"Sure. Over by the library. On McNabb Court."

"Good. Great. What's your phone number?" I stuck my hand in my tote bag and felt around for a pen.

"I gotta go, lady. Sorry."

He turned and fled, heading to a booth near the back, and I let him go. I had enough information so the police could find him. I tore into the envelope. Inside, I found a cell phone and a car key. There was a text message waiting for me on the phone.

PAY YOUR BILL. LEAVE ALL YOUR THINGS IN YOUR CAR'S TRUNK. KEEP ONLY THIS PHONE AND THE CAR KEY. GO NOW.

I flagged Cyndi down and got the check, left enough money on the counter to cover it and a tip, and went to the ladies' room. I locked myself in a stall and sent Ellis a text on the phone he'd given me, typing in the message I'd received. I ended it:

WISH ME LUCK.

Outside, I hurried to my car and opened the trunk. As I swung my tote bag inside, the phone I'd just received buzzed, alerting me to a text message's arrival. Someone was watching me. I scanned the lot but saw nothing unexpected. Two men were sitting in their cars with the engines on, one a Lexus, the other a Mini Cooper. Waiting for a friend or a spouse who went to the restroom, I guessed. A car pulled in and parked. Another car circled the lot coming from the rear and left. A woman stepped out of the diner, jogged to the Lexus, and got in, and they drove away. The man in the Mini Cooper turned off his engine and got out. He stretched, then glanced at his watch and hurried across the lot, as if he were late. Probably he'd wanted to finish listening to something on the radio.

The text read:

> **GO TO GREEN CAMRY PARKED AT BACK.**
> **SIT IN CAR. PUT OVERHEAD LIGHT ON.**
> **GO NOW.**

Just like that, the GPS devices we'd planted in my tote bag and car were lost. *At least I still have my boots,* I thought. I found the Camry in the last row of the lot at the rear of the building by pressing the UNLOCK button on the key and watching for the flashing lights. I slid in behind the wheel and turned on the overhead lamp, wondering if police were nearby, hidden in cars or in the surrounding woods. A jumbo-sized blue bath towel was folded neatly on the front seat. I turned back corners to find the label. It was part of the Room Essentials collection and was, I knew, sold at Target stores nationwide. I stared at it for a moment, then checked the phone's number. It had a 617 area code. The eastern part of Massachusetts. It buzzed. Another text.

> **DRIVE TO YOUR CAR. TRANSFER DOLLS**
> **TO CAMRY'S TRUNK. SIT IN CAMRY WITH**
> **LIGHT ON. GO NOW.**

I did as I was instructed, backing the Camry up to my car, leaving about two feet between them. I hoisted the tub up and into the Camry's trunk, then got back behind the wheel and turned the light on.

DRIVE TO FIELDSTONE INN. RT 1 NEAR HAMPTON. ON LEFT.

I knew the Fieldstone Inn. It was a new construction, all-suite residency hotel. I'd met the manager at the last chamber of commerce breakfast. It took about twenty minutes to get there, a straight shot down Route One. There was a steady stream of cars going in both directions, enough so I couldn't tell if anyone was following me. When I got there, I turned into the lot and stopped. Thirty seconds later, a message arrived.

DRIVE TO POOL IN BACK.

Lights were on in about half the rooms, including a ground-floor unit overlooking the pool. The blinds were up. A man about my age was sitting on the bed watching TV, drinking beer from a bottle. The kidnapper could be watching me from any room, a creepy thought. I rolled to a stop.

TAKE KEYCARD FROM GLOVE BOX. LEAVE CAR KEY ON FRONT SEAT. TAKE TOWEL AND PHONE. GO TO . . .

Another text arrived.

. . . HOT TUB. REMOVE BOOTS AND CLOTHES TO UNDERWEAR. SIT IN TUB AND SUBMERGE HEAD. GET OUT AND TOWEL OFF . . .

"What?" I said aloud. "Are you nuts?"

I looked around. The man on the bed seemed oblivious to anything going on outside.

"I get it—you think I might be wired."

It occurred to me that he might be listening in, that possibly he'd rigged the Camry with GPS, just as we'd done to my car, and added a listening device as well. He wouldn't need to follow me . . . he could track me. He could also hear if I was making unauthorized calls—but I could text Ellis from the new phone.

. . . DON'T GO OUT OF SIGHT. GO NOW.

He's watching me. My heart leapt into my throat at the thought.

I looked around. The place appeared to be deserted, but there were ample hiding places—stands of trees and bushes, a janitor's shed near the pool, any of the guest rooms.

I opened the glove compartment. A white keycard, the kind used to access hotel guest rooms, rested on the black plastic. The only marking was a blue arrow indicating which way was up.

The pool area was surrounded by a six-foot-high black iron fence. The gate was fitted with a silver lock, a boxy-looking thing with a slot near the top. I inserted the keycard into the slot, and a second later a green dot of light glowed on the top. I pushed, and the gate swung open. The pool was kidney shaped, covered with a sturdy tarp. The hot tub was positioned at the far end of the pool. A separate building housed the towel service, now closed, and changing rooms, also closed. Big red-and-white signs warned that the pool and hot tub had no lifeguard, that you used the facilities at your own risk.

I dropped the key and towel on a chaise, then sat to remove my boots and socks. I stood to take off my slacks and shirt. Goose bumps appeared on my arms and legs, and I hurried into the hot tub. The jets weren't on, but the water was hot. I eased myself in, sat for a moment, held my breath and dunked myself, then stepped out and ran through the chilly knife-sharp air and grabbed the towel. I wrapped it around myself and rubbed. The phone sounded, and I pounced.

LEAVE CLOTHES WHERE THEY ARE. TAKE KEYCARD. OPEN CAMRY TRUNK. CHANGE IN BACKSEAT. DROP YOUR UNDERWEAR OUTSIDE.

A second text arrived.

PLACE TOWEL AND KEYCARD IN TRUNK.

I ran to the car. Inside the trunk, I found a large clear plastic, kitchen-sized trash bag. I dumped the contents into the trunk. There was another towel, a match to the first, a pair of white briefs, a white bra, a black dress, and flip-flops. I stuffed everything back into the bag and got into the backseat area. Kneeling on the seat, glancing around to make sure no one was close by, I stripped off my underwear and slipped on the briefs, which were the right size, and the bra, which was too big. The dress was way too large, and shapeless. It hung like a potato sack to just below my knees. The flip-flops were too big as well. I wouldn't be able to run in them. Or kick an enemy. I felt exposed and vulnerable and cold.

I dropped my underwear on the curb, as instructed, then placed the towel and keycard in the trunk and slipped behind the wheel to wait for the kidnapper's next directive.

The man was still watching TV, still drinking beer.

I turned the heat up to high, and when the warm air began pouring forth, I held my hands up to the vent.

My boots were gone, and with them the last GPS devices.

The phone buzzed.

DRIVE TO SHAW'S IN NEWINGTON. PARK NEAR THE LEFT SIDE ENTRANCE. GO NOW.

I had to make a decision, and I had to make it now, except there was no decision to make, not really. I typed:

I WANT TO TALK TO ERIC.

I hit the SEND button before I could second-guess myself.

NO. GO NOW.

NO. A PHOTO OF HIM WITH TODAY'S PAPER OR I TALK TO HIM. NOW.

Time passed. Seconds stretched into minutes.

"Please," I whispered. "Please."

It got too hot, and I lowered the temperature. It was still too hot so I lowered the fan speed. The phone buzzed.

HE'LL LEAVE A VM. DON'T ANSWER PHONE.

I texted back: **OK.**

The phone rang six times before the automatic voice message system kicked in. I watched the display. The phone number was the same as the one sending the texts. The call lasted twelve seconds. As soon as the icon popped up, I pressed 1 and followed the prompts to retrieve it.

"Hi, Josie," Eric's message began. He sounded tired, more than tired, weary. "It's Eric. I'm okay, sort of. I got hit on the head. Do what they say, okay? Would you—"

I pounded the dashboard.

They. Eric said "they." More than one. I wasn't surprised. It would be next to impossible for one person to handle something this complicated, to manage so many moving parts, alone. A text arrived, a repeat of the last instruction.

**DRIVE TO SHAW'S IN NEWINGTON. PARK
NEAR THE LEFT SIDE ENTRANCE. GO NOW.**

I pulled out of the Fieldstone Inn's lot and headed back toward Portsmouth. The traffic was lighter, but not light enough to be able to spot a tail. Eighteen minutes later, I turned into the mega-grocery-store parking lot. A text arrived before I parked.

**GO INSIDE TO FLORIST SECTION. LOOK
UNDER PALM TREE FOR KEY. WHEN YOU
HAVE IT RETURN TO CAMRY.**

The plant and flower department was at the front on the opposite side of the store from where I'd entered. I walked past the checkout aisles. When I reached the area, I saw two five-foot queen palms in terra-cotta containers on the floor near a display of miniroses. Several smaller palms of various varieties were in plastic pots on tables. I lifted a four-foot fan palm, then a three-foot windmill, then a date palm about the same size. I found the key under a four-foot pindo palm tucked in a corner half-hidden by a chest-high stack of twenty-pound bags of potting soil.

I returned to the Camry, and in a minute another message arrived.

> **PARK CAMRY IN HIGH-HANOVER**
> **GARAGE, LEVEL 4.**

I drove back into Portsmouth's business district and turned into the High-Hanover parking garage. It was mostly deserted, and as I circled up, level by level, I saw fewer and fewer vehicles. This time my wait for the message was shorter.

> **PARK NEXT TO WHITE SONATA**
> **ON THIS LEVEL. PLACE ENTRY TICKET**
> **IN GLOVE BOX. TAKE NEW KEY AND**
> **PHONE AND NOTHING ELSE. MOVE**
> **DOLLS TO SONATA TRUNK.**

I backed the Camry up to the Sonata to make the transfer easier. When the bin was safely in the Sonata, I parked the Camry, put the parking ticket in the glove compartment, and got behind the wheel of the Sonata to wait for the next message. It came quickly.

> **TICKET, MONEY, WIG IN GLOVE BOX.**
> **PUT ON WIG. LEAVE LOT. DON'T TALK**
> **TO CLERK. TAKE SPAULDING TPK N.**
> **I'M WATCHING U.**

Icy fear threatened to take hold of me, but it faded quickly. In crisis mode, fear is acknowledged by some part of my brain, then dismissed. I looked left and right, seeing only the near-empty garage, and then I spotted a video camera attached to the outside hood ornament, its lens aimed right at me, the pinprick-sized dot of red glowing brightly.

"Okay, then," I said aloud. "Next up is the wig."

The wig was golden blond and chin length, with bangs. Tucked inside was what looked like a flesh-colored nylon stocking, except shorter. I'd never worn a wig before, and I had no idea what the nylon was for or how to put the wig on. I started the engine so I could turn on the heat. I pushed the ceiling light button, tilted the rearview mirror so I could see myself, and began experimenting. The wig was impossible to get on. I picked up the nylon piece and examined it. It was stretchy, and just for the heck of it, I tried drawing it over my head. It was tight but not uncomfortably so. It fit like a bathing cap. I worked loose strands of hair up and under the cap's edge. After several failed attempts at pulling the wig down onto my head, I discovered that if I leaned into the wig and eased it over my head, it fit as if it had been made for me. I smoothed it into place, then stared in the mirror. I was unrecognizable. Even if the police had managed to follow me, unlikely, I knew, they'd never think that the blonde in the white car was me. Without question, I was on my own.

I was heading north on the Spaulding Turnpike, as instructed, when a text message arrived. I pulled over and set my blinkers.

**TURN ON PISCATAQUA. RT ONTO RABBIT.
LEFT ONTO OLD GARRISON.**

I'd never been on Old Garrison before. It was narrow and winding and seemed to cut through a dense forest. There were no houses or cars that I could see, or if there were houses, they were set so far back not even a glimmer of light shone through. I stopped in the middle of the road to listen, in case someone was following me with his lights off. No one was. I started off again, flipping on my brights to check for side roads or turnoffs. Nothing. I could have been the last person alive in the world. If I hadn't been in crisis mode, I would have labeled what I was feeling as terror. As it was, mostly I was admiring the kidnappers' attention to detail.

A new text arrived. I rolled to a stop.

¹/₁₀ MI BEFORE SPRUCE, TURN ONTO DIRT ROAD ON RT. ENTRY HARD TO SEE. LOOK FOR NARROW PASSAGE BETWEEN TREES. GO TO END AND PARK FACING IN.

I missed it twice. I got to Spruce Lane and backed up, then did it again. The third time I lowered my window and inched forward, peering into the darkness. Calling the entry an opening was like calling a needle's eye a gaping hole. I turned in. Twigs and leaves dripping from the day's rain scraped the side of the car. The packed dirt road must have originally been some sort of cart track. The dirt was more sloppy mud than anything else, filled with gullies and dips. The road curved to the right, then left, and then, a quarter mile in, it dead-ended at a wide circular clearing, a kind of homegrown cul-de-sac. I parked as instructed, then picked up the phone, willing it to ring. Ten minutes later, just as I was about to jump out of my skin, it did.

STAY INSIDE. OPEN TRUNK.

Out of nowhere, I heard an engine. I looked into my rearview mirror and quickly turned away, momentarily blinded by dazzlingly bright white headlights.

I bit my lip. Gazing into the sideview mirrors, I had a sense that a vehicle was behind me, but I couldn't tell for sure. For all I knew the kidnappers were on a motorcycle holding klieg lights they'd mounted on a fence post to mimic a car's headlights. I knew what I needed to do, but Ellis's warning echoed in my ears. *We don't know how twitchy he is. Your demanding anything may send him over the edge.*

I hit REPLY, then typed: **NO. ERIC FIRST.**

As I hit the SEND button, my heart crashed against my ribs and my pulse began pounding in my ears. *Please, God,* I prayed.

LOOK TO YOUR RT BACK ABOUT 300 FT. STAY IN YOUR CAR OR I SHOOT HIM.

I leaned to the right, peering into the sideview mirror. Eric was sitting on the ground in stippled light, leaning against a tree. His wrists and legs were bound. His eyes were open. He was looking in my direction. He looked drugged or injured or both.

Another message appeared. OPEN TRUNK.

I replied, THEN WHAT?

He answered, I TAKE DOLLS AND LEAVE. DONE.

I thought it through. His plan was a good one. He'd be able to back out and disappear before I could get Eric inside the car.

I pushed the button, and the trunk door swung up, blocking my view. The lights behind me went out. I looked in both side mirrors but couldn't see a thing. The night was dark, and my eyes hadn't adjusted. I blinked several times, willing myself to see, but it didn't help. I got a sense of a man's shape, nothing more. I timed him. The bin bumped against the fender. Another bump. A dull pounding. Several seconds of silence. His trunk door slammed shut. His car door closed. His engine revved, not too fast. He was in control, neither anxious nor hurried. Motor sounds, receding. Four minutes from his final text message to his departure.

The second he began to drive, I threw open my door, kicked off my flip-flops, and raced through squishy mud and sharp-edged pebbles toward Eric. The kidnapper's vehicle was already out of sight, and within seconds it was out of hearing, too.

"Eric," I called as I ran. "Eric!"

Eric's mouth opened as if he wanted to speak, then closed as if he couldn't. He looked perplexed. Before I reached him, his eyes glazed over and he made a horrible rasping sound. His head lolled to the side and he slid sideways, collapsing onto the ground in a heap.

CHAPTER SIXTEEN

E ric!" I screamed as I reached him.

He lay motionless. Rope bound his hands. I wanted to check his pulse, but I couldn't force my fingers under the thick double-wrapped rope, so I pressed them against the side of his neck instead. I fell back on my heels, tears of relief running down my cheeks as I felt the reassuringly strong thump-thump-thump. As if on cue, the cloud cover thinned and silvery moonlight dappled the ground. I straightened his legs and head.

I had to get him to a hospital. I didn't know if I could lift him, let alone carry him to the car, and I was afraid that jostling him might make some unseen injury worse. I needed help. I ran back to the car, tripping on a knotty root, stumbled, and almost went down, but managed to right myself. I grabbed the phone from the passenger seat and punched in 9-1-1. I gave my location and the nature of the emergency, then dialed Ellis's cell phone and got him. He heard me out in silence, then said, "I'm en route."

I turned off the engine, plunging the scene into darkness, then changed my mind and turned the motor on again. I turned the car around so the lights would be on Eric and approaching vehicles. The headlights illuminated a pie-shaped wedge of impenetrable forest. Eric hadn't moved. The dirt in front of me was crisscrossed by tire marks, and I wondered if the technicians would be able to trace the kidnapper by the tread patterns in his tires.

I stepped out and scanned the area for something I could use as a pillow. There was nothing. I sat down beside Eric, leaned back against a tree, and lifted his head, placing it in my lap. It was all I could do for him. The mud was wet and cold, saturating my dress and chilling me. The tree bark was rough and uneven and poked at me. Drops of water fell from laden leaves, adding to my overall discomfort.

"You'll be fine, Eric," I whispered, stroking his arm. I prodded at the rope that bound his hands, trying to see a way to tackle undoing the knot. I couldn't, and I worried that my efforts might tighten, not loosen, the restraint, so I stopped. "Help is on the way. Hold on, just a little while longer."

I closed my eyes and shivered in the now-cold night air, wishing help would come already, thinking that the kidnapper was simultaneously bold and risk-averse, that kidnapping for ransom was a reckless act, yet he'd planned every move with astonishing attention to detail. Who, I wondered, fit that description? I had no idea.

"Hold on, Eric. Help will be here soon."

Three minutes later, the ambulance arrived. Two men, one younger than Eric and the other about my age, ran toward us.

"What happened?" the older man asked.

"He was conscious when the kidnapper released him, then he collapsed. Maybe he fainted. I don't know. His pulse seems strong. He told me he'd been hit on the head."

As we talked, he moved his fingers slowly over and around Eric's head and neck and back. When he was done with his physical exam, they recorded Eric's vital signs, and the younger man called in a report.

"What's wrong with him?" I asked the elder of the two.

"Too soon to tell," he said, which offered no comfort at all. To his colleague, he said, "Ready? On three."

He counted it out, and together they lifted Eric onto a gurney they'd carried to his side and strapped him in. Ellis pulled up as they were loading Eric into the back of the ambulance. He bounced along the forest edge and pulled up next to me in the clearing.

"Are you okay?" Ellis asked me, taking in my outfit and appearance.

"Eric's alive."

He nodded and approached the older man. I followed so I could listen in, but I learned nothing new. The EMT said he didn't know why Eric was unconscious, that they wanted to get him to the hospital ASAP.

"You, too, ma'am," the older EMT said. "You can ride with us."

"I don't need to go to the hospital."

"You look cold clear through. Cold's a dangerous thing."

"I appreciate your concern, but I need to talk to the chief. I'm their only lead."

"I'm putting it down that you're acting against medical advice."

"Where are you taking him?" I asked.

"Rocky Point Hospital."

"I'll talk to her about going," Ellis said.

The EMT nodded and jogged to the ambulance.

Ellis cocked his head and stared at my face. "I never would have recognized you," he said.

I touched the wig and shapeless dress. "A simple disguise."

"You okay for real?"

I felt my eyes fill, and I looked away. "No."

He nodded, then saw me shiver. "Let's get you inside," he said, "and warm you up. I've got the heat really pumping."

"I'm a mess. I'll ruin your seats."

"Removable seat covers. Not that it would matter."

I climbed into the cab.

"We'll leave in about ten minutes," he told me, "and get you a look-see en route to the station. I just need to get the techs squared away."

"Can I borrow a phone or use the one the kidnapper gave me? I want to call Grace."

"Sure," he said, scrolling through his BlackBerry to find her number and handing me the unit. "Use mine."

"Grace," I said, when I had her. "Eric's alive. He's en route to the hospital."

She screeched and dropped the phone.

"What? Who is this?" a man's voice demanded.

"This is Josie. Josie Prescott."

I could hear Grace howling in the background.

"Josie! This is Jim. Grace's brother. What's going on?"

"It's over. Eric is alive."

He asked question after question I couldn't answer until finally I interrupted him.

"I don't know anything more than I've told you, Jim. What you ought to do now is take Grace to the hospital."

"We'll leave right away."

"Do you want me to call his mom or will Grace want to?"

"Let me ask her," he said. The shrieks had stopped. I heard muffled voices. "She will, if that's all right with you."

"Absolutely," I said. "Call me if there's any news, okay? Anything. Call anytime. Use my office phone number for now. I'll check voice mail there. I don't have my cell phone with me." I gave him the number, and he promised that he'd call with updates.

Ellis's SUV was warm, hot really, but not too hot. I felt chilled clear through, the kind of cold that took more than heat to warm. I looked out the window. Ellis stood off to the side, his flashlight illuminating the road. I called Ty, and as soon as I heard his voice, I began to cry.

"What's wrong?" he asked.

I couldn't speak. A line of vehicles arrived, and Ellis walked to meet them.

"Is it Eric?" Ty asked.

"Yes," I whispered and managed to add, "he's alive."

"Injured?"

"I don't know." I gulped and forced myself to stop crying. I needed to talk more than I needed to cry. "I don't know what's wrong with him." I told him where I was and what had happened. "I'm freezing even though the heat is on high, and I'm tired, scared, and mad, all at once." Ellis opened the driver's door. "Ellis is here. I have to go."

Ty told me he loved me and that he'd call me later, and we hung up.

"You okay with a quick stop at the hospital?" Ellis asked. "As the man said, cold's a dangerous thing."

"Sure," I said.

I pulled off my wig and skullcap, ruffled my flattened hair, and leaned back with my eyes closed the whole drive to the hospital.

After I got an all clear at the hospital and changed into fresh clothes I borrowed from a stash the police kept, I gave my statement and answered scores of questions. By the end, I was so tired I felt as if I might topple over.

I trudged into my house at 3:00 A.M., beyond tired, beyond thinking. Ellis had directed an officer to retrieve my clothes and car, and after the technicians confirmed that no one but me had touched anything, it was all returned to me. I left everything except my tote bag in the car.

Ty had texted me at eleven that he was going to sleep, asking that I call when I got home, whenever that was, but I didn't. There was no point in waking him. I'd needed to hear his voice before, but I didn't now. Now I needed a hot bath. I started the water in the tub, and with the steam pouring from the faucet, encircling me, helping loosen my rock-hard muscles, I e-mailed him that I was home and safe and about to step into a bath. I told him that I'd gotten an all clear from the medical team and had given a detailed statement to Ellis. I added what Ellis had learned in a phone call from a doctor around midnight, that Eric had been drugged with they didn't yet know what. He was regaining consciousness, and all indicators pointed to his making a full recovery.

While waiting for the tub to fill, I sat on its edge and scanned my messages. Wes had called three times wanting to know what was up and offering to help. He'd texted twice and sent an e-mail, too. Jim, Grace's brother, had left a voice mail saying he had no hard news, but the doctors were optimistic. I texted Gretchen, Cara, Sasha, and Fred the good news about Eric, adding that they should feel free to tell everyone and anyone, and that I didn't know when I'd get into work. Done for the night, I tossed my BlackBerry into my tote bag and slipped into the soothingly hot water.

CHAPTER SEVENTEEN

I rolled over to see my alarm clock. It was nine fifty-seven. I closed my eyes and tried to go back to sleep but couldn't. I sat up in bed and called the hospital. The woman at the patient information desk would only tell me Eric was in good condition, so I asked to be transferred to his room. Grace answered. Eric, she reported, was awake and eating. He was feeling tired but fine.

"Do you know when he'll be released?" I asked.

"Maybe as soon as today," she said. I could hear the smile in her voice, then a man's voice in the background, the words indistinct. "He wants to talk to you."

"Eric," I said when he was on the line. "Grace tells me you're not feeling too bad."

"Yeah. A little woozy still. I got a concussion. And I was drugged."

"A concussion!"

"Yeah. He whacked me a good one, maybe with a gun, I'm not sure. The doctor tells me the dizziness is from the drugs, though, not the concussion."

"God, Eric. It's just horrific. Terrifying. Who attacked you, do you know?"

"No. Some guy ran me off the road, can you believe it? At first I thought it was a hot-rod guy trying to pass me, you know, who messed up. He swerved in front of me and jerked to a stop. I nearly crashed into him. When he didn't take off again, I thought he was having car trouble. I stepped out to see if I could help him, but he got out of his car before I reached him, and I guess he circled around the van, 'cause I was looking one way when bam out of nowhere he hit me, and down

I went. Next thing I know, I'm tied up like a pork roast, lying on a cot in a log cabin somewhere. After that, I only saw him wearing a Spider-Man mask. Except when he was driving."

"Oh, Eric. It's just awful to think of what you've been through."

"It's okay. I mean, I'm okay, you know?"

I did know. It's hard to remember the sharpness of pain or heart-pounding fear. Once you've endured an agonizing or petrifying epi-sode and come out the other side intact, most of what you feel is relief. When you think back, you recall that you felt pain or fear, but it's an intellectual, not a literal, recollection.

"I know you are . . . and thank goodness for that! Are you all right answering a few more questions?"

"I guess. The police were here already asking a lot of stuff. I couldn't tell them much. I don't know much."

"What did he look like? You saw him without his mask twice, right? When he ran you off the road and when he drove you to the exchange."

"Yeah, but I think he was disguised. He had red shaggy hair, and even at the time I thought it was a wig, you know, the kind you'd wear on Halloween if you were going as a clown. He wore aviator sun-glasses. He had a little mole next to his mouth, but maybe that was paint or makeup. All I know for sure is that he was white and thin, or at least not fat. I don't know how tall he was, but I figure he must have been somewhere in the normal range or I would have noticed."

"It's amazing, isn't it, how effective a simple disguise can be? You change one or two things, and everything changes." I paused for a moment. "When he drove you away from the log cabin, were you able to see where you were?"

"No. He had me drugged up by then. I wasn't noticing anything. I was in the back, lying down and blindfolded. I'm sorry I can't be more helpful."

"It doesn't matter, Eric. All that matters is you're safe and well. Grace tells me you're eating. Did he give you any food?"

"Yeah. He let my hands loose sometimes and let me eat out of a box of Cheerios. I had bottles of water, too. I guess he knew I wasn't any danger to him, not with all the drugs he gave me. Grace says that

I have about a million calories to make up, which is why even dizzy, I'm hungry."

"I'll tell Cara to make some gingersnaps. I know those are your favorites."

"Great! I hope they let me out of here soon."

"Don't hurry too much. You need rest."

"Yeah, and warm socks. I almost got frostbite. There was no heat in the cabin, and the nights were cold. Lucky for me it's May, not January."

We chatted awhile longer, and then I asked to speak to Grace.

"I know he's going to want to come into work over the weekend. Don't let him, okay?"

"If I can stop him. You know Eric."

"True. How are you doing, Grace?"

"Better. Thank you for everything, Josie."

"What about his mom? Is she all right?"

"Kind of."

"Is she there in the room with you?"

"Exactly."

I left it at that. Eric's mom was never happy, never relaxed, never kind. She wasn't evil. She was just sour, pickled in the brine of her bitterness.

I rolled into work, feeling semibattered and still upset, around one that Wednesday afternoon. I'd considered taking the day off, but I'd felt too restless to read or rest or even watch TV. I'd called Ty and Zoë. They were both supportive and loving and busy. I'd decided not to communicate with Wes, not until I felt more like myself. Finally, after realizing I hadn't eaten since Zoë's care package the evening before, I cooked myself a hamburger and decided to go into work.

The media was still out in force. I drove slowly past the barrage, waved at Officer Meade, who was stationed at my parking lot entrance, keeping them at bay, and parked near the front door. As I got out of my car, I scanned the reporters' eager faces and noted that Wes was nearly growling at me. Bertie waved and smiled as if we were old friends.

I parked near the front and stepped inside. Everyone looked up. I grinned.

"Yes," I said, "it's all true. Eric's fine. He may be released from the hospital as soon as today."

Fred leapt up from his chair and whooped, punching the air, wanting a high five. I laughed and returned the salute. Gretchen applauded, and Cara joined in. Soon we were all applauding, clapping until our hands stung and then clapping some more.

"Can you tell us what happened?" Gretchen asked. "If not, no problem, but you can imagine how curious we are."

"I'd better not, not until the police say it's okay. I don't know what they may be holding back. I can tell you this much. The kidnapper was clever. Very smart. Very detail oriented." I waved it away. "For now, I just want to celebrate the good news about Eric. Is there any coffee? I want to propose a toast!" When we all had our drink of choice in hand, coffee for Gretchen, Fred, and me, and tea for Cara and Sasha, I raised my mug and said, "To Eric's safe homecoming, and to us all. You're family to me."

Mugs clinks, we sipped, then Fred said, "One more toast: To Josie, our fearless leader, for doing what was necessary to win Eric's release."

"And for being the best boss ever," Gretchen added.

"Hear, hear," Cara said.

"Hear, hear," Sasha said.

I felt myself redden as their mugs touched, clink, clink. "Oh, gee, golly . . . enough of that . . . you're making me blush." I smiled. "Thank you." I placed my hand on my chest, over my heart. "Thank you so much. You are incredible." I paused and grinned. "One thing I should confess. Cara, I made a commitment on your behalf. I promised Eric you'd bake him gingersnaps."

"Oh, good! I'll make them tonight!"

"I don't expect him to come back to work until Monday. Maybe Saturday if Grace can't stop him."

"That's all right. I'll have them here in case he stops by, and I'll make a fresh batch for Monday."

"You'll need to," Gretchen said. "Your gingersnaps never last long around here!"

"I have another toast!" Fred said, raising his mug. "To Cara's gingersnaps!"

We clinked and laughed and called out "Hear, hear," and then the moment passed and people placed their mugs on their desks and began drifting back to their desks.

"It's such a relief, isn't it?" I asked. "Such an incredible relief. Fill me in, Gretchen. Is there any work stuff I should be aware of?"

"Cara and I will oversee the tag sale setup," Gretchen said.

"Excellent," I said.

Fred leaned back in his chair, pushed up his glasses, and grinned. "I've confirmed the witchcraft book—it was in fact owned by Boswell. Strafford's Autographs in London has a letter Boswell wrote, signed with one *l*. They've used a forensic examiner to authenticate it. They e-mailed me a scan of the letter showing the signature. It's a lock."

I leaned against Sasha's desk. "Holy cow."

"Exactly."

"So now we hire a forensic examiner of our own," I said.

"And make some history."

"Well done, Fred," I said.

"Thanks. I'm stoked."

"I don't blame you." I turned to Sasha. "Anything with Alice's dolls?"

"Nothing like as amazing as Fred's news," Sasha said. "There's only one new doll in Alice Michaels's collection since last year. Isn't that a surprise? She sure seemed focused on getting the Farmington collection, so I assumed she was in acquisition mode."

"Interesting," I said, nodding. "I'd like to see it."

We walked together through the warehouse to the side worktable where Alice's doll collection was laid out.

Sasha reached for a sock doll. "This is the new one. It's simple and pleasant-looking, but it's neither unique nor, from what I can infer from the age of the socks, rare. Isn't it strange that only this one doll has been added?"

So this is Hilda, I thought, *the doll Alice made for herself when she was a girl.* The blue of Hilda's eyes and the red of her mouth had faded over the decades, but the artistry was unmarred; the features had been drawn with flair. The brown yarn used for her hair was in excellent condition, with no unraveled bits. She wore a blue-and-yellow polka-dot pinafore. Her blouse was white.

"I'm certain that this doll," I said, "is not a new acquisition. This is Hilda. Alice told me about her. She made it herself when she was about seven. She named her Hilda after her favorite teacher."

"That's sweet, isn't it?"

"Very." I unbuttoned her blouse to examine the stitching. "Alice was a good seamstress. The workmanship in these set-in sleeves is flawless."

"How do you think I should appraise it? Traditionally, sock dolls are considered folk art, which, of course, makes determining value very tricky."

I nodded. "True. Still, even if we consider nothing more than the doll's age and condition, she's got to have some value—she's more than fifty years old and in pristine condition. See what you can find in doll auction records over the last year when a sock doll is part of a lot of rare dolls. Then compare the sales records of the other lots when no sock doll was in the mix."

"Good idea," she said, nodding. She reached for a wooden doll with delicately carved features. "Do you remember this one? Last year we couldn't trace the maker. I'd like to try again, if it's all right with you. Queen Anne dolls are so rare. If I can prove this is one . . . well, I don't want to shortchange the estate."

Sasha's point was well taken. It was extraordinarily unusual to see a doll that dated from earlier than 1850; further, most early dolls were crafted to look like children. Dolls from the seventeenth and eighteenth centuries that look like adults are among the rarest of finds, and thus the most valuable. Even though Queen Anne's reign ended in 1714, dolls that meet these parameters are known as Queen Anne dolls.

The majority of these early adult dolls were crafted in England by carpenters who carved the dolls out of hardwood and added paint to enhance their features. In excellent condition, they're nearly price-less. Last year, after sending the doll out for age verification and learning that the wood dated from the mid-seventeenth century, we valued it at fifty thousand dollars based on its age, subject matter, craftsmanship, and condition. Sasha had referenced an auction catalogue saying only thirty Queen Anne dolls with a known maker were extant.

"Am I remembering correctly that Alice had no idea about its provenance?" I asked.

"She knew a little, but it wasn't helpful. She bought it at an antiques store on Cape Cod twenty years ago. The store was called Elegant Antiques. She had no specific memory of how much she paid, although she thought it was in the hundreds, not the thousands. The shop closed when the owner died, ten years after that. The inventory was sold at auction. No records were retained by the estate once probate was granted."

A dead end. "Since Alice had impeccable taste and good instincts, and since she was attracted to early European dolls," I said, thinking aloud, "I agree that it's worth pursuing. Alice wouldn't have purchased it unless it met her standards."

"That's what I was thinking, too," Sasha said.

"How will you try tracing it?"

"Last year I examined photos of the dolls made by known carpenters of that era to see if I could identify any common elements of style. Since the photos are from online museum sites or auction catalogues, they're limited, and usually the dolls are dressed. This time around, I thought I'd ask the curators or owners to take more detailed shots for me to use."

"That's a great idea, Sasha," I said. "Since so few carpenters are known to have done that sort of work, that's a smart approach—you won't be overwhelmed with options." I paused, then asked, "Is the jewelry box from that same period?"

"No," Sasha said.

She unwrapped the box from multiple layers of bubble wrap. I expected her to add additional commentary, but she didn't. I picked it up. The box was roughly 18" × 6" × 6" and crafted from mahogany, with rosewood embellishments.

"This isn't rare," I said, my brow wrinkling.

"I know."

I lifted the lid. From the run-of-the-mill brass hinges and contemporary nails to the glue used to attach the red velvet lining to the wood, it was obvious that the box was modern and ordinary. It was attractive, but nothing special.

"What about the jewelry?" I asked, scanning the array of gold and silver earrings, necklaces, and bracelets. Most of the stones were blue, but I spotted red, pink, yellow, and green ones, too.

"I looked at each one. I think it's all costume and contemporary," Sasha said.

"She must have been pulling Darleen's leg when she told her it was her most valuable possession. I can see that happening. She would have loved to see Darleen make a fool of herself by offering it for sale to a New York City auction house or something."

"Not nice," Sasha said.

"No. Alice was often not nice—especially to Darleen." I shrugged. "We should ask Nate to take a look at everything, just in case."

"I'll get it all to him right away."

"Anything else I should know?"

"Not at this point," she said. "I'll let you know if I learn any—"

She broke off as the PA cackled. "Wes Smith on line one," Cara said.

"I've got to take this," I told Sasha. "Keep up the good work!"

I told Cara I'd take the call upstairs and ran for my office.

"We have to talk," Wes said, skipping hello, as always. "You should have called me back."

"Give me a break, Wes."

He sighed. "Okay, okay—but I've got a real shockeroonie. You're not going to believe it."

"What?" I asked, knowing he wanted me to draw him out.

"Not on the phone," he said, lowering his voice conspiratorially. "We've got to meet."

I glanced out the window. It was a dazzlingly bright day, warm and fresh after yesterday's cleansing rain.

"Really, Josie. It's important."

The time display on my computer monitor read 1:50. "Okay. Our dune. Ten minutes."

"Done!" he said, sounding both pleased and excited.

Wes, I knew, would plead with me to give him a blow-by-blow account of my experience. Probably he'd be upset that I hadn't surreptitiously taken photos. I shook my head. Wes was pushy and relentless, but he was also diligent and dedicated. In the hours since Eric had been rescued, Wes would have used his sources to piece together details about the kidnapper that I had no other way of learning. He had his agenda, but I had mine, and I was willing to make a trade.

CHAPTER EIGHTEEN

I arrived first and climbed the dune. Standing on the still-damp sand, I stared out over the ocean. The gentle sway of the tide was hypnotic. Toward the horizon, it looked as if golden stars were twinkling on sapphire glass.

I heard Wes's car before I saw it. He needed a new muffler. I watched him jerk to a stop, then turned back to the ocean and waited for him to scamper up the dune.

"You look okay," Wes said.

"Thanks. It's been quite a week."

"Yeah—a murder and a kidnapping. You're the girl of the hour, that's for sure."

"That's not how I would put it."

"Yeah, whatever. So fill me in."

"What's your shockeroonie?" I asked, cringing inside as I repeated one of Wes's favorite words.

"Eric's been released from the hospital," Wes said.

"Already? I spoke to him around ten."

"Did he tell you about his concussion?"

"Have you spoken to him?" I asked, ignoring his question.

"No. Why?"

"How do you know he had a concussion? Medical information is confidential."

"I have good sources," he said proudly, as if I'd been admiring him, not questioning his ethics. "The police are at his house now. So far, he doesn't remember anything useful. What about you?"

"How much do you know about what happened?" I asked.

"Just the basics. I'm counting on you to fill me in. I want to know everything."

"As soon as the police say I can, I will."

"Josie!" he whined. "That's not reasonable."

"If I tell you anything, you have to promise me you won't publish it until it's public."

"Or until I confirm it from another source. Like always."

"There is no other source. Just me—and the kidnapper."

"You know you can trust me," he said, sounding hurt.

"I know. I wouldn't talk to you at all otherwise. I'm not negotiating, Wes. I'll talk to you on my terms or not at all."

He sighed, a deep one. "Okay, then. Your terms and I get the info as an exclusive."

"I can't guarantee that," I said.

"Why not?" he asked, sounding shocked.

"Because I don't know who else might have information I want."

He pursed lips, upset and hurt. I knew that I probably wouldn't want to talk to another reporter. I never had, but this time, other considerations were at work. As far as I was concerned, kidnapping Eric was a personal affront, a slap in my face. You don't mess with my family and get away with it.

He sighed again. "Okay. Talk."

I did, and I knew I had Wes's full attention when he pulled a piece of ratty paper from his pocket and began jotting notes. I didn't embellish the story, but I didn't skip any details, either. Retelling it brought back tendrils of the anxiety and fear I'd felt during those agonizingly long hours. While I spoke I kept my eyes on the ocean, the steady ebb and flow of the incoming tide helping to calm my jagged nerves.

"How come you didn't push Eric more on things? Like in his phone message to you, whether he used 'they' because he thought there was more than one kidnapper or because it's just one of those things you say? Or how often he was untied? Or whether he ever heard people talking in another room?"

"Because he was in the hospital recovering from a concussion!"

"You said he was eating."

"God, Wes, you're ruthless."

He grinned. "Nah. I'm a pussycat."

I grinned back. Wes was one of a kind.

Wes asked me to e-mail him the scans of the Civil War currency, and I agreed. He said that he would try to get the digital X-ray showing the European doll's hollow head filled with money from his police source.

"That'd be off-the-chart cool," he said. "Spooky, too, like a dead doll."

"Have you heard anything about the keycard or the cars?" I asked, eager to change the subject.

"Why are you asking about them?"

"I was thinking there are a lot of leads for the police to work—like the stuff the kidnapper gave me, and maybe his car's tire tread, if they can isolate it in the mud. Of all the options, though, I thought the two that probably offer the best promise are the hotel keycard, which he either stole or got because he registered as a guest, and the cars, which he must have bought somewhere. I mean, buying a cash-and-carry phone, a simple black dress, run-of-the-mill flip-flops, and nothing-special towels is one thing. Getting your hands on a hotel keycard and purchasing two cars is another thing altogether. There have to be records."

"Good call, Josie! The keycard was issued to a man who checked in the day after Eric was kidnapped. He registered for three days."

"Three days? Why three days? Why not one? Or two? Why three? Oh!" I exclaimed before Wes could respond. "I know . . . because he didn't know how long it would take to work out the exchange, he guessed. He wanted to avoid having to contact the hotel to extend his stay if he could—figuring the less contact he had with anyone, the better. Am I right?"

Wes grinned. "No one can think of any other reason. Good going, Josie!"

"So who is it?"

"George Shankle. He used a California driver's license to check in. It has a fake Fresno address."

"Let me guess, no one remembers him."

"Right. There's a security camera at the front desk, which shows a white guy wearing a Red Sox baseball cap. He kept his head down and his back to the camera as much as he could, as if he knew it was there."

"Do you have the photo?"

"Yeah, two of them," he said, scrolling through images on his smart phone. "The camera takes shots every three seconds. These are the only ones that show any part of his face." He handed the unit to me. "Here."

The photos were black-and-white and grainy. The man was tall, or so it seemed. He wasn't overly thin or noticeably heavy. He wore a puffy down jacket, too warm for the season but effective at hiding his body's size. He stood with his chin almost resting on his chest, his cap's bill casting long, dark shadows over his face. In one of the photos, he was signing the registration card, and I looked at his hands. He wore no rings. His nails were neatly clipped. I saw no scars or tattoos or birthmarks.

"How on God's earth did you get these, Wes?" I asked.

"Cool, huh? Do you recognize him?"

"No. Did you steal the photos?"

"Josie!" He sounded outraged. "The police gave them to me. They want to publicize it. They're up on our Web site already and will be all over the news tonight. They hope someone will recognize him."

"Amazing. What about the cars?"

"The Camry was purchased for cash in Brookline, Massachusetts, by, wait for it, George Shankle. The Sonata was purchased from a used car lot in Quincy, Massachusetts, also for cash, also by Shankle."

"Wow," I said, thinking it through.

"There's more." From his tone, I could tell he was big with news. "The same guy, George Shankle, bought a third car—an Impala. This one came from a lot in Newton, Massachusetts. Same deal. Lots of used car lots have security cameras installed, but none of these do, so the police think maybe that's why he chose those three dealers over all the others."

I grew up in Wenton, outside of Boston, so I knew the area well. Brookline, Newton, and Quincy were all on the subway line. He could take public transportation to the dealers and drive away.

"Interesting . . . so he was driving the Impala."

"That's what they figure."

"When did he buy them?"

"All three were purchased yesterday—the day after Eric was kidnapped."

"The day *after*?"

"Yup, the same day he registered at the hotel. He bought the first car at eight in the morning, the second at noon, and the third at four."

I nodded, thinking. "What about the license plates?" I asked. "Can't they trace him from the tags?"

"Nope. They were stolen from vehicles parked in the long-term parking garage at Logan Airport, from three cars parked next to one another. The police figure he picked those particular cars because they were parked in a remote, dark corner, and there were no security cameras."

"A long-term parking garage . . . So there might be a good chance the owners wouldn't be back to their cars for days. Even then, who checks if your front plate is in place?"

"I know. Wicked clever, huh?"

"Yeah . . . wicked," I said, not rolling my eyes but wanting to. "Have they found the Impala yet?"

"Yup. Want to guess the first place they checked?"

"The long-term parking garage at Logan Airport."

"Hot banana, Josie! That's what I thought, too. So did the cops. It's logical, but no dice."

"Which means he didn't leave his own car in that garage."

"Right. There are security cameras at the cashier's booth. If he'd parked there, he would have had to exit in front of the cameras, and they'd have him for sure."

"So he walked into the garage to get the license plates," I said, thinking aloud, "and he walked out. Where did he park his car?"

"Who knows? He could have parked it in a commuter lot anywhere along the line and taken the subway to the airport. Lots of people do that."

"So if they didn't find his Impala in the long-term parking garage at Logan, where was it?"

"At the Round the Clock diner," Wes said.

"The Round the Clock? Why would he park there . . . oh! Got it. The express bus to Logan leaves from there. Wow . . . so the morning after he kidnaps Eric, he leaves his car at the diner and takes the bus to the airport. He takes the T, the subway, to Brookline and buys a car. He drives it back to the diner in Rocky Point, about a ninety-minute drive, maybe two hours, if there's traffic. The diner is so busy all the time, no one would notice a car that hadn't been moved, at least for a few days. Were there any dolls in the car?"

Wes frowned. "I don't know. The police aren't talking."

"Okay, then. The kidnapper hops the bus back to the airport, takes the subway to Newton, and buys the second car."

"Actually Quincy was second. Newton was third."

"The bus drivers can't ID him?"

"Nope. Working backward from the time the cars were purchased, they can estimate when he boarded the buses. If they're right, there are three different bus drivers involved, and none of them noticed anything. My request for other passengers to come forward is already posted on our Web site. The police think community cooperation is their best shot for ID'ing him. They have his schedule and his photo—don't you think there's a good chance it will work?"

I shook my head and handed back his phone. "No one notices other people on a bus or train. Even when you sit next to someone for hours, like on an airplane—unless you had some kind of meaningful conversation or something weird happened—by the time you've collected your luggage, they're gone from your brain. Plus, I figure he wore a disguise."

"Like he made you do, huh? I hear you look good as a blonde."

"Wes! Who said that?"

"I'm not telling," he said, grinning.

The young EMS guy, I thought. Neither Ellis nor the older paramedic would comment on my appearance to a reporter, but I could see the young guy getting into it with Wes. I didn't want to know the details.

"What about the car dealers?" I asked, changing the subject. "Can't they ID him?"

"Not really. A middle-aged white guy. Crazy red hair and glasses, and a mole. The police artist took one of the photos and extrapolated what the guy would look like straight on, then Photoshopped it to add the red hair and so on." He punched a button on his phone. "Here, take a look."

The photo was unrecognizable. "It could be any of them—Lenny, Ian, or Randall," I said.

"Yeah. They all have motives, right?"

"Right, and you could make a case that Alice told any one of them where the money was. In other words, the more we learn, the less we know." I sighed. "What about fingerprints?"

"None. They're certain he wore gloves the whole time."

"They're tracking the purchases of the phone and clothes and so on, but I bet they're not going to find anything."

"Probably not. They're hoping Eric will remember something, anything, that might help them. Like how long it took to drive from the log cabin to the meet off Old Garrison. Like the view from the window where he was kept. Like whether the kidnapper spoke with any kind of accent or used any unusual words. Anything."

I nodded. "The devil's in the details, and Eric might remember a detail that causes the kidnapper's whole plan to unravel."

"Yeah. So when is Eric coming back to work, do you think?"

"When he's ready. I don't expect him before Monday."

"When he comes in, take a photo," Wes said.

"Wes! Don't be crass."

"What's crass about that? He's hot news, Josie. Let him have his fifteen minutes."

"I'll see. I doubt he'll want me to. Eric's not a chasing-celebrity kind of guy."

"Take it when's he not looking."

"Forget it, Wes."

He sighed, a to-his-toenails indictment of my discretion. He glanced through his notes. "The kidnapper sure thought of everything, didn't he?"

"A detail-oriented risk taker. Or someone desperate enough to risk everything."

"Who fits that bill?"

"I don't know."

"What else you got?" Wes asked.

"Nothing. You have it all."

"Great! Thanks! Catch ya later!"

I watched him slide-walk down the dune and jog to his car.

Wes was always in a hurry.

When I got back to work, surviving another pass through the media gauntlet, Cara handed me a message. Barry Simpson, the numismatist, had called. I climbed the steps to my private office and dialed his number, eager to hear his findings.

"I hate to be the bearer of bad news," he said, "but some of the currency you sent me is counterfeit. Are you sure you sent the right packages?"

My mouth fell open and my heart sank, inch by inch, to the pit of my stomach. I stood up, then fell back down. Was it possible that I'd given the kidnapper the genuine bills?

Dawn and I had laid out four bills from what was supposedly the real stash on the photocopier's glass. I recalled extracting them from the pile. As soon as we had a good-quality make-ready, I'd placed those bills in the safe with the others. She and Fred had meticulously cut and trimmed the photocopied bills. The currency I removed from the Chatty Cathys went in envelopes. The fake currency went into the dolls. What I'd sent Barry was the currency I'd intended to send him.

"You said 'some.' Which part?"

"All from one envelope, three hundred bills."

"All of them?" I asked, stunned.

"Yup. It looks that way."

"I'm shocked, Barry. Really shocked. I thought all the bills I sent you were real. What about all the others?"

"They look promising."

Relief washed over me. I'd taken bills from the stash of one hundred to create the make-ready. Whatever was going on, it wasn't my mistake. "What can you tell me about the three hundred you think are phonies?"

"Here's what I know: The currency is printed, not photocopied, and printed well—it's a complicated, detailed design, and it's in perfect registration. Specifically, the money was printed on an offset press using Pantone inks, which if you want to ID the counterfeiter doesn't help much because both of those components, the press and the ink, are about as common as it gets. What I can say is that you're looking for a master printer. A real craftsman created the plates used to print these bills. Which narrows the field a little, but not all that much. There are lots of good printers here and around the world. The paper is called Elegance. It's good quality, archival, appropriate for the purpose, manufactured in Minnesota by Penterman & Sons. Elegance features a quill pen watermark. The paper was introduced in 1965 and discontinued four years ago when the company was acquired by Eastham. It was never sold overseas."

"So the counterfeits were made in this country and more than four years ago?"

"Most likely on both counts. It's possible someone shipped the paper to another country, just as it's possible there are some reams of Elegance still knocking around, but that would be a fluke. Based on the materials used and the old-school printing quality, my guess is that someone created these bills years ago."

"I don't have a clue about what's going on, Barry—but I know I have to report this to the police right away. Can you e-mail me your report?"

"I have a hard copy of it here. Let me fax it over. Do you want me to send out an alert to dealers, a BOLO?"

I recognized the acronym: Be on the lookout. "Yes, please, and ask them to report any sightings to Police Chief Hunter."

I gave him Ellis's contact information and our fax number, asked him to ship the counterfeit currency back for next-morning delivery, and told him to send his invoice. I added one more thank-you, then hung up and dashed downstairs. I wanted to get the fax myself before anyone else saw it. I didn't want to take the time to explain Barry's findings; the situation was too urgent and the potential ramifications too dire to risk any delay in reporting it to the police. Jamie and Lorna had to be told—I only hoped they'd believe me when I assured them I hadn't tried to pull a fast one.

I knew Ellis would want me to give an official statement, so I made a photocopy of Barry's fax, filed the original in a locked drawer of my desk, and called Ellis from my private office.

"I have something to tell you and something to show you that can't wait. Can I stop by now?"

"Yes. I'm in the middle of six things, as you can imagine, but I'll fit you in for sure."

Downstairs, I told Cara I'd be back in a while and left.

Cathy, the Rocky Point police civilian admin, showed me into Ellis's office. The office furniture and the layout were unchanged from when Ty had been the police chief. The desk, bookcases, and guest table and chairs were crafted of ash. From where I sat, I had a good view of Ellis's framed Norman Rockwell posters that lined the walls.

The door opened. "Thanks, Cathy," Ellis called over his shoulder. He smiled as he closed the door. "It's nice to see a friendly face."

"You look harassed."

"I feel harassed."

"What's going on?" I asked.

He sat down and arched his back a little, stretching, maybe trying to loosen taut muscles or ease an ache.

"I guess it's all right for me to tell you," he said. "The attorney general wants the world to know, and it'll be all over the news in about an hour anyway. The attorney general, in cooperation with the federal prosecutor, has issued warrants for Lenny Einsohn and Randall Michaels. He's calling a press conference on the courthouse steps at four thirty, just in time for the evening news. Our part in the production is to organize the perp walk. We'll be marching them up the stairs during his presentation."

"Holy cow! What are the charges?"

"Racketeering and fraud are the big ones." He took in a breath. "Various charges related to financial improprieties at Alice's company."

"Are you happy to cooperate? Or are you feeling dragged into a media circus?"

"A little of both. The AG is a good man. He wants to reassure the victims that law enforcement is on the case and making progress, and he wants to warn other scammers that they're not going to get away with it on his watch, and this is a good way to do it. Yet it does feel a little staged." He shrugged. "I'm just a cop. It's not my place to judge."

"You're such a good man, Ellis." I paused. "Lenny I expected... but Randall?"

"Yeah, I think the evidence is a little slim myself, but the AG is confident. According to his theory of the crime Randall's business is just a front, a tax dodge. He thinks it operated as a department of ADM Financial Advisers Inc., not an independent entity, and that as Alice's chief marketing strategist, Randall knew or should have known about the Ponzi scheme. Essentially, they're saying Randall was his mother's puppet."

"Yikes."

He glanced at his watch. "Yikes, indeed. We have to leave in about forty minutes. What can I do for you?"

I slid Barry's report across the table. Ellis's eyes dropped to the paper. He scanned it, then raised his eyes to meet mine.

"Counterfeit?" he asked.

"Yup."

He read the report, taking his time, then rubbed his nose, thinking. He tapped the paper. "So the currency from the doll we X-rayed and two of the Chatty Cathys is fine, but the currency from the third Chatty Cathy, all three hundred bills, is fake, is that what he's saying?"

"Yes—and that it was printed between 1965 and four years ago, although the four-year mark isn't set in stone since a store or printer might have had some leftover reams in inventory."

"Would you agree that in all probability Jamie and Lorna don't know the currency is phony?"

"Yes. Which means that probably Selma, their mom, didn't know either."

"So someone replaced the real stuff with fake bills sometime between 1965 and a few years ago. Is there any way to narrow the timeline?"

"Absolutely. Paper's perishable. Even though it's archival, we have tests available to date it. We can get to within a year or so, but no closer. As to the ink, we can date that, too. Barry's shipping the currency back to us today. We'll get started as soon as it gets here. Barry's also sending out a BOLO to alert dealers so any sightings come to you."

"Thank you," he said.

He stood up and placed Barry's report on his desk, tucking it into a corner of his blotter. I joined him as he walked to the door.

"Good," he said, pausing with his hand on the knob. "Except before you do anything, check with me. I'll talk to the county attorney and get his read on the situation. We might need to call the Feds in on this one. Counterfeiting money is definitely not a local crime. We'll need to inform the owners, too. One more thing. We found the kidnapper's car, and the dolls are inside the trunk. I'll need to notify the owners that damage to their property occurred."

"The owners? What kind of damage?"

"The Chatty Cathys were smashed, Josie."

"Ouch," I said.

"Yeah, but only them."

"He knew where to search," I said, "and how much money he was looking for. Once he found it, he stopped."

"That's a reasonable theory. When we catch him, we'll ask."

"When he jacked the van and there weren't any Chatty Cathys there, he thought maybe the money had been moved, so he looked in all of the dolls."

"That's what I think, too," Ellis said.

I nodded. "Can I get my dolls back?"

"Yes. As soon as the lab is done with them, which shouldn't take all that long."

I stood in the lobby for a moment watching him stride down the corridor, then waved good-bye to Cathy and pushed open the heavy wooden door. The sky was a delicate shade of pale blue. The tall grasses that edged the dunes swayed in a gentle breeze. One of God's days, my mother would have said. I walked to my car and sat with the windows down, listening to the waves roll into shore, thinking about Civil War currency and printing craftsmanship and dolls. Alice had been murdered, but I didn't know why. Except for the timing, I had no reason to think her death was in any way related to the dolls. It seemed obvious that Eric had been kidnapped to get the dolls, but the kidnapper was really after the money, not the dolls, so someone must have known that the dolls contained rare currency. Who? After a while, having had no new thoughts and having reached no conclusions, I decided to take a brief detour. I wanted to hear the attorney general's press conference and witness Lenny and Randall being marched up the courthouse steps.

CHAPTER NINETEEN

I parked on Thistle Lane, a short, narrow road off Main Street, across from a bookstore named Briscoe's and about two blocks from the Rocky Point Courthouse. I walked across the green, pausing for a few seconds to watch an orange monarch butterfly flit from one lilac blossom to another, its wings fluttering.

As the courthouse came into view, I saw that I was not the first person to arrive, or even the tenth. A small crowd had congregated near a makeshift podium that had been positioned at the top of the steps in front of the main entry doors.

The setting was certain to communicate the kind of gravitas the attorney general hoped to convey. The courthouse, half a block wide and made of local granite, with a gold cupola and fluted columns, was a relic from a different era. An owl, an ancient symbol of wisdom, perched on the roof, encouraging all who entered to bring their individual best in the common pursuit of justice.

Wes, I noted, was already in position, standing directly in front of the podium, with his feet spread wide apart, guarding real estate. Two young men and a young woman were fussing with the microphone hook-up, saying, "Test. Test. Test," over and over again, but the mic wasn't on. I counted eight other reporters standing near Wes and three cameramen, their video units resting by their feet. As I mounted the forty-five steps, four flights of stairs, two satellite vans pulled up, followed by Bertie.

"Hey, Wes," I said as I approached.

He turned and chuckled. "I thought it wouldn't be long before you showed up. I knew you'd want to be in on the action."

"May I share your space?"

He glanced over his shoulders, eyeing his competition, and lowered his voice. "Guarantee me an exclusive about the story you told me today."

Wes, I thought, was as relentless and irresistible as a hurricane. "Deal." I paused, then added, "Which doesn't mean you can publish it now."

"I know, I know." He stepped to the left to make room for me. "This is Mickey." He nodded toward one of the cameramen. Mickey, older than Wes by a generation, was short and thin, with arms as muscular as Popeye's. "He's shooting footage for our Web site."

Mickey and I exchanged hellos; then I turned around to scan the crowd. No one seemed to be paying any attention to me, a good thing, until Pennington Moreau arrived and zeroed in on me like a cat spotting a bowl of cream. He stepped out of a blue van with his station's call letters stenciled on the side, followed by a cameraman. He smiled at me, tossed a comment over his shoulder to his colleague, then took the steps two at a time heading straight toward me. Bertie, following his gaze, spotted me, too, and I knew I was done for.

"Your competition is about to try to wrest me away from you."

Wes spun and eyed them. "Don't let them," he said.

"I won't."

"Josie," Penn said when he was half a dozen steps away, his voice a soothing mix of graciousness and sympathy. "We keep meeting under such difficult circumstances. I heard the good news about your employee."

I smiled. "Good news doesn't even begin to describe it. It's spectacular news!"

"How about a quick on-air comment to that effect?"

I felt Wes, facing the other way, bristle.

"Do you know Wes Smith?" I asked.

He said he didn't, and the two men shook hands.

"I'm not doing any on-air anything, Penn."

"It would be good exposure for you, Josie. My segment is seen from Cape Cod to Bar Harbor."

I shook my head and looked away. "No, thanks," I said.

"Josie!" Bertie called. "What an experience for you. Tell me, woman to woman, were you terrified?"

You're not a woman, I thought. *You're a she-devil.* I pretended I hadn't heard her.

Bertie kept chattering at me, closing in as if she could force me to talk to her if she intruded far enough into my space. I planted my feet on the granite step and continued to ignore her.

A dozen or more reporters arrived and began their climbs. I recognized several of them, then noticed that several nonreporters were in attendance, too. Some people seemed merely curious, like me; others had a vested interest in the situation, like Ian Landers.

Ian stood off to the left, parallel to the podium, leaning against a column. His fiery bright blue eyes and cocky grin made me suspect he had a plan, and whatever it was, it would be ugly. He looked threatening, like a pit bull showing teeth. I wanted to call Wes's attention to him, but I didn't want Penn, or any of the other reporters, to think I was cozying up to Wes or excluding them. I dug my phone out of my bag and texted Wes. **LOOK @ IAN.**

I pretended not to notice as Wes pulled his vibrating phone from his pocket and read my message. I turned my back to the podium, watching as the crowd swelled.

Wes texted back, **NASTY.**

HAWK?

NO.

I suggested, **TIGER?**

YES. ABOUT TO POUNCE. LOL.

I nodded. Wes was right. Ian had homed in on game and wasn't going to let it escape. Penn jostled his way into a prime spot a little to the left of where Wes and I stood, out of earshot, so I risked whispering a comment to Wes.

"Ian looks positively gleeful."

"In spades," Wes said. He turned to Mickey, standing on my other side, and whispered, "Do you see that guy? I don't want to point. Tall and big, leaning against the column?"

"Yup."

"Make sure you include him in the shot. He's up to something."

Mickey nodded, picked up his gear, and headed to the left and down a few steps. From that angle he'd have both the podium and Ian in view.

"Do you know when the attorney general is supposed to start?" I asked a woman I didn't know standing to my right.

"Any minute, from what I hear."

One of the men who'd been fiddling with the microphones tapped it. It was live. "Test, test, test," he said, and his voice carried up and over us, probably reaching all the way to the green. He nodded over his shoulder, and New Hampshire's attorney general, Frank Harson, strode forward. He was about forty pounds overweight, but tall enough so he didn't look fat. He had thick dark hair and wore glasses. At a guess, he was around fifty. Another man, leaner and younger, walked beside him.

Reporters surged closer, and he paused, letting them get their cameras in place.

"Thank you for coming," he said. "I'm Frank Harson, New Hampshire attorney general. I'll make a brief statement, then federal prosecutor Christopher Almonte, standing here beside me, and I will answer your questions. Earlier this morning we issued arrest warrants for Lenny Einsohn and Randall Michaels. The charges include racketeering, securities fraud, investment adviser fraud, mail fraud, wire fraud, money laundering, and perjury, among others. A complete list has been prepared and is being distributed now." He pointed at the two young men I'd seen working on the sound system. They were making their way down the steps passing out sheets of paper. Ian smiled as he took one. His smile broadened as he read it.

Frank Harson looked into a cable news station's camera for three seconds, his expression earnest and grave. He shifted his gaze without changing his expression to a network camera. One by one, he stared into all the cameras. Even though I knew it was staged to provide each news station with its own content, it didn't feel cynical or manipulative.

From everything I'd heard and observed, and confirmed by what Ellis had just told me, Frank Harson was a straight shooter. He was outraged that criminals would victimize citizens while he was the attorney general, and he wanted everyone to know it. I glanced at Ian. He stood with his arms crossed, grinning, enjoying the show.

"Here they are!" someone behind me called.

I swiveled to face the street. Ellis and Griff led Lenny up the steps. Detective Brownley and Officer Meade did the same with Randall. The police officials' expressions were consciously unconscious. Lenny's face was ashen, his eyes wide with shock and disbelief. He looked as if he might faint. Randall looked smaller than he had in my office, maybe because he walked with his rounded shoulders hunched forward and his head bowed. He seemed stunned and mortified and frightened. I glanced at Lenny in time to see Griff's grip on his elbow tighten, not in punishment or fear that he would flee, but in support. Lenny, it seemed, was close to collapse. Randall moved slowly, but he was able to climb the stairs under his own power. Out of the corner of my eye I saw that Ian had started down the steps, his expression menacing.

"Where's the money?" Ian shouted. "Huh, Lenny? Where'd you stash it? Do you know, Randall? Be smart, guys. Trade up and get yourself a plea deal."

Neither man replied. Neither man reacted, which seemed to heighten Ian's fury.

"You think you can blow me off?" he asked, his hands forming fists. He was closing in on Lenny. "Is that what you think? You're wrong. Dead wrong."

Ellis's arm shot out, palm up, like a traffic cop signaling a car to stop. "That's close enough," he said, his words carrying on the soft spring breeze.

"You're going to tell," Ian said, continuing to close in, ignoring Ellis. "It's just a matter of time. Tell now. Make some news."

Ellis said something to Griff, then dropped Lenny's arm and stepped in front of Ian, blocking him. Ian stopped short, but from his raised chin and hard-eyed glare, I could tell he wasn't the least bit intimidated. Griff hustled Lenny up the remaining stairs toward the massive iron doors. Just before the two men disappeared from view, Ian leaned around Ellis to shout out his parting shot.

"Alice kept a diary. Did you know that, loser? She kept a journal of all the details of her life. The cops are going to find it, Lenny. Then your goose will be cooked good. Make a deal now, while there's still a chance. Once they find the diary, they won't need you anymore. You too, Randall. The first one of you to talk wins. Be the first, Randall."

Reporters fired questions at Ian. "What diary?" and "How do you know about a diary?" and "Why hasn't a diary been found up until now?" and then the overlapping shouts made it impossible to distinguish one question from another. Ian didn't reply to any of them.

Randall cast his eyes around looking for someone, Darleen perhaps, and when he didn't see her, his expression changed from fearful to dejected. He scanned the steps one more time, then looked at me—his eyes aimed at my cheeks.

"Where's Darleen?" he mouthed.

I shrugged and shook my head and turned my hands palms up.

"Why is he looking at you like that?" Wes whispered. "Why did he ask you where his wife is?"

"I have no idea, Wes. I agreed to appraise Alice's dolls for them, to give them a benchmark in case the collection is confiscated to repay her victims, that's all."

"Out of everyone here, it's you he reached out to."

"Maybe it's because I'm the only civilian here he knows, the only one who isn't out for blood."

Ian watched the two men with predatory eyes until they disappeared inside. Ellis said something to Ian I couldn't hear. He shook his head, angry and impatient. Ellis said something else, and again Ian shook his head, then turned and ran down the steps. Ellis watched him until he hit the sidewalk, then continued up the steps.

"If I could have your attention," Harson said into the microphone.

One reporter, a blond woman wearing more makeup than I used in a year, started after Ian, but at Harson's next words, she stopped to listen, then, with one last glance at the fast-receding quarry, resumed her place close to the podium.

"Let me be clear," Harson said. "We have not offered either man a plea deal, and we don't expect to offer any. Mr. Almonte and I are confident that our cases are strong. In addition, we are actively pursuing several lines of investigation to locate the missing funds. Various governmental agencies are cooperating in this endeavor. We'll take your questions now."

"What do you know about Alice Michaels's diary?" Wes shouted.

"Earlier this morning, we received a court order authorizing us to freeze Ms. Michaels's assets, including all of her personal possessions," Harson replied, "pending authorization to seize them. If there's a diary, we'll find it."

"Will you pick up Ian Landers for questioning about it?" another reporter called out.

"We'll do everything appropriate in our vigorous pursuit of justice for the victims and to protect the interests of the citizens of the state of New Hampshire."

"What's the role of the federal government in the investigation?" a TV reporter I recognized from a Boston station asked.

Harson stepped aside so Christopher Almonte could answer. "Once Mr. Harson learned that money and mail had been moved across state lines, that changed the nature of the crime. He correctly called us in. The legal principle is simple: You cannot use the United States banking system or the United States Post Office for illegal activities."

I didn't hear the next question. I was wrestling with a dilemma. Not a dilemma, an unpleasant reality. If I knew Darleen, the minute she heard that a court order freezing Alice's assets had been issued, she'd run, not walk, to my company demanding Alice's dolls back. Given her propensity for running roughshod over anyone who disagreed with her, I could only imagine the snit fit she might throw.

I sidestepped past the reporters and trotted down the steps. I needed to contact my staff before she got her teeth into them.

"Yes," Cara said, and from that one word, I could tell she was upset. "Darleen Michaels called about half an hour ago. She's canceled the appraisal and is coming to pick everything up. Sasha is packing the dolls now."

"Tell Sasha to put everything in the safe. Don't give Darleen anything. If she arrives before me, tell her I'll explain why we can't turn the dolls over to her when I get there."

"Okay," Cara said, her anxiety at having to endure Darleen's fury apparent.

"I'll be there in about ten minutes."

Back at my car, I slipped in my earpiece and called Max Bixby, my lawyer. Max was a rock and an ally. Over the years he'd been an unflappable source of strength and a bottomless fount of knowledge.

"Josie!" he said when his assistant put me through. "What's up with my favorite antiques expert?"

"I'm in a quandry." I explained how I'd just heard the attorney general say they'd received a court order freezing Alice Michaels's assets and personal possessions. "I'm in possession of some of them, and I just found out that the woman who brought them in for appraisal, Alice's daughter-in-law, called and told us to pack everything up. She wants them back, probably so she can hide them from the Feds. What do I do? I'm in a heck of a position, Max."

"Not really. It's simple. You call the attorney general's office to report you have some objects relevant to their court order. They'll take it from there."

"Clients will never trust me again."

"You have a lot of clients trying to hide things from the law, do you?"

"Good point," I said.

"Do you want me to call the AG on your behalf?"

"Yes, please. Tell them to send someone right away. I don't want Darleen to have any reason to harass us. Once it's a fait accompli, there'll be no point in her raging around my office."

"Raging around your office? Sounds like a fun time. I'll call you as soon as I speak to someone."

I thanked him and spent the rest of the drive planning what I would say to her and hoping she wouldn't be too awful.

·   ·   ·

To my surprise, there was still a strong media presence at Prescott's. I figured they'd all be on the courthouse steps, but I was wrong. I ignored the questions being shouted at me and drove straight to the front door, stepping inside just in time to hear Darleen demanding to see me, her voice strident.

Fred was standing, his eyes signaling frustration.

Gretchen was seated at her desk, but she wasn't working. She was leaning forward, her elbows on her desk and her chin resting on her hands, absorbing every dramatic detail.

Cara was cowering by the warehouse door.

"Oh, there you are!" Darleen said. "Tell him to get me my dolls. Now."

"I can't," I said, closing the door, the chimes' soft tinkling serving to highlight her shrill braying.

"Excuse me?" she said, dripping sarcasm.

"I spoke to my lawyer, and he instructed me not to release any of Alice Michaels's possessions."

"How dare you? This fight is between us and the government. It's none of your business."

"I wish that were true, Darleen, but it's not. Obeying court orders is everyone's business."

"Are you working for the cops now?"

I felt the hairs on the back of my neck rise. Her tone implied that working for the cops was one step below selling drugs to school kids.

"Are you suggesting that cooperating with law enforcement is something to be ashamed of?" I asked in a level tone.

"I'm suggesting that a businesswoman should focus on keeping her clients happy, not on doing law enforcement's dirty work."

"Darleen, I think you ought—" I broke off as the door opened and Christopher Almonte stepped inside.

"Ms. Prescott?" he asked, taking in the office with one sweeping glance.

"Yes," I said.

"I understand you're in possession of some of Alice Michaels's possessions, specifically a doll collection."

"That's correct," I said. I turned to Darleen and smiled, allowing myself that guilty pleasure. "Darleen, this is Federal Prosecutor Almonte. Mr. Almonte, this is Alice Michaels's daughter-in-law, Darleen Michaels. She was just trying to get me to release the objects to her."

"Really . . . then my timing is good." He handed me a court order, then turned to her. "Seems like you and I should have a talk, Ms. Michaels."

Darleen stormed out. She didn't say a word, but if looks could kill, Christopher Almonte would be very sick, and I'd be dead as a doornail.

I called Max, and he asked me to fax the court order to him for review. While we waited for his callback, I asked if anybody wanted some lemonade.

"There's Cara's gingersnaps, too," Gretchen said, heading for the minifridge.

We'd barely poured the lemonade before Max called back.

"Give the man what he wants. Get him to sign a detailed receipt. Also, the AG asked me to ask you if you'd consult for them and appraise Alice's household goods."

"Of course," I said, flattered to be asked.

"I'll take care of the paperwork. We want to be certain your liability is limited. We can finalize everything tomorrow."

"Thanks, Max," I said, glad to be back on solid, familiar ground with Max by my side, not stumbling along Darleen's rocky road.

It was nearly five thirty, and I told everyone to leave, but Gretchen said she was fine to stay and help. She prepared the receipt, and Fred loaded the tub containing the dolls into Mr. Almonte's trunk. After he had gone, I realized I was trembling. I was adept at handling difficult personalities. In a consumer business where megadollar sales and competing agendas were routine, coping with anger, jealousy, and envy were all in a day's work. Darleen was something else altogether. She was mean and spiteful, and I hoped I'd never have to interact with her again.

Upstairs, I sent Wes the scans of the currency as promised, then turned to face my window. I looked out over the forest, into the cerulean sky. I couldn't think of anything I could do to help find Eric's kidnapper, not at this point. The police were gathering facts and reinterviewing Eric, and the media were issuing calls for citizen cooperation.

My thoughts gravitated to Randall. How could a skilled and successful businessman be unable to look a person in the eye? I knew well what it took to oversee a small business—Randall had to be able to take calculated risks while simultaneously creating workflow procedures. He had to be able to sell, make decisions, and lead. The man I'd met, the man I'd witnessed climbing the courthouse steps, possessed none of those qualities. Either someone else was running the business or Randall was different at work than he was at home. Lots of people, I knew, were like that, bringing forth different parts of themselves in different environments. It was possible that Randall was competent at work and a milquetoast the rest of the time.

I called Wes.

"Is Randall's business really a success?" I asked.

"Why are you asking?"

"He doesn't strike me as the successful entrepreneurial type. I got to wondering if maybe Darleen's the power behind the throne. Can you check with some employees?"

"Done."

Unlike Randall, whose subjugated demeanor seemed at odds with how he'd need to act at work, Ian behaved as expected and completely in character. Even so, that was quite a performance he'd put on at the courthouse. I considered the possibility that he'd invented Alice's diary in an effort to force Lenny's and Randall's hands. If they, on their own, or in a conspiracy of Alice's making, were guilty of even darker crimes than fraud, crimes like blackmail, Ian might hope to tempt them with a way out. If they came clean about the missing money, maybe they could frame a deal that would allow them to escape graver punishment for the more serious charges. Ian might have been teasing them by hinting that he had knowledge relating to their alleged crimes. Or Ian could have fabricated the whole thing for reasons only he understood.

I could think of only one way to find out if Ian's claims about the diary were real, and that was to ask him.

CHAPTER TWENTY

I didn't have Ian's cell phone number, so I decided to call his wife, Martha, at the day spa. I picked up the phone to dial but changed my mind before the call connected and hung up. I didn't know what she thought of Ian's behavior. For all I knew, she was egging him on, but it was possible she'd distanced herself, that she was acting as if she didn't know him. Better, I thought, to talk in person so I could see her eyes and gauge her attitude, and better to just show up, instead of giving her time to prepare.

Lavinia's Day Spa faced the village green. It was housed on the ground floor of a two-hundred-year-old former chocolate factory. Stepping inside, I was immediately immersed in the subtle and familiar aroma of lavender and peppermint, Lavinia's signature scent. The inside walls were original redbrick, mellowed to a muted terra-cotta color. The flooring was original, too, wide oak planks polished to a golden sheen. Thick aubergine area rugs were scattered here and there. The lighting was recessed and subdued. I felt myself relax the moment I entered.

I waited for a woman in front of me to check in, then said hello to the receptionist.

"I'm Josie Prescott. Do you know if Martha Landers is around, and if so, if I could see her for a minute or two?"

"She's here somewhere, probably in three places at once, if I know her. Let me check for you."

I leaned against the counter, orange granite flecked with gold, and waited as she called someone named Patricia, then Sylvia, then Deb.

"I found her!" she said, hanging up. "Her assistant will be right out to lead you through the labyrinth."

I thanked her again and stepped aside as two customers approached the counter. A moment later, a young woman with a ponytail, wearing a miniskirt and high-heeled sandals, popped her head out of a door marked PRIVATE.

"Josie?" she asked, and when I nodded and stepped forward, she added, "Follow me, please."

I'd never seen the back offices before, and I was surprised at their plainness. Whereas the spa conveyed warmth and calmness, this section was completely unadorned. The wall-to-wall carpet was industrial gray, the lighting was fluorescent, and from what I could see by peeking into rooms and cubicles as we passed, the walls were stark white and undecorated. The overall feel of the place was utilitarian, even unwelcoming, and certainly not inspiring. It wasn't a place I'd want to work. When we reached the end of the corridor, the young woman knocked twice at a closed, unmarked door, then opened it without waiting for a reply and held it for me, so I could enter ahead of her.

Martha Landers looked up from her computer monitor and smiled at me. She looked thinner than I recalled, and tired, with purple smudges under her eyes that makeup couldn't conceal.

"I'm sorry to barge in on you like this," I said.

"Are you kidding me? You're more than welcome! I'm always glad to take a break from budgeting, and I'm also always glad to see you. How are you doing, with all that's been going on with you?"

"Amazingly well, I must say. Once I knew that Eric was safe, I felt the weight of the world lift off my shoulders. It's terrible about Alice, too, of course, but Eric was alive, and—" I stopped midsentence. I didn't need to relive the horror.

"Understood. Is this a social call? Or can I do something for you?"

"Mostly, I wanted to say hello and see how you're doing. I know this has been a tough time for you, too."

She leaned back in her chair, and her shoulders sagged. "Yeah, you could say that."

"Ian's sure been all over the news."

"What now?"

"You haven't heard what happened at the attorney general's news conference just now?"

Martha cocked her head. "Let's skip the two-step, Josie. Assume I know nothing."

"Sorry," I said. "I was trying to be subtle, not sneaky. If I were married to Ian, I'd be worried. He seems a bit like a loose cannon, if you know what I mean. I was just wondering what your take is on the whole situation."

"Ian who?"

I stared at her.

"We've split up." She shrugged. "I thought you knew."

"Oh, God, Martha, I had no idea. I'm so sorry."

"Don't be. I stuck with it as long as I could, but even I, Miss Goody Two-Shoes, has a limit. I can tell from your expression that you don't know what I'm talking about. You're thinking I'm upset about the money thing. Or I guess I should say the lack of money thing. I am. Of course I am. Who wouldn't be? I don't care about money, though, not in that way. I walked out on Ian because I caught him screwing around on me. Nice, huh?"

I shook my head sympathetically. "You must be crushed, Martha."

"Actually," she said, sounding drained but not embittered, "I am. That's a good word for it. Crushed, like a steamroller ran over me. You know the worst part? Ian didn't even try to hide it all that hard. I caught him dead to rights because he didn't even care enough to fake it. It was a few months ago, in February. I was pulling together all the receipts and everything we need for taxes. I noticed a charge for lingerie on one of our credit card statements. I hadn't received any lingerie, thank you very much. It was like he wanted to get caught."

"What did he say?"

"'Damn—I thought I'd thrown it away.'"

"That was it?" I asked, shocked.

"No. He came clean. He told me he'd been unhappy ever since the kids graduated college, and that's what? About five years ago now. He'd been having an affair that whole time. Five effing years, Josie, and I was just too stupid to notice."

"Oh, God, Martha. You must be insane."

"I was. I'm better now." She took a deep breath and smiled, a weak one. "You come to say hello and get an earful. Sorry about that. For the first couple of months, I did the stoic thing. Then I realized that *I* was suffering for his sins—and screw that. Now I talk about if I'm so inclined." She flipped a palm. "Believe it or not, talking about it makes me feel better."

"I believe that a hundred percent. Talking about things always makes me feel better, too. Have you filed for divorce?"

"Yeah. Alice did us one favor. Not having any money means there are no assets to fight about."

"Awful. Is he still seeing that other woman?" I asked, hoping my direct question wouldn't offend her.

She snorted. "Ian's mistress was Alice Michaels."

"Alice?" I shook my head, staggered. "Alice? I just can't imagine it. She had to be, what, a dozen years older than him?"

"Seventeen, to be exact."

"Oh, wow. Martha, you must have been out-of-your-mind upset."

"To tell you the truth, Josie, mostly what I am is mad. I feel like such a fool. After we broke up, two so-called friends said they'd wanted to tell me they'd seen Ian out with Alice doing the hot and heavy but hadn't known how."

"Yeah, I had friends like that, too. I promise you that if I ever see anything you'd want to know or that you'd need to know, I'll tell you about it."

"Thank you, Josie," Martha said, smiling. "Believe it or not, that means a lot. I promise you the same thing."

"Deal. On a separate but related subject, I need to talk to Ian about something he said today. I won't mention this conversation to him."

"Don't mind my nosiness—what do you need to talk to him about?"

"He said Alice Michaels kept a diary. Actually, he taunted Lenny and Randall with it. I don't know if he said it because he was trying to goose Lenny and Randall into talking, or if it's true, but I want to ask him. I've been asked to appraise Alice's household objects, and the more I know about the diary, the better the likelihood I can find it. Since Ian wants it found, I'm hoping he'll talk to me about it."

Martha unscrewed a bottle of water and took a long drink, then took her time screwing the cap back on. "It's true. Alice kept a diary. Ian told me about it. It was that same night, when I confronted him about the lingerie. He said he was just as glad his affair was out in the open, that it was bound to come out sooner or later because Alice kept a diary. As soon as you put something in writing, he said, you're screwed. It's not if you're screwed, it's when. He told me he tried to get her not to write about him, but she just laughed it off."

"Well, that answers that. I wonder where it is."

Martha ripped a sheet from a memo cube, wrote something on it, and handed it me. "Here's his phone number. Ask him."

I sat in my car with the windows down and called Ian, but I didn't reach him.

"This is Josie Prescott, Ian," I said after his voice mail beeped. "I'm hoping we can talk soon. As you may or may not know, it looks like I'll be the one going through Alice's possessions, so any information you can give me about her diary to help me find it quickly would be appreciated."

I looked out over the green, watching a woman roll a ball for a toddler. It was still warm, with the sun an hour or more from setting. I didn't want to go home. With Ty out of town, there was no reason to hurry, and I wanted to try to clear my head. Something about Ian's rant was tickling a memory, but I couldn't seem to capture it. It was like the thought was there, right in front of me, but so thoroughly shrouded in fog, I couldn't see it.

I drove to the beach. Leaving my car at Rocky Point Taffy, not yet open for the season, I crossed the two-lane street, pushed through rambling roses, just in bud, clambered up a dune, the sand shifting under my feet, and crab-walked down to the beach. Ribbons of slick green seaweed littered the sand. To the north, a man and a woman were playing Frisbee with a golden retriever. I headed that way.

After a while, the couple and dog left, and I called Ty.

"Hi," he said. "How are you?"

"Okay. Confused. Upset. How are you?"

"I'm okay. Why are you confused and upset?"

"Nothing seems to make sense," I said. "It's hard to tell the sharks from the minnows. Three hundred out of a thousand bills I sent Barry were counterfeit, and no one knows where the real money is. I have no idea who killed Alice or why, which means a murderer is probably here among us. Ian Landers, you don't know him, but you've heard me talk about his wife, Martha—she's the manager at Lavinia's Spa—anyway, Ian had a five-year affair with Alice, who was, by the way, just about old enough to be his mother."

"Five years? That's not a one-night stand."

"No."

"You sound like you need to spend time with a special fella, someone who'll give you a little back rub and tell you how beautiful you are, and how he'll never cheat, never think about cheating."

I smiled. "That would be wonderful—exactly what the doctor ordered—except the man of my dreams isn't here . . . wait a minute . . . yes, he is. I'm talking to him!"

"I miss you, Josie. I wish I was there. Don't get me wrong—the training here is good, and the meetings aren't running too long, so work is okay. I'm just tired of being away from home."

"Today's Wednesday. It's only two more days."

"Two days that will feel like two weeks."

"We need a vacation," I said.

"Where do you want to go?" he asked.

"Norway."

"Really? Why?"

"I've never been."

"There are lots of places you've never been. Why Norway?"

"I don't know. I read a book once in which a couple went to Norway and cruised along the fjords. It sounded romantic."

"Okay. When do you want to go?"

I smiled. I was going to Norway! "After Gretchen's wedding and before tourist season really kicks in."

"Late June. Consider it done."

We talked awhile longer, and then the sun lowered toward the horizon and a chill set in. I told Ty I was ready to go home and that I'd call him at bedtime.

As I drove, I slipped in my earpiece and called Zoë.

"May I invite myself over later?" I asked. "I'll bring a pitcher of Blue Martinis."

"Oh, please. You're the answer to a prayer. I've had such a day."

"What's wrong?"

"If have to watch one more animated cartoon I'm going to run screaming into the woods."

"Ready for some adult conversation, are you?"

"Desperate. Hurry."

"I'm on my way!"

I turned on the flat-screen TV Ty had installed in the kitchen for company and mixed a pitcher of Blue Martinis. I was cutting pineapple wedges for the garnish when the TV anchor said, "And now our Legal Eagle, Pennington Moreau, will discuss the arrests today that have rocked the Seacoast region."

"Thanks, Mitch," Penn said. "Lenny Einsohn and Randall Michaels were arrested today on a laundry list of charges stemming from the alleged Ponzi scheme being run by Alice Michaels, founder of Rocky Point–based ADM Financial Advisers. One of the investors who alleges he lost more than a million dollars in the scam is Ian Landers. Mr. Landers has been extremely vocal in condemning the company's principals and demanding they reveal what they know."

I heard Ian's voice and looked up in time to view a video clip of his in-your-face confrontation with Lenny and Randall.

"In an exclusive off-camera interview conducted after this episode," Penn continued, "Mr. Landers was a changed man. Instead of yelling, he was somber. He explained that he was despondent over his financial losses and heartbroken over a recent romantic breakup. He stated he'd been romantically involved with Ms. Michaels for more than five years and that she ended the relationship about a month ago."

Poor Martha, I thought.

"The police and state and federal prosecutors are certain to follow up by looking at what, if anything, Mr. Landers might have learned from Ms. Michaels about her firm's alleged financial irregularities during the course of their relationship. According to a high-placed official on the prosecutorial team, who would only speak on condition of anonymity, Josie Prescott, owner of Prescott's Antiques and Auctions, has been retained to appraise all of Alice Michaels's household goods. It's hoped that she will discover among Alice's possessions enough objects of value to compensate the alleged victims.

"If you have any knowledge of anything related to this case, the police and the prosecutors want to hear from you. Call the toll-free tip line number you see at the bottom of your screen.

"I want to leave you with one last thought. Let this increasingly distasteful situation serve as a cautionary tale. Choose your friends and associates with care. Are they looking out for your interests—or their own? This is Pennington Moreau, the Legal Eagle, soaring high and signing off."

I muted the TV just as the phone rang.

"Why didn't you tell me you were hired to appraise Alice's stuff?" Wes asked, sounding hurt.

"You were listening to Penn."

"Weren't you?"

"He's wrong. Nothing's been finalized, Wes, and he didn't even call me to confirm the report. Sloppy journalism."

He snorted. "He's not a journalist. He's a wannabe."

"Good point. Let me ask you something. Do you know if Ian Landers or Randall Michaels has an alibi for when Eric was kidnapped?"

"Why are you asking?"

"Alice saw the Civil War currency in one of Selma's dolls. If she and Ian were as close as Penn says they were, it's reasonable to think she would have told him about it. As for Randall—if Alice confided in her lover, it's not out of line to think she would have confided in her much-loved son. I don't know, Wes. I just figure it can't do any harm to check."

"I'm on it," Wes said. "Give me a quote about being hired."

"I haven't been hired."

"You will be. Give me a quote I can use if and when."

"Okay. Are you ready?"

"Shoot."

"Keeping in mind that this is all if and when, 'Prescott's looks forward to working with the authorities to ensure a comprehensive and impartial appraisal.'"

"Jeez, Josie, that's a little white bread, don't you think?"

"It's all I've got under the circumstances."

"Okay. Catch ya later."

"Wait—what about Randall's company?" I asked. "Did you find anything out yet?"

"Yeah. According to two employees and a client it's like the AG said. Randall was his mother's errand boy. Alice ran the business and he did as he was told. All three said it wasn't a problem for them because Alice was easy to work for and with and Randall never interfered."

I nodded. "Thanks, Wes."

"Talk soon." He hung up.

I turned off the TV and finished preparing the pineapple wedges, placed the pitcher and plate on a tray, then picked my way across the little lawn that separated my place from Zoë's, thinking that you could never tell, you just never could tell. I'd thought that Randall was merely a shadow of a man. Then I learned that he had evidently lied and cheated like a champ at his mother's behest. Now I wondered just how far he'd go for the woman in his life. Would he have kidnapped Eric if Darleen told him to? Would he have killed his mother?

Likewise, I'd thought Ian was just bombastic. Then I learned he was a philanderer. Now I wondered what other crimes he might have committed.

CHAPTER TWENTY-ONE

At seven thirty the next morning, Thursday, I sat at my little round table eating cereal and orange slices and watched the local TV channel's anchor rip Randall's and Ian's characters to shreds. It was painful and embarrassing to watch, but I couldn't look away. He alternated between locally relevant news stories, like the planned lane shutdowns on Route One due to emergency pothole repairs, and innuendo-laced speculations about the two men's roles in ADM's collapse and Alice's murder. Since the anchor had no facts, he quoted anonymous sources, which for all I knew were his in-laws. Watching him made me respect Wes more. Wes was frequently irritating, but he never skimped on facts and never repackaged gossip as news.

The anchor presented Randall as a co-conspirator, a hapless man manipulated by a stronger personality into a life of crime. That was bad, but what he said about Ian was worse. He actually referred to Ian as a shark. He talked over live video showing reporters staked out in front of Ian's condo. I recognized some faces from their recent siege of Prescott's, including Wes. Bertie was there, too.

While the anchor was saying something about how the police were drilling down into Ian's alibi for Alice's murder, implying they were taking a harder look at him than anyone else, which, as I thought of it, might actually be true, Ian charged out of his unit. He didn't look despondent. He looked as angry as ever. Instead of welcoming the reporters' attention, he ignored their questions and stomped past them to his car, a white SUV. I could almost see the steam pouring out of his ears. Several reporters, including Wes, jumped into their vehicles to follow him. The TV cameramen swung the shot wide, and the chase began. When Ian turned onto a side street, with the horde of reporters following close behind, the station returned to a standard in-studio shot. I wondered if Ian would be able to get free of the onslaught. I was almost sympathetic, but not quite.

Ten minutes later, Ian called me.

"I got your message," he said. "Sure, I'll tell you what I know about the diary. Not on the phone, though. What with Penn implying that Alice spilled the beans during pillow talk, I figure there's a fair to middling chance the Feds have tapped my phone."

"You might be right. When should we meet, and where?"

"I've got some business to deal with out of town. How's four this afternoon?"

"Four will work, but is there any way we could meet sooner?"

"No can do," he said. "Let's meet at North Mill Pond. Do you know Fenter Lane?"

"It's off Maplewood, right?"

"Yeah. It dead-ends at the pond."

I knew the short road from when I'd first moved to Rocky Point seven years earlier and had spent hours driving around town trying to get the lay of the land. Fenter Lane was off one of Rocky Point's busy main streets, about a quarter mile from Route One. It was quasi-industrial, mostly deserted, and a good choice if you wanted to have a private conversation.

The courier carrying the currency, including the three hundred counterfeits, arrived about nine thirty.

"I'll be in the back," I said.

"Before you go," Sasha said, "I heard from Nate Blackmore."

"He discovered a priceless treasure among Alice's costume jewelry."

She smiled. "No such luck. It's all costume. There's nothing valuable or remarkable in any way. He'll drop everything off soon."

"Got to love Alice's sense of humor," I remarked.

While Sasha started in on the dolls, I took charge of the currency, carrying the package to a worktable near the safe. Wearing latex gloves, I extracted two bills, one from the middle of the hundred-bill stack and another from the middle of the three-hundred-bill stack Barry reported was counterfeit, and held them up to the light. In the first sample, the light seemed to radiate through and around the paper. There were no watermarks or mars or noticeable threads. The second sample was obviously printed on different paper. As clear as day, on a spot to the right of Salmon Chase's portrait and above the *U* in "United States" was a sweep of feathers, the kind found on a quill pen. I was looking at Elegance's watermark.

I locked the box of currency in the safe and went upstairs to call Ellis.

"Well, all right, then," he said. "I'll call the Secret Service."

"I still can't believe it, Ellis. Do you want to call the Farmington sisters or shall I?"

"Let's tell them together, and in person. I'm sure they'll have questions that can only be answered by an antiques expert."

"Okay, although I'm certainly not a numismatist. Shall I bring a bill as an example?"

"Better not. We'll give them the bad news, I'll ask my questions, and that will be that. From then on, they'll be dealing with the Feds. The Secret Service will sort out who owns what. Which means you shouldn't turn anything over to the Farmingtons, neither the three hundred counterfeits nor the seven hundred genuine bills. I'll call them now and try to set something up. What does your day look like?"

"I have an appointment in Portsmouth at four that shouldn't last more than an hour. Anytime up until then is fine. Or after."

"I'll see what I can do. So I hear you're getting on the government's payroll."

"I am?"

"That's what the AG tells me. They've hired you to appraise Alice Michaels's household goods."

"I knew it was in the works. I didn't know it was a done deal. My lawyer had some questions about liability."

"I guess they straightened it out. If you find that diary, call me."

"If I'm working for the state or the federal government, shouldn't I call them?"

"I'm not telling you *not* to call them. I'm just asking you to call me. If you could call me first, that would be even better."

"You're a tricky devil, aren't you?"

"Nope. I'm just a cop working a couple of unsolved cases, you know, a murder and a kidnapping."

"I understand," I acknowledged. "Yes, I'll call you if I find the diary—first."

"Thank you. Any idea where it is?"

"No, but I feel as if I ought to have one."

"Why?" he asked.

"I just have a sense that I should. Like déjà vu in reverse. Don't you ever get that feeling? Like you've heard something or seen something that should register with you, but for whatever reason it's slipped away or faded away or something?"

"All the time, actually. I thought it meant I was getting old."

"Ha, ha," I said. "It doesn't. It means your brain is full. That's what I figure, anyway. I stupidly filed the memory in the wrong drawer of my mental filing cabinet, and I can't find it. All I can do is keep poking around and hoping I run across it." I laughed. "This must sound bizarre to you."

He chuckled. "That's one way of putting it." He added that he'd call after he spoke to the sisters, and we hung up.

I checked the time display on my computer. It was just after ten. I picked up my accountant's report and settled back to read about revenue streams. About forty minutes later, Cara called up. Max Bixby, she said, was downstairs and asked if I had a minute.

Max sat on the love seat and laced his hands behind his head.

"I was in the neighborhood," he said, "so I thought I'd stop by. I see the reporters are gone."

"They've moved on to other stories, I guess."

"Sometimes stonewalling works."

"Is that what I was doing?" I asked. "I thought I was simply ignoring them."

He smiled, a lopsided grin. "A rose by any other name . . . I've hashed out the details with the attorney general and the federal prosecutor.

All I need to do at this point is confirm your rate, and we're good to go. Your contract will be with the federal government. They wanted to split your time between the two agencies, but I refused. This is cleaner from our perspective, and it doesn't matter whether they divvy the charges up before or after you do the work. There are no liability issues. You're to use your best efforts. Period."

"You're a magician, Max!"

I gave him my rates, and he said he'd call when I could stop by and sign the contract. I could send someone to retrieve the dolls from the federal prosecutor's office anytime. I thanked him again and escorted him downstairs, then told Sasha the good news about our new appraisal contract.

She smiled and tucked a strand of hair behind her ear. "Oh, that's great news—especially since I haven't been able to get that wooden doll out of my mind." She rifled through a stack of papers on her desk. "Look at this."

Before I could take the paper she was handing me, Ellis called to tell me that the Secret Service was sending someone from Boston to pick up the currency.

"It's now officially out of our hands," he said.

I turned back to Sasha and reviewed the stapled document she handed me. There were three pages, each showing a different angle of a finely crafted wooden doll. I flipped through the pages, then looked at Sasha.

"These photographs come from a doll dealer in Berlin named Oskar Streinfeld," she explained. "I posted photos of Alice's wooden doll and put out a call for sightings same as I did last year, but this time Oskar came through! I think it's the same maker. Look at her ear. Do you see the bulbous lobe? That's an unusual shape. Alice's doll has the same lobe. Also, there's a subtle indentation directly above the clavicle. It's hard to see in the photo, but I confirmed it directly with Mr. Streinfeld. He said to look at the doll's ankles for a signature. The maker, Thomas Whitley, carved his initials on the inside of his doll's left ankle. Apparently, the initials are so small they're barely noticeable. Can you imagine?"

"Sasha, this is terrific news! Fabulous! But why didn't Mr. Streinfeld respond last year when you put out the call?"

"He just acquired his doll a month ago from an estate sale."

I nodded. Timing wasn't all, but it was a lot. "What do we know about Thomas Whitley?"

"He owned a fine cabinetry shop in London. He died in 1680."

"Wow."

She grinned. "Yeah."

"Do we know that he made any dolls besides Mr. Streinfeld's?"

"Yes. He kept detailed work records. Mr. Streinfeld has put me in touch with a university professor who wrote his thesis on seventeenth-century entrepreneurs. He has copies of all Thomas Whitley's work records. From those documents, we know he carved a dozen dolls. Alice's doll, if we can verify its authenticity, will be the third extant example. So when I say I'm a little excited, I mean it!"

"Well done, Sasha."

Fred walked in, setting the chimes jingling. "What's well done?" he asked.

Sasha recapped her research coup, and I added, "I'm glad you're here. I was just about to suggest we try calling Eric."

Cara dialed, and when Eric was on the speaker, she said, "I have gingersnaps for you, Eric."

"Great! I'm still hungry all the time. I'll be in tomorrow."

"What?" I couldn't believe what I was hearing. "No way!"

"The doctor said I was fine. All my tests so far are good. I'd have come in today, but I need to go back this afternoon for a final all-clear checkup."

I squelched the anxiety-fueled protest I was about to utter. Eric was a grown man and needed to be guided by his own judgment, not my fretfulness.

"Well, you know best. If you change your mind, just give us a call."

I listened to my staff's enthusiastic questioning about his condition and was reassured by Eric's commonsense replies. He'd slept a lot and eaten a lot and was eager to get back to it. He had lots of questions, too, about the status of the tag sale setup, and whether Gretchen had scheduled the gutter cleaning, and how the new bushes he'd planted were coming along.

"How's Hank?" Eric asked.

I smiled at the thought of dog-loving Eric asking about Hank.

"He misses you," Gretchen said.

Ellis called just after eleven.

"I spoke to Jamie Farmington. They can see us at one if that works for you. I can pick you up."

"The time is good, but let me meet you there. I have errands afterward."

"Okay. Can you stop by here en route? Like maybe at noon? I'd like to talk to you."

"Am I in trouble?" I asked.

"No. Why would you ask that?"

"A visceral reaction to a police chief saying he wants to talk to me."

"I want to consult you," he said. "I need your brains and antiques expertise."

"Oh . . . in that case, sure."

I parked in the police station lot about quarter to twelve, crossed Ocean Avenue, and climbed a high dune. Looking out over the ocean, I saw dots of white froth whipping across the midnight blue water. The sky to the northeast was gray and seemed to be darkening in front of my eyes. A storm was brewing.

I hadn't finished saying hello to Cathy when Ellis poked his head out of his office and smiled.

"Come on in." He stood until I took a seat at the guest table, then sat across from me. "We've got a bite. A numismatist in Portsmouth named Vaughn Jones called, responding to the alert your friend in New York posted. A man with blond hair wearing a cowboy hat and sunglasses just tried to sell him some Union currency. Our Union currency, it looks like. Jones asked to keep the money so he could research it, but the seller said no, he was leaving town for his home in California and wanted to make the sale right away. Jones passed, and the customer left."

"That's terrific news, Ellis. A real lead."

"How so?"

I felt my brow furrow and thought it through. "Oh, I get you . . . not so terrific a lead after all. He was in and out of there in a minute and a half, and in all likelihood he didn't touch anything, so there aren't any fingerprints and he didn't leave any DNA behind. Got it. Did he give a name?"

"Mitchell Davidson. Do you recognize it?"

"No. Should I?"

"No. What else do you want to know?"

"That's a funny question to ask me. Usually you avoid answering my questions."

"No, I don't," Ellis said. "I avoid revealing confidential information. This isn't confidential. I've already released it to the media. I'm hoping the public can help us identify this man. We did the same thing with Eric's kidnapper."

"Have you got any good leads on either so far?"

"No. Ask me questions."

"Does the dealer have any security cameras?" I asked.

"No. He works out of his house, which is in a mostly residential neighborhood. The closest camera is located at a bank down the street. They have outside cameras for their ATM."

"Did he call or just show up?"

"He called. From a disposable cell phone, not a number we've seen before. Then he knocked. I thought maybe he pushed the doorbell and we could capture a print, but no such luck."

"Anything odd in his speech? An accent or anything?"

"No."

"Did he say how he found Jones?"

"Yes, through an online search."

"So you can expect him to try other dealers who advertise there, too," I said.

"Detective Brownley is on the phone now, calling them all—all we found by Googling relevant keywords."

"What about industry associations? There's probably an online directory."

His reached to his desk for a pad of paper and took a pen from an inside pocket. "Good idea," he said. "What else?"

"Does Ian Landers have an alibi?"

He cocked his head. "What's your thinking?"

"Nothing, not really. Just that he's involved—or he's involving himself for some reason."

"True. So are Lenny and Randall."

"Also true."

"Who else are you wondering about?" he asked.

"No one."

"Why did Mitchell Davidson pick Jones, do you think?" Ellis asked. "Proximity?"

"Are there other numismatists close by?"

"No."

"Then I guess so. Still, it doesn't seem very smart to me. If I were him, I wouldn't try a dealer anywhere from Boston to Portland. There's been way too much publicity about the kidnapping and too much speculation about the dolls and whether they contain contraband for comfort. To say nothing of Barry's BOLO about the counterfeit bills, which, while he might not know about it, he should expect." I shrugged. "Plus, locally, Eric's kidnapping and the money hidden in the dolls . . . well, it's all most people are talking about. Like that print." I pointed to Norman Rockwell's *The Gossip*. "If it were me, I'd stay way clear of the seacoast. I'd go to New York."

"Maybe he can't leave Rocky Point. Any ideas why not?"

"Maybe he's a caregiver who can't leave the person he's taking care of. Or he's a professional whose absence would occasion remark. A doctor just can't cancel appointments on the fly, for instance, without everyone in his office talking about it."

"Perhaps. What else?"

"I can't think of anything else," I said, thinking that in all probability Mitchell Davidson was an invented name, just like George Shankle, and this lead, which had seemed so promising when Ellis first told me about it, was just another dead end.

. . .

As soon as we were seated in Selma Farmington's Victorian-influenced living room, Ellis turned to me.

"Please tell Lorna and Jamie everything we know," he said.

I recounted Barry's assessment, adding that I'd seen the watermark that indicated modern paper.

As soon as I uttered the word "counterfeit," Lorna began to cry, and she didn't stop the whole time we were there.

"I wish I had better news to report," I said.

Jamie was made of sterner stuff. She heard me out in silence, but her expression made it clear she wasn't staying quiet because she had nothing to say. By the time I was done, her lips had thinned to one invisible line and her eyes had narrowed to slits.

"We gave you currency that had been in our family for a hundred and fifty years," she said

"I'm afraid not," I said.

She turned to Ellis. "I want to call my lawyer."

CHAPTER TWENTY-TWO

D riving from the Farmingtons' to Max's office, on streets that followed three-hundred-year-old cart tracks, passing row houses built just after the Revolutionary War, and hardwood forests far older than that, I thought of how confusing and frightening things must seem to Jamie and Lorna. Tradition and stability were gone. Their mom had just died, they had the depressing and onerous job of cleaning out a fourteen-room house where their family had lived for generations, and they'd just learned that someone had stolen more than half a million dollars' worth of rare currency.

I parked in the small lot in back of the old mansion that housed Max's firm, along with an architectural firm and an insurance agency. Every time I entered Max's private office I felt a jolt of delightful surprise. Although not much older than me, in appearance and demeanor, Max was old-world courtly, yet when it came to furnishings, his taste was completely contemporary, an inexplicable contradiction. His desk was a slab of black granite perched on stainless steel legs. Black solid surface and stainless steel bookcases lined one wall. The guest chairs were black leather and slouchy. The carpet was a red and gray block print. The art was abstract, mostly oils, all black and white geometric shapes slashed with red or purple or gold.

"First things first," Max said, handing me two copies of the one-page letter of agreement from the federal government retaining my company to appraise Alice Michaels's household goods. After I signed with a pen from the silver holder on Max's desk, he handed me an envelope containing a set of keys and a letter authorizing me and my staff to enter Alice's house and remove anything we choose.

"Is there an alarm?" I asked.

"No."

"Really? That's odd."

"Lots of houses don't have alarms," he said. "Rocky Point isn't exactly crime central."

"True . . . and I bet she doesn't have a lot of antiques around."

"Except her dolls."

"Which don't figure on most thieves' top ten lists," I said, nodding. I slipped the envelope into my tote bag. "We'll get started right away. There's something else, Max. I think I'm about to be sued." I described the situation with the counterfeit currency and Jamie's reaction.

"If and when," Max said, "I'll take care of it."

"I don't think they're malicious. I think they're overwhelmed and confused."

"I'll be certain to point that out to their lawyer."

I smiled as I thanked him, relieved, as always, that Max was on my side.

I decided to treat myself to a late lunch at Ellie's, a long, narrow restaurant on the village green. Ellie makes crepes far better than anything I can make at home. Her chicken with asparagus in Mornay sauce is my favorite. As I walked across the green I called Wes.

"You know about Mitchell Davidson, right?" I asked. "How he tried to sell some Union currency to a dealer named Vaughn Jones?"

"Yeah. It was on the police scanner. Whatcha got?"

"I saw you take off after Ian this morning. Where did he go?"

"I lost him," Wes said, chagrined. "We all did. You should have seen him. He pulled stunts straight out of a James Bond movie, spinning sideways down an alley I didn't even know existed . . . pulling a whoopee in the middle of the street. Jeesh!"

"'Pulling a whoopee' means what, exactly?" I asked.

"You know, a U-turn, but faster."

"So he was determined to lose you."

"Not just me. All of us. He definitely didn't want any company. Why are you asking?"

"We need to know if Ian, Lenny, and Randall have alibis for the visit to Mr. Jones's house. I'm betting one of them is Mitchell Davidson."

"How come?"

"Because there's no one else."

When I got back to my office, I asked Fred if he could be ready to leave in ten minutes, and he said sure. He also told me, with a gleam in his eye, that Sasha had news.

I hurried to join her in the warehouse. "So?" I asked.

She smiled, a big one. "Look at this." She handed me a loupe and pointed to the wooden doll's inner left ankle.

"Well, well," I said. Without strong light and magnification, the maker's mark was impossible to see. With them, it was impossible to miss. It was as if Thomas Whitley had been a humble man, a simple carpenter who didn't want to put himself forward by highlighting his accomplishment.

"I should have noticed it without prompting," Sasha said. Her tone conveyed her embarrassment.

"I'm amazed you found it even with prompting."

"It's a lesson to examine every inch of everything."

"Maybe. Or it's a lesson that we're only human and we're going to miss things sometimes."

"Thank you, Josie."

I smiled and tilted my head at the doll. "So we have a genuine Queen Anne doll dating from the mid-1600s." I noticed Alice's jewelry box at the back of the table. "When did this reappear?"

"With the dolls," she said. "When Mr. Almonte took the dolls, he took it, too. When the dolls came back, it returned as well. I've roped off a section for Alice's goods; I figure you and Fred will be bringing some objects back here. Anyway, I took it out so everything would be together." She picked up the doll. "I can't wait to hear Mr. Streinfeld's thoughts about valuation."

I raised my right hand, fingers crossed, then glanced at the wall clock. It was after three. I needed to hurry.

"Fred and I are going to head over to Alice's now and get started recording everything," I said, starting to rush back up the center aisle. Then, changing my mind, I veered to the right.

I wanted to say hello to Hank. As I passed the rows of angled shelving filled with antiques and collectibles and the roped-off sections containing consigned goods or objects under review, the niggling feeling that I was missing something continued to taunt me.

"I don't know," I said aloud, frustrated. "So close, and yet so far away."

Hank was curled in his basket, asleep, his right front leg draped over the edge, as if he'd started to get up but hadn't quite been able to make it before a nap took him away. I sat down next to him and petted him gently so I wouldn't wake him, and he began purring in his sleep.

"What is it, Hank?" I whispered. "What did I see or hear?"

He didn't even wiggle.

"I know the kidnapper is someone who's both a risk taker and methodical. He's someone who knew how to get fake IDs. He has enough cash on hand to buy three used cars. What else? He was after the currency. He knew that Selma Farmington had Union currency and that she stashed the money in her Chatty Cathy dolls. He didn't know that someone had already stolen some of it from Selma and replaced it with counterfeit. Hmmm... that might exclude Randall, don't you think, Hank? I just don't know, Hank. What a good boy you are, that's right... You're *such* a good boy. I still think it might be Ian, don't you, Hank?"

He stretched and turned his head to lick my hand, four sandpaper licks, then repositioned himself into a tight little ball.

"You don't know any more than I do, do you, Hank? Never mind... you're a good boy. A very good boy." I stood up. "Sleep tight, baby boy. You're a good friend, too, Hank. Just being able to sit here for a few minutes and talk to you... well, thank you, sweet boy."

Alice Michaels had lived in a twelve-room Colonial on the ocean. Old stone walls marked the property line, and woods of scrub oak, pine, and sycamore blocked the ocean view from the street and flanked each side of the property, providing Alice, and her neighbors, privacy. Across the street, on the inland side of Ocean Avenue, a half acre of woods completed the panorama. The property was as private as anything I'd seen along the shore. The closest side streets were Astor Road, the cut-through from Main Street that Fred and I were on, and the more distant Raleigh Way.

Fred and I took separate cars and parked at the end of the long, winding driveway. We entered through the side door, and I stood and looked around as Fred unpacked the video camera. We were in the mudroom. I lifted the lid of a wooden bench positioned along an outside wall. Four pairs of boots of various styles and colors stood next to one another. They were all size seven, and presumably they were all Alice's. Across the small room coats hung on hooks. Cabinets revealed piles of hats and scarves and mittens and gloves.

"Ready?" I asked Fred.

"Ready," he said, and I unlocked the kitchen door.

Prescott's appraisal protocol requires that we create an annotated video recording before we begin appraising individual objects. I planned on a quick walk-through just to see if anything stood out as special, leaving Fred to do the actual recording. Fred decided to begin in the basement and work his way up.

"I think I'll head upstairs first," I said.

The attic was accessed by a door in a small bedroom at the rear of the second floor. I climbed the narrow staircase and found an unfinished, unused space. A single low-watt lightbulb dangled high overhead. The space was gloomy and stuffy.

I walked to a small south-facing window and took in the beach view. A woman was power-walking on the soft sand, her auburn hair streaming behind her. The water was choppy and nearly black. The storm was blowing closer.

By the time I'd returned to the main floor, it was clear that Alice's taste ran to British Colonial. The furnishings appeared to be modern reproductions and of good quality, but there was nothing that stood out as noteworthy. Her furniture was a mix of heavy, dark wood and rattan. The only custom piece was an empty display case, where, I presumed, Alice's doll collection had been housed. The key was in the lock. Two rooms on the upper floor were wallpapered, one with a grass-textured paper, the other with a pattern featuring monkeys and coconut palms. The rest of the rooms were painted in neutral tones, taupe and sand and straw. The artwork was also reproductions. The Queen Anne doll would go a long way to reimbursing investors, but based on my quick once-over, I didn't see anything else that would contribute much to the cause. I saw lots of places where a diary could be stored, desks and bedside tables and bureaus, but I didn't bother opening any of them. If Alice had kept her diary where it was easy to find, the police would have already found it.

A room on the ground floor that Alice had obviously used as an office was stripped nearly to the bones. The desk drawers were open and empty. Phone and fax machine cords lay across the desk, but the units themselves were missing. A wireless router sat on a bookshelf, but there was no computer. A mahogany file cabinet was barren. I scanned the book titles that filled the shelves. They were all contemporary and business oriented: investor guides, industry analyses, and economic reports, that sort of thing. There was nothing that appeared to be a diary, but I supposed it could be secreted in a hollowed-out book, which would, as I thought of it, be a great way to hide it in plain sight. We'd need to examine each book individually.

I found Fred recording the contents of the kitchen pantry.

"Anything interesting?" I asked.

"No," he said, lowering the camera. "No antiques at all." Fred didn't wrinkle his nose, but from his tone, he might as well have.

I nodded. "All right, then. I'm going to take off. If you find a diary or a journal or anything that could serve as a diary, like a notebook or something, let me know right away, okay?" I handed him the keys and the letter of authorization. "Don't feel obliged to do everything today. We can finish up tomorrow."

"I'll see how it goes."

I told him good-bye and left, pausing on the wraparound porch to enjoy the view. Whitecaps swirled close to shore, and the tall grasses near the house lay nearly sideways in the now-strong breeze. The sun was still out toward the west, but looking east, the cloud cover was thick.

• • •

When I pulled to a stop at the end of Fenter Lane, right on time, Ian was nowhere in sight. I parked by the side of a rusted corrugated Dumpster large enough to hold a car and looked around. The packed dirt road was pitted with potholes. Thick tangles of weeds grew along the sides. A decrepit one-story building stood to the north situated on a low rise. The windows were boarded up, and a sign, its paint cracked and peeling, swung from a broken chain. I squinted to make out the words. It read KAT'S BODY SHOP. The wind had died down, and the sun was trying hard to poke through the clouds. The dark green water on North Mill Pond was glassy. Pussy willows, cattails, vines, and thorny bushes grew in wild abandon around the perimeter. Three ducks dipped their opalescent teal heads into the water, then swam past in perfect alignment, as if they were part of a synchronized swim team. I leaned against my car and watched them frolic.

I checked the time on my cell phone and was surprised to see it was ten after four. I thought I'd only been watching the ducks for a minute or two. I decided to wait until twenty after, then call him. At twenty-two after four, I left him a cheery I'm-here-where-are-you message. At four thirty, I decided to leave.

Rather than try to turn around in the narrow lane, I pulled up Kat's packed dirt and gravel driveway. I was about to back out when I noticed a reflection—the now-bright sun was bouncing off something white. I drove in another ten feet.

Ian's SUV was parked at an angle, as if he'd driven up the driveway intending to parallel park behind Kat's but had messed up. I left my car idling in park and stepped out.

I was standing on a slight rise, maybe fifty feet above the pond, in a cleared dirt area, roughly rectangular in shape, about a hundred feet square. A couple of wooden horses stood off to one side amid a thick knot of weeds. A rake rested on a patch of crabgrass. A green plastic chair, with all but one of its back slats missing, sat next to a heap of old tires. I looked down toward the pond. The ducks were nowhere to be seen. A gray rabbit ran across the dusty road and disappeared into the brush.

I approached the SUV gingerly, worried about what I might see. I cupped my eyes and peered inside. The keys were in the ignition. The car was empty. I frowned and walked toward the hood. I saw a shoe.

"Oh, God," I said. "No."

I took a step and then another. The shoe was of cordovan leather, a man's loafer. Slacks came into view, khakis. One more step and I would see the man's face. I closed my eyes and took a breath, then another. I opened my eyes and took the step. It was Ian. He lay on his back, his left arm by his side, his right arm bent, his legs straight, his eyes open, his mouth forming an O, as if he were surprised. A river of blood, glittering in the sun, streamed from his head toward the weeds. A target pistol rested near his right hand. My stomach leapt into my throat, then plummeted. Little gold flecks spun in front of me, and I thought I might faint. I stumbled a few steps away, then ran for my car.

CHAPTER TWENTY-THREE

I nside my car with the heat on high and the doors locked, I dialed Ellis's cell. I got his voice mail.

"Ian Landers is dead," I stated. "His corpse is behind an old body shop, Kat's, on Fenter Lane. A gun is by his hand. I'll call nine-one-one now."

I repeated the message to the 911 operator, then settled in to wait, the warm air streaming at my face providing a measure of comfort. Twelve minutes later, Ellis's SUV and two Portsmouth police patrol cars roared down the road, their red and blue rooftop lights spinning and their sirens piercing the air. Ellis slammed to a stop halfway up the driveway, in back of my car. I pushed the button to lower my window.

"Are you okay?" Ellis called, stepping out.

"Shaken, but intact."

"What are you doing here?" he asked.

"I was supposed to meet Ian at four. I waited until four thirty, then used the driveway to turn around. I saw his car . . . then a shoe. It's horrible, Ellis, just horrible."

"Stay here," he ordered.

I watched him jog to where Griff and Officer Meade stood waiting for instructions. Ellis said something I couldn't hear, and I stopped trying to pay attention. Instead, I raised my window and called Ty.

"Hi," I told Ty's voice mail. "If my voice sounds all quivery, it's because I'm a mess. I just discovered a dead body. Ian Landers. I think he shot himself. I was supposed to meet him at four. Why would he kill himself, Ty?"

Ellis tapped on the glass, startling me.

"Oh!" I said. "Here's Ellis. I've got to go."

I sat in Interrogation Room One, a small room with a scarred wooden table and metal straight-back chairs. I'd opted to face the two-way mirror, so my back would be to the human-sized cage. The cage, which Ty had told me was necessary for an occasional unruly guest, unnerved me. A video camera sat on a tripod, the pinprick-sized red dot signaling it was on.

"Do you think Ian killed himself?" Ellis asked.

"I can see it," I replied. "If he felt things closing in on him, he might have decided he had no choice. Is it definite that it was suicide?"

"Definite is too strong a word. The angle of the entry wound is right, but we're considering all options."

Which meant nothing. Either Ellis didn't know or he wasn't telling.

Since my meeting with Ian never took place, my statement was mercifully short. I explained that I'd hoped to get a description of Alice's diary and, maybe, information about its contents. I provided a detailed timeline and recounted finding the body. I refused to speculate about what might have happened, and that was that. Ellis thanked me for cooperating and said he'd be in touch. By seven thirty, I was home.

I changed into jeans and a long-sleeved T-shirt, and when Ty called I was mixing a Blue Martini.

"Oh, it's so good to hear your voice!" I said. "What a day."

"So I gather. First some good news—I'll be home tomorrow by two. I have one meeting, early, then I'm outta here."

"Yay! I can't tell you how much I've missed you."

"Me, too. Are you okay?"

"Not really. I'm still all weirded out."

"Do you have any idea why Ian would have killed himself?" he asked.

"He was an angry man, Ty, sarcastic and mean. It was the kind of anger that's out of proportion to the incident at hand, and maybe even unrelated to whatever was going on. Whatever was driving him, it ran at high velocity. I could see him spinning out of control. Anger outward turning inward, leading to depression and hopelessness."

"You know that's pure conjecture."

"Yeah, and I also know that when I try to interpret out-of-whack behaviors, I'm often wrong."

"Not always. Sometimes you're right."

"True." I shifted position, stretching out my legs, resting my heels on the coffee table. "Tell me about your day. I don't want to think about Ian anymore tonight. I want to listen to you talk."

"I came up with a new exercise," he said, "and it looks like it'll make the short list."

I could hear the pride in his voice, and the pleasure. We were two lucky people, and I knew it. Too many people I knew hated their jobs or their bosses or both. Ty and I were the exception, not the rule. After he finished describing his idea, he asked how I was feeling.

"Better since I'm talking to you, but still not great. All I want to do is hear about good news things. Or at least not bad news things. Do you have anything mundane you'd like to discuss?"

"Emotionally, you're full up."

"That's exactly right, Ty. If I were a teacup, I'd be spilling over."

"So," Ty said, "did you find those Hawaiian thingies you were looking for?"

After Ty and I had finished our conversation, I sent Martha Landers a brief e-mail.

I struggled to find the right words to express sympathy when I wasn't certain whether she would perceive Ian's death as a loss or a blessing. I settled on a simple message.

Hi Martha,
I can't imagine how you're feeling . . . I wanted you to know I was thinking of you. If I can do anything, please let me know.
Your friend,
Josie

Wes had sent an e-mail asking me to call him. I deleted it. I checked my voice mail and listened to his two messages. I deleted them, too. I didn't want to talk to him. I wanted to read a chapter or two of my current book, Rex Stout's *Plot It Yourself*, and go to sleep.

Wes called my landline as I was rinsing my martini glass, and I stared at the phone as it rang. I wondered if he was calling with news or for news. If I spoke to him, I'd have to relive the horror, but if I didn't, I might miss out on getting up-to-the-moment information. I needed to quell the chaos more than I needed quiet. I answered the phone.

"You should have called me back," he said, as usual.

"I just got your messages, Wes. It's been a full day."

"In spades, huh? You're in the thick of it, that's for sure."

"I just found the corpse, Wes," I protested. "I'm not in the thick of anything."

"Did you get any photos?" he asked.

"Of course not!"

"I don't mean of the body, although that would have been rad. I mean of anything, like the police showing up and doing stuff."

"No," I said. "No photos."

He sighed. "So why were you meeting Ian?"

"Is that why you called? To get me to tell you what happened?"

"Of course—but I also have a major league info-bomb."

"What?"

"You first."

"Ian said he'd tell me about the diary."

"Why was he willing to talk to you about it? He wouldn't tell me squat."

"I've been hired to appraise Alice's household goods. The more I know about the diary, its size, color, and so on, the more likely I am to find it. He wanted it located, so he agreed to meet me."

"If he wanted the diary to get to the police, it must be loaded with dirt. The question is, dirt on whom? Do you think he was killed to stop him from telling you?"

"Killed? What are you saying, Wes? I thought he killed himself.

The police told me the entry wound was at the right angle for a self-inflicted wound."

"Yeah, that's what I hear, too. I was just asking."

"So what's your info-bomb?" I asked, wincing as I repeated his made-up term.

He chuckled. "It's a doozy! The weapon found next to Ian's body is the same one that was used to kill Alice."

"You're kidding!"

"Nope," he said, tickled that I was astonished. "His prints are on it, in all the right places—and no one else's."

"That's incredible, Wes." I thought for a moment. "Do you have any info on where he was all day?"

"Yup. He had a long meeting with some Boston lawyers. They've issued a statement saying that due to Alice Michaels's position in Rocky Point society, Ian was concerned he wouldn't be able to find an impartial lawyer. Which may be true, no matter what anybody says. Anyway, he was at the law firm from ten to one. Then he went to a coffee shop around the corner and had a sandwich. He charged it so they know the exact time he left—one forty-five. If you figure it took him fifteen minutes to get to his car and he headed straight back to Rocky Point, he'd have gotten here between three thirty and four. But . . . hold on to to your umbrella . . . there's more . . . according to Ian's cell phone record, someone called him from a disposable unit—a unit the police haven't run into before—at ten fifteen, twelve fifty, and three forty. The first two calls were only a few seconds long. The last one took five minutes."

"So while Ian was with his lawyer, the calls went to voice mail, and whoever was calling didn't leave a message. Afterward, when the call came in, he answered the phone."

"Exactly. I'm thinking that he was already at Fenter Lane when he took the call. Whoever he spoke to told him something so upsetting, he killed himself then and there."

"When did he die?" I asked. "Do they know yet?"

"The preliminary report says three to four. They think it's on the later side. They're still analyzing his stomach contents."

"So the timing works." I paused. "What could the caller possibly have told him?"

"What do you think?"

I stared out the kitchen window into the blackness. I knew there was a meadow there, and woods beyond, but all I saw was nothingness.

"That he knew Ian had killed Alice," I said.

"Good one, Josie! That would explain everything! Ian murdered Alice because from where he sat, and it looks like he was right, Alice stole his money and then dumped him. Ian offered her a deal—repay me and I'll keep quiet about your Ponzi scheme. She wouldn't—or couldn't—repay him, so boom, he killed her. He felt righteous. Then someone starts in after him. He can't stand the thought of prison, so he folds."

"You're making a boatload of assumptions, Wes. Who started after him? Why?"

"That's what we have to find out." Wes said, exhilarated. "The police aren't stopping there, though. They're busy checking alibis, too. They're not ready to write it off as suicide, not by a long shot. So far, nobody's clear. Lenny and Randall both made bail by noon. Lenny says he was at home, but he lives in Greenland with no near neighbors. His wife was at her mother's, and his kids were doing after-school stuff. He didn't make any calls or anything, so essentially, he has no alibi. Randall picked up his daughter from school and took her to her ballet class. Then he ran a few errands, which covers the entire window of time we're looking at, but there are gaps. Theoretically at least, he could have made all the stops he says he did, gotten to Fenter Lane, and still picked up his daughter on time. He says that just because he shopped at a leisurely pace, that doesn't mean he's a murderer, that he wasn't in any hurry since he was just killing time until his daughter's class was over, at five. The police haven't found anything to contradict his story. No one remembers seeing him. There aren't any security cameras in the stores he visited. He paid cash for everything and kept no receipts, but who does for a small container of threepenny nails and a jug of laundry detergent, right?

He can't recall exactly when he was where, so for all intents and purposes, he's open, too."

"What about Darleen?"

"At a salon getting stuff done to her hair and face. She's covered."

She could still be the brains behind everything, I thought, *issuing the orders while staying out of sight.*

"What about the gun?" I asked.

"Stolen from a gun shop in Los Angeles two years ago. It hasn't been associated with any crimes."

"So what you're saying is that so far as is known, Lenny and Randall *could* be involved, but there's no reason to think it's *not* suicide." I thought for a moment, then asked, "In your gut, Wes . . . do you really think Ian killed himself? Do you really think he's a killer?"

"Maybe . . . why not? Things are usually just what they appear to be."

"Except when they're not."

I woke up the next morning, Friday, with a fully developed idea on how to find out if Alice's diary was pivotal to what was going on. It was six fifty. I reached for the phone to call Ellis, but as I dialed, I realized it would be far easier to explain in person than it would be on the phone, so I hung up and padded to the window to see if his SUV was parked in Zoë's driveway. It wasn't.

I dialed his cell phone and counted rings. I got to six before he answered, sounding groggy.

"It's Josie. I woke you up. I'm really sorry."

"I'm not awake yet. Keep trying."

"I have an idea."

"Shoot," he said.

I told him my thinking, and when I was finished, he said, "Congratulations . . . you did it. I'm awake."

I awakened Wes, too.

"I have an on-the-record statement to make," I said. "If you hurry, you can scoop everyone and get yourself on the morning news."

"Let me grab my pencil . . . okay . . . I'm ready."

"Ask me the status of our appraisal of Alice's household goods."

"What's the status of your appraisal of Alice's household goods?" he asked.

"Prescott's has finished our initial inventory of Alice Michaels's household goods. I know her company's former investors are interested in how much money is likely to be raised from their sale. It appears that besides her home, her doll collection was her most valuable possession. At first glance, we didn't find any other antiques, but we didn't expect to. We'll know more once we begin our on-site examination, which will happen later today."

"Is that it?" he asked.

"Don't you want to know our role in finding the diary?"

"What about the diary?" Wes asked. "Have you found any hint that it might be somewhere in her house?"

"No, but there are scores of places she could have hidden it."

"Like where?"

"I'll give you one of many possible examples. There's a wall of business books in Alice's home office. We need to examine each one to see if it's really a business book, or if Alice used a business book jacket to disguise her diary, or perhaps if she placed the diary inside a fake book."

"Interesting idea," Wes said. "Going back to something you said a minute ago—why didn't you expect to find any antiques?"

I smiled. Wes had just asked one of the two important questions I needed him to highlight in his article, and he'd done it without prompting. "Ms. Michaels's house isn't alarmed, and in our experience, when homeowners have valuables in their houses, they install some sort of a security system."

"What about the dolls?"

"Dolls aren't attractive to thieves; they're too delicate to transport and too hard to sell. Plus, they were displayed in a locked cabinet. As an aside, they're no longer at her house. We have them secure at Prescott's."

"What's your next step?" he asked.

I smiled again. There was question two. "We've already made a video of her possessions. We'll spend the morning reviewing it to prioritize where we should search for the diary. We'll begin that phase of our work this afternoon."

Cara arrived about quarter to eight, more than an hour earlier than her regular start time, a platter of gingersnaps in hand.

"I wanted to be here when Eric arrived," she said, smiling.

Eric's start time was eight.

"Me, too," I said.

So, it seemed, did everyone, even Fred. Gretchen and Sasha arrived about five of eight, followed closely by Fred.

"Wow!" I exclaimed in mock amazement. "Look what the wind blew in!"

"Getting ready for bed, Fred?" Gretchen asked, giggling.

"Just because none of you has ever seen me up and about this early before doesn't mean it can't be true."

I smiled broadly. "You seem so... I don't know... what's the word... oh, I know! Awake."

"That part's an illusion," Fred said. "All you can say for sure is that I'm vertical."

Gretchen giggled again and said, "I'm going to get Hank. He wouldn't want to miss seeing Eric."

She pushed into the warehouse as Fred said, "So what do you say, Cara? Can I try one of the new batch?"

"Not until Eric has some."

"You're being unreasonably cruel to a vulnerable man!" he said.

"I know," she said, smiling. "It bothers me a lot."

"Did you find anything worthy of remark at Alice's?" I asked as he poured himself a cup of coffee.

"No. It's all nice enough stuff, but nothing special."

Gretchen returned with a sleepy-eyed Hank in tow, cradling him like a baby. His head rested on her shoulder. One paw was wrapped around her upper arm.

"PTK," I said, reaching for him, using Prescott's shorthand for "Pass the kitty." She handed him over, and I gave him a little hug and kissed the top of his head. "Good boy, Hank."

Eric walked in, setting the chimes jangling.

"Yay!" I said.

Gretchen shouted, "Yay!" and her arms shot up, forming a wide V. She began her happy dance, a high-energy performance filled with high jumps, low kicks, sideswiping hand motions, and bouncing spins, circling him and saying "Yippee!" over and over again.

Eric looked the same. His color was good, his eyes were bright, and his demeanor was as reserved as ever. He looked pleased and embarrassed and awkward all at once. I plunked down at the guest table, Hank still in my arms, and rubbed his little tufty ears as I watched the fun.

Eric told us he was fine, really, fine as he ate half a dozen cookies in quick succession and drank about a quart of sweet iced tea.

As the excitement began to fade, I stood up, placed Hank on the floor, and said, "All right, everyone. Let's give Eric some breathing room."

Eric looked troubled as he leaned over and gave Hank a pat. "Do you have a minute?" he asked me.

"Sure," I said, hoping nothing was wrong. "Let's go upstairs."

Eric perched on about an inch of the wing chair, staring at the carpet. After several seconds' silence he raised his eyes to mine.

"Chief Hunter told me about what you did," he said. "I wanted to say . . . I mean . . . well . . . thank you."

"I did what anyone would do, Eric."

"You think?" He stood up, looking uncomfortable. "Anyway, thanks."

I nodded and let him go, which he did without saying another word.

Wes's online article was perfect. The headline read:

ALICE MICHAELS'S DIARY:
WILL IT BE FOUND TODAY?

The text used my quotes along with one from an unnamed police source whom I suspected was Ellis, stating that the police had the utmost confidence in Prescott's abilities. *Nice,* I thought.

●   ●   ●

I drove along Greenview Street, a two-lane road that ran parallel to Ocean Avenue, one block inland from Alice Michaels's house.

When Ellis had told me to stay clear, not to go anywhere near the stakeout, he'd spoken in as dictatorial a tone of voice as I'd ever heard him use. I understood his point of view. If the trap we'd set sprang as we hoped, we'd have a killer cornered. I didn't want to interfere, and I wasn't foolhardy, but I hated half a story, and I was committed to staying out of their way. I remembered how Wes said he wasn't surprised to see me wherever there was action. Curiosity was a powerful motivator.

I passed a bungalow on the right, closed for the season. Shutters covered the windows, and tarps were tethered to the porch railing to protect the outdoor furniture. A couple of rocks had fallen from the stone wall and sat on the crabgrass curb, a sign the owners or their gardener hadn't yet made their annual spring walk-around. Memorial Day weekend was Rocky Point's unofficial start of summer, and most part-time residents didn't drive up from the city to ready their houses for the season much before then. An old Chevy sat in the driveway, pointing toward the street. To my left, a half acre or so of scrub oak, sycamore, and pine blocked the ocean view, accounting for the bungalow's second-story porch. From there, the vista would be unobstructed.

I turned right onto Astor Road, heading away from the beach. Through the rearview mirror, I spotted Officer Meade in an unmarked vehicle closer to Ocean than Greenview, her vehicle pointing inland. Detective Brownley, in another unmarked car, faced the dunes. I turned right on Marlow, one block inland from Greenview, saw no signs of human life, and turned right again, on Raleigh Way. The police officer I thought was named Daryl sat in his unmarked vehicle a hundred yards from Ocean, also facing the beach. I suspected that Ellis, along with at least one additional officer, would be inside Alice's house, lying in wait.

I turned into a driveway across from an unmarked, private lane, closer to an alley than a road, that ran between Astor and Raleigh, halfway between Ocean and Greenview. The alley served the half-dozen houses that backed onto it, allowing trash to stay out of sight and deliveries to be more convenient. Griff stood partly hidden by an old maple tree, facing Astor. There were no vehicles parked in the alley, unless you counted an old red wheelbarrow sticking out from behind a wood-enclosed trash bin. I wondered why Ellis hadn't stationed a vehicle here, but only for a moment. The answer was obvious: From the lane, there was nowhere to go except Astor or Raleigh—and he had those streets covered. You could hide in the woods, but not well and not for long. A half acre sounds like a lot of land, but it isn't, not when you're trying to hide.

I backed out, headed up Raleigh away from the beach, driving two blocks past Greenview, and parked next to a weathered wooden fence. I walked back along Raleigh, then turned onto Greenview for ten paces, glanced around to check that no one was watching, and entered the patch of woods that ran from Greenview to the alley. I was twenty paces in, walking on a thick carpet of pine needles, before I realized that out of habit, I had taken my tote bag with me. I shrugged and continued on. My steps made a soft shush-shush sound. After several minutes, I reached the lane where Griff was stationed. I peeked to my right, waited until his back was to me, then ran on tiptoes across the lane. I was into the section of woods abutting Ocean Avenue in less than thirty seconds. I ducked under low-hanging branches and pushed through clumps of bushes and ferns until finally I glimpsed slivers of asphalt and dune. After another minute I saw a shimmer of water. I stopped five feet back of the stone wall that ran the breadth of the woods along Ocean Avenue and looked around.

I saw no one on the street or beach, and I doubted that anyone passing by could see me, but looking diagonally to my right, I had a clear view of Alice's driveway and her woods. If I looked up, I could see her chimneys. The bits of ocean I could see were as choppy as yesterday, but the sun was out. It was warmer than yesterday, too, a comfortable sixty-eight. Not far from where I stood, poison ivy grew amid a thick knot of Boston ferns, and I stepped a little further into the woods, knowing poison ivy was as common a ground cover in New Hampshire as grass was on a golf course.

I waited and watched and listened. Waves crashed against the rocky shore, then quieted as the tide drew back, only to charge forward and crash again, a rhythmic, deceptively peaceful song. A large brown bird circled overhead, gave a high-pitched *craw-craw,* then disappeared heading west. As the minutes passed, I began to feel as if I were the only person on earth, an eerie sensation. I dug my phone out of my bag to check the time. Before I could look, the silence was shattered by Ellis's call of "Stop! Police. Stop!"

A tall, thin blond man wearing a Padres baseball cap and wraparound sunglasses sprinted across Ocean Avenue straight at the stone wall, straight at me. Instinctively, I stepped back, tripping on a root and toppling sideways, landing hard. As I stretched out my arm to break my fall, my phone crashed to the ground and my tote bag slid off my shoulder, the contents spilling onto the pine needles. The man leapt over the wall like a gymnast vaulting a horse fifty feet away from where I lay in a heap, then pushed into the forest as if there were a pathway only he could see. Seconds later, he was out of sight, lost in the northern jungle. *It could be Lenny,* I thought. *Or Randall.* I stood up, rattled, but unhurt, in time to see Detective Brownley race by heading the wrong way, driving north on Ocean. If I didn't do something, he was going to escape.

I dashed to the wall, jumped up and over it, and ran into the middle of the street, heading toward Alice's house, certain that Officer Meade or Ellis would soon be in pursuit. Moments later, Officer Meade barreled onto Ocean from Astor. I waved my arms like a windmill, and she slammed on her brakes.

"You're heading the wrong way!" I yelled, running toward her. "He ran through the woods toward the alley, and probably to Greenview beyond."

She nodded and took off, whip-turning onto Raleigh. After standing in the street for another few seconds, waiting to see if Ellis or someone else was going to drive by, I ran back into the woods, found my phone amid the jumble of my possessions half buried under pine needles, and started off toward the alley, jogging fast, trying to make up time. I ducked and wove and stumbled through the forest, heading more or less straight, until an unseen branch scratched my cheek, drawing blood, and I froze for a second, crying out in pain and covering the wound with my palm.

"Go," I said aloud and took off again.

Moments later, the trash enclosure and wheelbarrow came into view. Griff was nowhere to be seen. I ran across the alley and entered the next section of woods. When I reached Greenview, I was nearly out of breath. I looked every which way and spotted the man in the Padres baseball cap. He was behind the wheel of the Chevy I'd seen in the bungalow's driveway, pulling out. In five seconds, he'd be gone. I called Ellis and got him.

"The man you're looking for is in a Chevy," I said, my chest heaving, "just about to pull out of a driveway on Greenview, near Astor."

"Stay where you are," he snapped and hung up.

Ellis's SUV spun onto Greenview from Astor, heading south, which meant the Chevy was behind him. Officer Meade's vehicle, followed closely by Daryl's, with Griff in the passenger seat, came flying by, sandwiching the Chevy between police vehicles.

The Chevy's driver, accelerating fast, veered left, trying to pass Ellis, but Ellis wouldn't let him. Ellis kept to the center of the road, swerving to keep the Chevy trapped in place. Ellis anticipated the Chevy's driver's moves as if they'd been choreographed and rehearsed, pulling left just as the Chevy did, then right, until, without warning, the Chevy's driver seemed to lose control and the car careened toward a stone wall on the right side of the street. Before it reached the wall, it jumped the curb and crashed into a tree, an old elm.

Still breathing hard, I ran full tilt toward the crash scene. Detective Brownley whizzed past. Ellis, his weapon out and pointed at the driver, sidestepped toward the vehicle. Even from this distance, I could see through the rear window, and what I saw told me that Ellis wasn't in danger—the driver was dead. He'd fallen against the steering wheel, his head resting on his shoulder at an impossible angle.

All at once, I ran out of breath and slowed to a walk. I was trembling from exertion and anxiety and fear. I stopped walking and bent over, placing my hands on my knees, trying to catch my breath. I heard Officer Meade call for an ambulance. As I stared at my bloody hand, the one that had touched the cut on my cheek, an unexpected thought came to me: Con men succeed because they're able to convince you that the alternate reality they create is genuine. If two people tell contradictory stories, either one of them is mistaken or one of them is lying. Ian hadn't sounded despondent when I'd spoken to him that morning. He'd sounded angry. I was willing to bet that when Penn had reported that Ian had sounded despondent, he'd been flat-out lying.

"It's Penn," I said aloud, standing up, my eyes on the man in the car. Ellis, standing by the driver's door, and the others, standing nearby, turned to look at me.

I took a step closer, then another. I kept walking until I reached Ellis. Penn's dark glasses were askew, and his eyes stared unseeing at a place about a foot to my left. His wig, or perhaps his own hair dyed with a rinse-out blond wash, was natural looking. His baseball cap lay on the passenger-side floor. I heard sirens approaching. The ambulance, I assumed.

"Step away, Josie," Ellis said.

"Why?" I asked Penn, knowing he couldn't answer. "Just for money?"

"Now, Josie."

I did as he said, crossing the street to the sidewalk.

Ellis opened the driver's door and leaned in. He looked at the man, then the car's interior. After a moment, he backed out and popped the trunk. Griff and Officer Meade aimed their weapons into the space and, standing off to the side, took a long, measuring look inside. Satisfied, Griff closed it, then squatted at the rear, trying, I guessed, to read the tag number through the mud.

Ellis walked over to where I stood.

"Tell me what happened," Ellis said. "From the beginning."

I recounted what I'd heard and done and seen from the minute I'd driven up to when I'd run down Greenview, and he listened without interrupting.

"You could have been hurt, Josie," Ellis said, "or worse."

"I stayed out of sight. Penn never knew I was there."

He shook his head. "I worry about you."

I met his eyes and saw concern. "Thank you, Ellis."

"How did you know it was Penn? Why didn't you—" He stopped himself and raised a palm, like a traffic cop. "Don't tell me now. You'll just have to repeat it at the station anyway."

"Can I take a shower first?" I asked. "I fell in poison ivy."

"Sure."

After promising to present myself at the police station in an hour, I traipsed back to the woods to gather up my wallet and keys and everything else that had fallen out of my bag when I'd tripped, then drove myself home to shower and change.

CHAPTER TWENTY-FOUR

A s I stood under the steaming water I thought about lies and liars and what I knew for sure and what I only thought was true. I knew Penn fit the profile I'd developed. He was both a risk taker and methodical, a man who'd cross an ocean in a hot air balloon. He was an athlete, an iron man, well able to run and vault. Through his investigative reporting, he had access to fake IDs and stolen weapons. It wasn't a stretch to think he knew how subtle changes in a person's appearance were a more effective disguise than over-the-top modifications. Or that he'd don a clown's wig if he thought that would serve his purpose, perhaps to let his victim know there was no point in trying to identify him, that he was disguised. He couldn't travel far to sell the federal currency, because of his regularly scheduled on-air live performances. What I didn't know was why a man of his prestige would lie and cheat and kidnap and kill. I knew the questions and, standing under the stream of hot water, staring at nothing, I knew where I'd find the answers—Alice's diary. Except that I didn't have a clue where it was.

It was nearly three by the time I got back to work after spending more than an hour giving my statement. Wes had called twice, e-mailed once, and texted three times. I wasn't ready to talk to him, not yet. I needed time to process all that had happened, to think. I was stunned that Penn had so completely snowed me. I hadn't known him well, but still, I felt snookered. I was also furious. How dare he kidnap Eric? How could he kill his friend, Alice? How could he kill Ian?

None of it made sense. Ty had called, too, to let me know he was home and worried about me.

"Whoa," Fred said, standing up as I entered. "It's sure good to see you. We heard about the chase and crash and that you were somehow involved."

"We were so worried," Gretchen said, her lustrous green eyes dimming at the thought of danger.

"Are you all right?" Cara asked.

Sasha leaned forward, looking anxious, listening.

I smiled, touched by their worry. "I'm fine. Thank you all." I explained that I didn't want to talk about anything and that they should just carry on.

"I'll call Eric," Cara said. "He asked me to let him know as soon as we heard from you."

"All right," I said.

I walked around my business, catching up with what was going on, the normalcy of my workplace a relaxing counterpoint to the horror I'd just witnessed. I found Eric in the tag sale venue directing the temps on how to display a collection of clocks. He greeted me with such fervor, I understood how upset he'd been. When I got to Hank's area, he was eating. Back in the front office, Gretchen was on the phone with someone about cleaning the carpet in the auction room. Cara was on another line, giving someone directions from Portland, Maine. Fred and Sasha were reading on their computer monitors. Upstairs, I called Ty.

"You're home," I said.

"Home and glad to hear from you. The news reports were daunting."

"The experience was daunting."

"Are you all right?" he asked.

"Better now that I'm talking to you. What are you doing?"

"Laundry."

"You're a man in a million," I said, meaning it.

"Just a man in love who likes clean clothes."

I laughed and then smiled, relieved I was able to appreciate the humor tucked into an everyday conversation. After the anxiety of the past week, I hadn't expected to laugh for a while.

"What do you want for dinner?" he asked.

"I want to go out. Surprise me."

"Done."

I returned to Hank's corner.

"Hi, Hank," I said, sitting on his carpet, leaning against the wall, watching him. "How's my baby boy?"

He mewed between bites.

"You don't say."

Another mew. I fluffed his pillow, the one Gretchen had ordered to custom-fit his basket.

"You know, Hank, I've been thinking. What if Alice hadn't been joking or setting Darleen up when she told her the jewelry box was her most valuable possession? What if she'd meant it, Hank? Have you considered that possibility?"

He mewed again, then crunched. I leaned back on my calves watching him as he lapped some water. All at once, the memory that had been flitting around the edges of my consciousness for days burst forth with a whoosh that almost rocked me.

"Alice said that when she was a kid she hid her diary key in the doll she made so her sister wouldn't find it. You know what, Hank? I bet she still did."

I leapt up and ran to the worktable where Alice's dolls were lined up. I lifted the sock doll named Hilda and gently squeezed her, starting with her head and neck, then moving to her torso and legs, trying to locate the key by touch. All I felt was cushiness. If the key was hidden in the doll, it had been placed deep inside. I lifted Hilda's dress to examine her tube-sock thighs and bottom. The seams were sewn with neat, small stitches; there was no opening. I raised the dress higher, and even though I was concentrating, I just about missed it. The ribbing aligned so precisely that the 2" × 4" inch flap was nearly invisible. I peeled it back. A slit had been carved into the stuffing, and a tiny linen envelope had been slipped inside. I used a pair of long-handled tweezers to extract the envelope. Inside was a shiny silver key with a heart-shaped finial at the top. I held it up and smiled, then placed it on the table.

The jewelry box rested nearby, still shrouded in bubble wrap. I unwrapped it and measured the height—it was 6¼" tall. I opened the lid and measured the depth. The red velvet inner compartment was only 5¼" deep. Somewhere in that inch was Alice's diary, I was as sure of it as if I'd stood alongside the cabinetmaker as he'd crafted the hidden compartment. Once again, I was reminded how looks can be deceiving. The jewelry box wasn't an antique, so I'd dismissed it out of hand.

There wasn't any visible looseness or gaps in the velvet lining. I used a sharp probe to try to locate an opening under the velvet, but failed. I turned the box upside down and examined the bottom and sides. An inlaid rosewood border ran around the edge. I slid my finger along it, taking my time, applying pressure. On the right side, about halfway back, my finger pushed in about half an inch, and a drawer popped out.

"Clever," I said aloud. "It's like those spring-loaded data ports on some computers."

I opened the drawer, and there was Alice's diary. It measured ¾" × 5" × 8" and was bound in black kid leather with matching leather ties formed into a neat bow on top. A silver keyhole was surrounded by a heart-shaped escutcheon. Next to it sat a small red flowered satin pouch, its drawstring pulled taut.

Hank mewed again and rubbed my leg. I hadn't realized he'd joined me. "Good boy," I said. "You did it again, Hank. You helped me think. We're a good team, you and me."

I used tweezers to loosen the bag's strings and opened it, but all I saw was darkness. I unlatched the flashlight I keep hooked to my belt and aimed the beam inside. I saw another key, this one flat and dull silver. I knew the style. I had one like it; it opened my safety deposit box. I pulled the bag's strings tight with the tweezers, then toyed with undoing the diary's ties. *Just a quick peek,* I thought. I shook my head. I'd never be able to replicate Alice's neat bow, and I couldn't risk mucking up evidence. Plus, I didn't need to read her entries to know what she'd written.

I used the wall-mounted phone to call Ellis. While I waited for him, I took a bunch of photos for Wes.

• • •

The rain I'd been expecting all day arrived with a thunderous blast about six, just as I was getting home. The temperature had dropped from sixty-eight to forty-two in an hour.

Ty opened the front door as I rolled to a stop and stood just inside the hall, silhouetted by the amber glow of the porch light. He was smiling at me. My heart began pounding as it always did when I first saw him. He was tall, just over six feet, and broad, with muscles earned by splitting logs and hiking, and lately by working out in hotel gyms. He had dark, thick hair and brown eyes. He was smart and funny and kind and tender. I adored him.

"Hey, good-looking," he called as I ran for the porch.

A clap of thunder sounded, and I ran faster.

"Hey, yourself," I said.

He pulled me inside and embraced me, holding me against his chest, lightly resting his chin on the top of my head.

"I'm all wet," I said into his chest.

"I've known that for years."

"Ha, ha. Seriously, you'll get damp."

"I don't mind getting damp. I want to hold you."

I smiled and hugged him, and after a minute, he leaned back to kiss me.

After a kiss that weakened my knees and sent my heart racing faster, he said, "You should go change into something dry."

"I can't wait . . . I'm so ready to relax. I changed my mind about going out. I want to stay home and cook. What are you in the mood for? Do you want barbecue chicken?"

"Sure. Always. You don't want to grill outside, though. Not in this weather."

"True. We can try the new grill pan."

I changed into my pink velour lounge-around pants and top, then joined Ty in the kitchen. While I mixed the marinade of olive oil, lemon juice, garlic, shallots, salt, pepper, and Italian peppers, Ty leaned against the kitchen wall drinking a beer, a Copperhook, and telling me about his training coup.

"It sounds goofy," he said, "but I read this article about the importance of discovery. To really learn something, there has to be discovery. That's how I came up with the idea. You can't just tell someone what to do. They have to discover how to do it for themselves."

"Experiential learning. We do that with appraisals, too."

"And it works?"

"Better than anything else we've come up with."

He nodded. "That's how I positioned it. Not that it's faster or cheaper, because it's not. That it's better."

As he was placing the Cooperhook empty in the recycling bin and getting another from the fridge, he said, "So, I've booked our flights to Norway. We leave on the Monday after Gretchen's wedding."

"Just like that?"

"I'm a can-do sort of guy," he said.

"I love you, Ty."

"I love you, too, Josie."

"It's all there in black and white," Wes said. He lowered his voice, his eyes searing ino mine. "Alice's diary is one hot potato!"

I stirred sugar in my tea. We sat in a back booth in the Portsmouth Diner early the next morning, Saturday, tag sale day. I ordered tea, a fruit salad, and an English muffin. Wes ordered his regular, a double side of bacon and a Coke.

"She wrote about everything—her affair with Ian, her business going down the tubes, Penn blackmailing her, learning that Salmon Chase had purchased a thousand of those Union bills, even seeing the Civil War currency in Selma's doll."

"She admitted running a Ponzi scheme?" I asked, astonished that Alice would put such a thing in writing.

"Not exactly. What she wrote was that Penn caught on to what she called her 'business difficulties.'" Wes punctuated the words with air quotes. "Can you believe that? 'Business difficulties!' Jeesh! Anyway, she wrote that her business difficulties affected cash flow, and that she had to cover her losses in unconventional ways. She didn't specify what that meant, just that she expected to make a recovery. Then Penn started demanding money as a courtesy for keeping quiet, and she paid and paid and paid until she couldn't pay anymore. She wrote that he was on a tear, the way gamblers get sometimes. How do you figure he latched on to her scam in the first place?"

I shook my head, saddened and stunned at how adroitly Alice had lived a lie. I thought I'd known her well. Now I realized I hadn't known her at all. "Penn was a lawyer and an astute businessman. If nothing else, he had to know that the returns Alice was offering were unrealistically high, and he had to know what that implied." I sighed. "You said she wrote about the Civil War currency?"

"Yeah. When she was over at the Farmington house, she saw a letter President Lincoln had written to Salmon Chase mentioning that Chase had bought a thousand bills."

"That explains why Alice was so hot to get her hands on Selma's dolls. She didn't admit to stealing the three hundred, did she?"

"Nope, but the cops opened her safety deposit box and bingo! There they were! All three hundred bills. One thing's for sure— Alice's investors will be clamoring for the currency to be included in her estate. I figure the courts will have to sort it out."

"I'm so glad to hear the money was found. The Farmington sisters may have to sue the estate, but eventually, I'm sure they'll get it all back."

"Maybe. You ready for a real gotcha? Guess what else was in the safety deposit box . . . printing plates. And guess whose fingerprints are all over them? Randall's. Gotcha!"

"So they have Randall cold. How about Penn? Is there any evidence he knew about the Civil War currency, and that it was in the dolls?"

"Uh-huh. From what Alice wrote, you can tell that she was kind of kicking herself for telling him about it. It came up at dinner one night last week when they got talking about how some people are so cynical about banks, they hide money under their mattresses or in the backyard, that sort of thing. She mentioned that she'd seen three hundred bills hidden in one of Selma's dolls and that President Lincoln's letter proved they were real."

I nodded. "I can picture that. She told him as a curiosity, but he heard it as an opportunity. What with Selma dead, her daughters' car gone, and our van parked out of sight in the back, the way it probably was so Eric could load it easily, he probably thought he could sneak into the house easily and get the dolls. He was a desperate man."

"Desperate enough to kill Alice?" Wes asked, sounding dubious. "Why?"

"If Alice threatened to turn him in for blackmail, he would have known the jig was up. He'd lost everything, and he was a very prideful man. I think he stole and kidnapped and killed not because he was busted flat but because he couldn't bear the shame of being busted flat. He joked about his losses, saying he lost his shirt. There was also a story about how he went on some gambling cruise and lost more than anyone in the history of the ship. Do you remember that, Wes? It was on your Web site the same day you wrote about the dolls. I didn't think about his comment at all, but if I had, I would have assumed he was exaggerating for effect. Now I think it was literally true—he lost everything and he was truly desperate . . . yes, for money, but more for a way to save face. Think of Penn, a local celebrity with a lot at stake. A gambler, with a gambler's belief that his luck was about to change, that the next big break was just around the corner. Once he got the idea that he could latch on to Selma's money, his optimism would have soared. Instead of breaking into Selma's house and finding the money, though, he found Eric. I bet he waited for Eric to leave. When he saw Eric behind the wheel of Prescott's van, he must have guessed that Eric had packed up the dolls and flipped out. In his head, he'd already been spending the proceeds."

"Are you saying that he jacked the van on impulse?" Wes asked.

"Yes. Remember, he didn't check into the hotel or buy the other cars until afterward."

Wes nodded. "Which he was able to do because he'd done a segment on local makers of fake IDs, so he could get new paper easily. He must have had a stash of cash, enough to buy the cars."

"Right—and he did another segment on how to get illegal weapons." I thought for a moment. "He must have tried to break into my place, too, also probably on impulse, but saw the bolts on the door and the security cameras and knew it was too risky. Have they found that remote, by the way?"

"Yup. In his car's glove compartment," Wes said, nibbling bacon. "His real car, the only one registered under his actual name. They also found the red wig and aviator glasses he wore with Eric and the phone he used to call Ian."

"With both men dead, we'll never know what they talked about."

"Which means we'll probably never know for sure if Ian's death was suicide or murder," Wes said. "What do you think?"

"Why do you suppose Penn didn't kill Eric?" I asked, delaying answering his question. "Wasn't he taking a risk Eric could ID him?"

"Apparently not a big one. Eric couldn't. Neither could you. Despite all the publicity, no one could."

"True. Still . . . you'd think that once you murder one person, the rest would come easy."

"Jeez, Josie, that's cold."

"I'm a realist," I said, shrugging, "and it's possible he did kill a second time . . . Ian."

"I think he did it."

"Me, too," I said. "Penn lied in his broadcast when he said that Ian was despondent. The implications didn't occur to me at the time, but when I spoke to Ian the next morning, he didn't sound the least bit despondent. He sounded angrier and more determined than ever. Penn hoped the police would believe that Ian, in the throes of despair, turned the gun on himself. He also hoped he'd find the diary before I did."

"I can't believe Penn fell for your trap, which, by the way, you should have told me about in advance."

"I couldn't tell you. I promised Chief Hunter I wouldn't."

"You promised him you wouldn't show up, too, but you did."

"No, I didn't. He told me to stay away. I never agreed that I would."

Wes sighed. "Whatever. Wouldn't you have thought that Penn was smarter than that?"

"No. Actually, I'm not surprised at all that Penn gave it a try. Desperate men do desperate things."

"Hard to believe his desperation was all about money," Wes said, shaking his head. "Money and maintaining his position. Do you care about money that much?"

"Well, yeah. Sure, I care about money. Don't you?"

"Not really. I care about work."

"Doing good work leads to money," I said.

He chuckled. "Not at the *Seacoast Star,* it doesn't. I figure my attitude toward money is why I don't have a girlfriend."

"What happened to that girl? You know . . . it was a while ago. You asked me to recommend a restaurant."

"Sue . . . yeah, she was nice. She moved to Florida to go to school."

"You'll find another girl, Wes."

"Whatever," he said, waving my comments aside. He chomped a piece of bacon. "So, Alice wrote that as soon as she told Lenny not to worry about certain bookkeeping entries, he stopped asking about them. Clearly Lenny turned a blind eye to accounting irregularities, but the Feds aren't blaming him much. They say that turning a blind eye is what employees do."

I didn't, I thought. When I'd blown the whistle on how my boss at Frisco's was colluding with the competition to fix commissions, I'd been naive enough to expect to be treated like a hero; instead, I'd become a pariah and learned an important lesson: Doing the right thing is lonely work.

"Randall's a different case altogether," Wes added. "They're probably going to up the charges because his involvement was more active—he created those printing plates."

"What about Darleen?"

"There's no mention of her at all, so it looks like she's off the hook."

"It's all so sordid, Wes."

Wes pushed his empty plate to the side. "You think so? It's just people being people, right? So what else you got?"

I shook my head at Wes's jaded view of human nature. "The police ran tests on my phone lines. There was no tap."

"You really got your paranoia going with that one, huh?"

"There were moments."

"Anything else?"

"No."

Wes double-tapped the table and said, "Thanks for breakfast. Catch ya later."

After Wes left, I sat awhile longer sipping tea and thinking about Alice. She'd misappropriated funds, had a long-term affair with another woman's husband, submitted to blackmail, and stolen her best friend's treasure. My dad had been right, as usual, when he'd warned me to be careful about the people you trust. No one else, he'd said, could get close enough to do much damage.

CHAPTER TWENTY-FIVE

The rain had stopped, but the temperature hadn't risen. It was raw. When Zoë called around eight and offered hot homemade blueberry pie and a fire, neither Ty nor I hesitated. Ty and I sat on huge pillows in front of Zoë's fireplace. Ty leaned against her ottoman, and I leaned against Ty. His arms encircled me.

"Ty and I are going to Norway," I said.

"That's great," Zoë said. "Why Norway?"

"Fjords," Ty said. "Josie wants to see fjords."

"Very romantic," Zoë said. Ellis reached over and took her hand in his.

"Do you want to go to Norway?" he asked.

"I wouldn't mind," she replied, "but my dream vacation is Italy."

Ellis nodded thoughtfully.

"How about you, Ty?" I asked. "Where's your dream vacation?"

He smiled at me. "Wherever you are."

I skewed around and reached up to touch his cheek. "I feel the same."

The morning of Gretchen's shower, I woke up early, filled with pleasurable anticipation. I showered and dressed and tiptoed out of the house, not wanting to wake Ty, then ran across to Zoë's.

Jake, age ten, and Emma, age seven, were seated at the farmer's table by the window with plates of French toast in front of them. Jake, as blond as Zoë's ex-husband, was tall for his age and lean, like a runner. Emma, who shared her mom's coloring and delicate features, had grown three inches in the last few months, without gaining any weight; her baby fat was disappearing almost in front of our eyes. A large box of cornflakes lay on its side in the middle of the table. The French toast was smothered in the maple syrup Zoë put up from the ancient maples that ringed the property, and it smelled wonderful.

"I'm here!" I said.

"I'm so excited!" Zoë said. "Gretchen is going to be so surprised!"

I grinned. "I sure hope so."

"Ellis will be here at eleven to take over babysitting duty. Are you still okay to hang for ten minutes while I grab a shower?"

"You bet! Take fifteen."

She shot me a grin and ran for the stairs.

"How's school?" I asked the kids.

"Good," Jake said.

"Good," Emma said.

"How's Mary-Rose?" I asked Emma. The monkey sat on the chair next to her.

"Good."

"Watch this," Jake said.

He tiddlywinked a cornflake, using a spoon as a catapult device, into a bowl perched on the window ledge about seven feet from where he sat. He landed one, a money shot, and air-pumped his accomplishment.

"Good job!" I said. I poured myself a cup of coffee and sat down to watch.

His next attempt banked off the window, sprinkling crumbs onto the floor.

"Too bad," I said.

"My turn!" Emma called.

Wielding the spoon with unsure hands, she sent her cornflake straight up three feet, then twirling onto the table near her plate. Her second try flew to the right and landed on the floor. She pursed her lips. From the set of her jaw I could tell she was mad. She took her time, aimed, and shot the cornflake. This time she hit the bowl's rim.

"That was good," Jake said kindly.

"No, it wasn't," Emma replied.

She tried again, and again she missed, her cornflake spiraling toward the corner of the room, ten feet from the bowl. She slapped her spoon down in frustration and resumed eating her French toast.

"Shooting cornflakes is too hard," Emma complained to me. "Can you do it?"

"I don't know. I'll try." I balanced a cornflake in the spoon and let 'er rip. I missed by a mile, my flake slamming into the kitchen door a good two feet to the right of the bowl. "Oops."

Emma giggled.

I tried a second time and hit the door again.

I turned to Emma. "You don't feel so bad now, do you?"

She giggled again. "No."

I gave it one more try. This time, I even missed the door.

"Well, what do you know!" Zoë said, stepping into the room. "You're worse than I am, Josie, and I didn't think that was possible."

"I'm a novice," I replied. "Give me practice time and I'll leave you all in the dust."

"Even me?" Jake asked.

"Well, maybe not you." Zoë went for coffee, and I added, "FYI, some crumbs hit the floor. I'll clean them up."

"Don't bother. Cleaning them up is part of my morning routine."

I smiled. "You're such a good mom."

A soft pink flush colored her cheeks. "Thanks . . . I try."

Wes called as Zoë and I were driving to the restaurant. I slipped in my earpiece and took the call.

"Darleen's filed for divorce," he said.

"I'm not surprised. It can't be any fun being married to a criminal. Randall's going to have a terrible time in jail."

"That's the whole idea of jail, Josie," Wes said. He didn't add "Duh," but it was in his voice.

"True," I said. "What about Lenny?"

"He insists he was acting under duress. My police source says they expect it to go to trial, and he may get off. A working man doing what the boss man tells him, you can hear the lawyer now, right?"

"I'm not so sure he's wrong," I said. "He was in what must have felt to him like an impossible situation."

"Maybe. Or he just lacked character." He paused. "Got anything else?"

"No," I said.

"Today's Gretchen's shower, huh?"

"Yeah. I'm en route now."

"Say hey for me to her, okay?"

"Sure," I said.

As I hung up, I wondered how he knew Gretchen well enough to want to say hey to her, then realized with a jolt that Gretchen might well be one of Wes's sources. Wes's reach was growing by the day.

As soon as Gretchen stepped onto the Bow Street Bar & Grill's porch, we all yelled, "Surprise!" and she shrieked. Her hands flew to her cheeks; then she spun toward Jack, who stood in back of her, grinning.

"You knew about this!" she said.

"Yup. We all did. It's called collusion."

She laughed and ran to me. She hugged me, then hugged me again, whispering, "Thank you, Josie." She turned back to face the crowd. "I can't believe it! I just can't believe it! This is so wonderful of you all."

"Aloha, everybody!" I called. "It's time for a luau!"

CHAPTER TWENTY-SIX

T y and I stood on the deck of the *Azura* as we sailed through a craggy glacier-carved inlet, a fjord near Oslo. To my right, water cascaded from a rocky cliff. To my left, emerald green grass and yellow, blue, violet, pink, and white wildflowers transformed the jutting rock formation into a heavenly garden.

"What do you think?" he asked.

"I think I'm the luckiest girl in the world."

Ty reached his arm around my waist and drew me close, and we stood that way, my back against his chest, his arms around me, for a long, long time.

ACKNOWLEDGMENTS

S pecial thanks go to Leslie Hindman, who, with her team at Leslie Hindman Auctioneers, continues to appraise antiques for me to write about. Please note that any errors are mine alone.

Thanks to Christopher Kerezsi for helping me sort through the legal implications of finders-keepers, to Sheila York for listening to my early plans for the book, and to Katie Longhurst for her careful reading of the manuscript.

As a former Mystery Writers of America/New York chapter president and the chair of the Wolfe Pack's literary awards, I've been fortunate to meet and work alongside dozens of talented writers and dedicated readers. Thank you all for your support. For my pals in the Wolfe Pack and fans of Rex Stout's Nero Wolfe stories everywhere, I've added my usual allotment of Wolfean trivia to this book.

Thank you to Jo-Ann Maude, Christine and Al de los Reyes, and Carol Novak. Thank you also to Dan and Linda Chessman, Marci and James Gleason, John and Mona Gleason, Linda and Ren Plastina, Rona and Ken Foster, Liz Weiner and Bob Farrar, Meredith Anthony and Larry Light, and Wendy Corsi Staub and Mark Staub. Thanks also to Harry Rinker for his invaluable assistance about antiques.

Independent booksellers have been invaluable in helping me introduce Josie to their customers—thank you all. I want to acknowledge my special friends at these independent bookshops: Partners and Crime, Front Street Books, The Poisoned Pen, Well Red Coyote, Clues Unlimited, Mostly Books, Mysteries to Die For, Book'em

Mysteries, Legends, Book Carnival, Mysterious Galaxy, M is for
Mystery, Murder by the Book in Houston, where David Thompson
will be forever missed. Manhattan's Black Orchid Bookstore is also
still sorely missed; I remain grateful to Bonnie Claeson and Joe Gug-
lielmelli for helping launch Josie. Thanks also to Murder by the Book
in Denver, Murder by the Book in Portland, Schuler Books, The
Regulator, McIntyre's, Quail Ridge Books, Book Cove, Remember
the Alibi Mystery Bookstore, Centuries & Sleuths, Mystery Lovers
Bookshop, The Mystery Company, The Mysterious Bookshop,
Booked for Murder, Aunt Agatha's, Foul Play, Windows a Bookshop,
Murder by the Beach, Books & Books, Moore Books, The Bookstore
in the Grove, Uncle Edgar's Mystery Bookstore, Seattle Mystery
Bookstore, Park Road Books, and Once Upon a Crime. Thanks
again to Linda and Bobby from the now-gone Mystery Bookstore in
Los Angeles. Many chain bookstores have been incredibly supportive
as well—thank you to those many booksellers who've gone out of
their way to become familiar with Josie.

Thanks also to the Jane Austen Society of North America, Linda
Landigran of *Alfred Hitchcock Mystery Magazine*, Barbara Floyd of
The Country Register, and Wilda W. Williams of *Library Journal*.
Special thanks also to Molly Weston and Jen Forbus. Thank you as
well to The Samaritans of New York, a wonderful organization dedicated to suicide prevention with whom I've been affiliated for more
than fifteen years.

Special thanks to my librarian friends David S. Ferriero, Doris
Ann Norris, Sally Fellows, Mary Russell, Denise Van Zanten, Mary
Callahan Boone, with whom I share a love of theater, Cynde Bloom
Lahey, Cyndi Rademacher, Eleanor Ratterman, Jane Murphy, Eileen
Sheridan, Jennifer Vido, Judith Abner, Karen Kiley, Lesa Holstine,
Monique Flasch, Susie Schachte, Virginia Sanchez, Maxine Blei-
weis, Cindy Clark, Linda Avellar, Heidi Fowler, Georgia Owens, Eva
Perry, Mary J. Etter, Paul Schroeder, Tracy J. Wright, Kristi Calhoun
Belesca, Paulette Sullivan, Frances Mendelsohn, Deborah Hirsch,
Sharon Redfern, and Heather Caines.

Thank you to my literary agent emerita, Denise Marcil. I remain
grateful for her support and encouragement. Special thanks go to my

fabulous literary agent, Cristina Concepcion of Don Congdon Associates, Inc. Thank you to Michael Congdon, Katie Kotchman, and Katie Grimm as well.

My editor, Minotaur Books' executive editor, Hope Dellon, continues to provide insightful feedback about the manuscript. Special thanks also go to Silissa Kenney, editorial assistant, for her thoughtful comments. I'm indebted to them, and to the entire Minotaur Books' team. Thank you also to those I work with most often, Andy Martin, Hector DeJean, Sarah Melnyk, and Talia Ross, as well as those behind the scene, including my copy editor, India Cooper, and my cover designer, David Baldeosingh Rotstein.